WHEN

DARKNESS

ENDS

USA TODAY BESTSELLING AUTHOR

MARNI MANN

Visit my website at: www.MarniSMann.com
Cover Designer: Hang Le, By Hang Le, www.byhangle.com
Editor: Jovana Shirley, Unforeseen Editing, www.unforeseenediting.com
Proofreaders: Judy Zweifel of Judy's Proofreading, Kaitie Reister, and
Chanpreet Singh

ISBN-13: 979-8738808074

I know you're dancing across the stars tonight, Nana, and shimmying your shoulders in the clouds.
I love you.

PLAYLIST

"My Own Prison"—Creed
"drivers license"—Olivia Rodrigo
"I Alone"—Live
"wipe your tears"—Halsey
"self crucify"—Bea Miller
"Use Me"—PVRIS, featuring 070 Shake
"Buzzcut Season"—Lorde
"Still Sane"—Lorde
"i wanna be your girlfriend"—girl in red
"Blue on Black"—Kenny Wayne Shepherd
"Loveless"—PVRIS
"Silence"—FLETCHER
"Broken Bones"—KALEO

ONE

BEFORE

ASHE

2000

There was beauty all over Boston, but not a single woman compared to her.

That was the only thought in my head as she came rushing out the door of her classroom, focused on the notebook in her hands, heading straight toward me. She never glanced up, never slowed her pace. She stayed fixated on whatever she was reading, rushing as though she was late.

Just leaving class myself, I should have moved to the other side of the hallway, giving her more space to walk.

But I couldn't take my eyes off her, allowing her to crash right into me instead.

Our bodies collided, the books flying out of her hands.

Panic covered her gorgeous face as she wobbled, losing her balance, her body threatening to take her down.

I grabbed her waist, holding her steady. "I've got you," I said. "I won't let you fall."

A long piece of her dark hair was now stuck to her lip, her sapphire eyes glimmering as though they were a cluster of carats set in a ring. The scent of fall came from her skin as I clutched the narrowness of her hips, the feel of her like the start of a thousand-piece puzzle.

"I'm sorry." The fear dissolved from her expression, her cheeks now reddening. Once she began to breathe again, she immediately took a step back, causing my hands to drop. "I should have been looking at where I was going." Her voice was as smooth and gentle as a song.

Rather than admitting it had been just as much my fault, I knelt to the ground and picked up the books she had dropped. *Rehearsal and Performance* was on the front of one, and I placed it on top of the stack and handed it to her. "That class sounds like hell."

She glanced at the book's cover and then back to me, holding the small pile against her chest. "It's actually my favorite course this semester." Her lips spread, showing teeth that were perfect enough. "I'm a theater major."

I laughed, lifting the flap of my bag that hung on my hip. *Organic Chemistry* poked out of the top. "Premed—different worlds."

"Now, that's what I would call hell." Her grin slapped against my chest like a crack of lightning. "I wouldn't survive two seconds in your major."

That smile was going to land her an Oscar—I was positive of that. It wasn't fake or over the top, just genuine and charming, filled with the warmth of a summer campfire.

She looked toward the end of the hallway, reminding me that we weren't alone even though it felt that way, and once again, I heard the students passing us on both sides.

"I've got to go," she said, her stare finding mine. "I'm going to be very late." She glanced at her watch. "Shit, I already am."

2

Her smile was gone, and in that moment, I would have done anything to make it return. "Thanks for not letting me fall."

Before I could say another word, she was rushing down the corridor toward the stairwell, disappearing into the thick crowd.

I gripped the strap of my bag and walked in the same direction, taking the stairs to the bottom floor and opening the heavy door to the outside. I glanced around the open space, searching for that beautiful, brown-haired girl. But there were hundreds of students rushing across Boston University's campus, making it impossible for me to find her.

Giving up, I walked across the leaf-covered lawn in the direction of my off-campus apartment and stopped at a coffee shop a few blocks away. Once I reached the front of the line, I requested their darkest roast in their largest to-go cup.

Only two weeks into the fall semester, and I was already coming here twice a day, placing the same order each time. I had a feeling that wasn't going to change until the summer. Premed was getting more challenging every day, and I had no idea how I was going to make it through my junior year.

Or tonight.

There was no way around the fact that I would be studying until the early hours of the morning.

I grabbed a cardboard sleeve on my way out, slipping it over the cup, and continued the rest of the way to my building. Instead of waiting for the elevator, I hustled up the three flights, and as I unlocked the door, I heard voices coming from our apartment.

I vaguely remembered when I'd left for class this morning, my roommate, Dylan, saying something about hosting a study group. Once I stepped inside, I saw they were in the midst of one. Both couches were full, and several people were sitting on the floor.

"My man," Dylan said from the recliner. "Welcome to

Sexuality and Social Life." He smirked. "This is"—he circled his hand around in the air—"everyone. Everyone, this is my roommate, Ashe."

All eyes shifted in my direction.

But a gaze so fucking intense, like an earring piercing through a virgin lobe, was the only thing I felt in that moment. As I glanced toward the couch, I saw exactly who it had come from.

And this time, I was the one taken by surprise as those sapphire gems stared back at me.

"Hey, everyone." My words were to all of them, but my focus was only on her.

I wanted to sit on the armrest she was squeezing and start up our conversation where we had left off, but I knew the timing wasn't right. She was in the middle of studying, and I wasn't going to interrupt.

"You guys have fun," I said, taking her in for a final few seconds before I went to my room.

Once I shut the door behind me, I tossed my bag onto the bed and arranged my pillows in a comfortable position. *Organic Chemistry* sat on my lap, and I opened to the chapter that we had gone over in class. I was just bringing my coffee up for a sip when there was a knock at my door.

"Come in," I said, glancing up to catch that blue stare on the other side.

That hadn't taken long.

I liked that about her.

She clung to my doorframe, those slender fingers gripping it so tightly. "Dylan had to make a phone call, so we're taking a quick break. I just wanted to come and say ... small world."

"Had I known you were in such a rush to come to my place, we could have walked here together."

A heat moved across her skin, cheeks flushing. "I was running so behind; they had to start without me." She stepped in farther, still staying by the door but putting her back against the frame. "I'm Pearl, by the way."

"Ashe—you already know that."

"Ashe," she said as though she were trying it on for size. "I like that. Is it short for something?"

"It's my mother's maiden name. She has six siblings, all sisters. She didn't want their last name to die out."

"I love that."

"And you?"

"You mean, is Pearl short for something? Or what I'm named after?"

I didn't know what the hell I was asking. I just wanted to hear more of her voice and see the way those plump lips moved and to keep her eyes on me, so I answered, "Both."

She glanced toward the window, her arms circling around her stomach. "One of my mother's boyfriends once told me that if I had been a diamond, she would have sold me, but I had unfortunately come out as a pearl."

"He sounds like a fucking dick."

"That's all she ever dated." She was trying to hide how much that admission hurt, but her eyes wouldn't let her. They were as loud as a scream. "You're not going to school to be a shrink, are you?"

"No." I shook my head. "A surgeon."

"What kind?"

"Heart, I think. But I have a lot more years and what feels like a million more classes to complete before I make that decision. Premed is only the very beginning."

A smile replaced the emotion. One that was so alluring that I would agree to anything she asked. "The amount of studying and term papers and exams you have in your future kinda makes me want to die." She laughed, and it was just as captivating as her grin. "I want to graduate as quickly as possible and start my career."

"And go where?"

Her arms dropped, and she tucked her hands into her pockets. "New York or LA—whichever city will take me."

"That's an interesting way to put it."

Once again, her eyes were seeking out the window, like the answers were written on the glass. "My industry doesn't welcome you with open arms. I'm going to have to find a crack and squeeze my way in."

There was something so intriguing about Pearl. Different. Deeper. Like a wild bird that wasn't supposed to be made a pet and that was what college was doing to her. Humble to the core but far too talented for Boston.

"I don't think I've ever met anyone like you," I confessed.

Her smile didn't reach as far as her eyes this time. It stopped at her nose and slowly faded. "Something tells me you won't ever again." She moved into the hallway and added, "Maybe we'll cross paths again one day. See you around, Ashe."

The door shut before I got a chance to say another word.

Several seconds passed, and I finally looked at the textbook in my lap. I scanned the words, not retaining a single one. Knowing that she was in my living room, I couldn't concentrate. I just wanted my eyes on her, my body in her presence; something unfamiliar tugged at me to get closer to her.

I made a promise to myself that I wouldn't leave my room until I finished the chapter. I counted the double-sided pages and had eight to go, taking notes as I read to force myself to pay attention. When I reached the final sentence, I got up and went down the short hallway. But as I reached the opening of the living room, Pearl was nowhere to be found.

Where's the hot girl? I mouthed to Dylan, the room loud, as several people were speaking.

He shrugged and replied, *She had to go.*

She had found her crack, and she had squeezed her way out.

TWO

BEFORE

PEARL

"You're late. Again." My boss seethed as I rushed into the bar. He was leaning against the bar top with a tumbler in his hand, the whiskey a permanent fixture that I never saw him without. "Pearl, I won't tolerate your tardiness anymore."

"I'm sorry."

I had known I was cutting it close, but I'd needed the extra studying for the exam we had on Friday, and Dylan's apartment was only a few blocks from here.

My boss blocked me from the back entrance, standing several inches over me, the booze on his breath making my stomach churn. "Your good looks will only get you so far." His eyes were on my lips while he licked his own. "You know, average-looking girls show up on time, and they're hungry for the attention my customers give them. Maybe I need to fire you, trade you in for an average girl, someone who isn't such a diva."

Divas didn't work six nights a week, begging for the seventh shift. I didn't say that to Frank. Instead, I apologized again and sidestepped around him, rushing into the break room.

I set my bag on the bench, digging through it to find my

uniform. Once the clothes were in my hands, I stripped out of the ones I was wearing, hurrying to put on the tight black cotton skirt and see-through white tank top. The bra that happened to be clean today was bright blue, so that was the color eyeliner I would soon swipe over my lids. I added a pair of fishnets and tied my apron around my waist. As I stood in front of the mirror, I repositioned the curls that hung down to my chest, spraying them with hairspray, and once my eye makeup was done, I added some red lipstick.

Finished with the look, I shoved my bag into my locker and opened the door to the hallway, instantly greeted by Frank, who had been waiting on the other side.

Sipping his drink, he eyed me up and down. "Took you long enough." He waited for a response, but I didn't give him one. "Pearl, take this as your final warning. I'm up to here with your bullshit." He pointed at his throat.

"They're not excuses—"

"What did I just tell you?"

His voice was full of threats, ones I'd heard many times before. His eyes told an entirely different story as they continued to travel across my body, pausing at the spots I wished were more covered up.

"Frank, I promise to do everything I can to be here on time. But you know the full load of classes I take each semester, and I'm heavily involved in the theater, which causes my schedule to be even tighter."

He handed me his empty glass. "The only thing tight I want to hear you talk about is your pussy."

Half of my coworkers slept with him. The thought made me sick.

He put his hand on my chin, lifting it so my lips moved closer to his. "Don't do it again. Understood?"

If I wasn't short six hundred dollars on rent, I would knee

him in the balls and walk out, never returning. But he ran one of the most successful bars off campus, and none of the others in the area could pay me what I earned here.

I nodded hard enough that his hand fell, and I walked away.

"My God, I hate that man," I said to Erin, the bartender, stopping at the bar as she was cutting up limes.

"That makes two of us."

Erin had interviewed me almost two years ago after I came home from school that afternoon, finding an eviction notice on the door. She promised the money would be worth the bullshit. At the time, I didn't know what she meant.

I'd learned fast.

If I wasn't dealing with a drunk customer trying to shove his phone number into my tank top, I was putting out a Frank fire.

"I think I can make this shift a little better for you." She smiled, lifting a clipboard from behind the counter and turning it toward me. The schedule showed that I'd been assigned the front of the house—the best section in the bar.

I reached over the cutting board and hugged her. "Thanks for having my back."

"Girl, I've always got you—you know that."

As I pulled away, grinning, I pointed at the two high-tops by the door. "Have they been helped?"

She shook her head. "I told them you'd be right over."

I thanked her again and went up to the first table. "What can I get you?" I asked the two men.

"Two shots of Jameson," one of them answered. "And a Jack and Coke for me."

"Bud Light," the other man replied.

I wrote down their order and moved on to the four-top, asking those customers the same question.

And I repeated those words over and over for the next five hours until Frank came up behind me and said, "You're cut."

I was at the bar, waiting for Erin to finish making a round of drinks I had ordered, when I felt his breath on the back of my ear. I looked at him over my shoulder, his stare making my stomach turn. "Now?"

"We're slow tonight. You're lucky I didn't send you home hours ago."

"But my tables are still full."

"I'm the boss; I give the orders. You? You're barely holding on by a thread." The whiskey he sipped made his lips wet, and he didn't bother to lick it off. "Collect your tips and get your ass home." I was just turning away when he said my name, gaining my attention again. "Do yourself a favor and be early tomorrow."

I had another study group after class, followed by play rehearsal.

Tomorrow would just be an echo of today.

As he left, Erin placed the drinks on my tray and said, "One day, when you're a famous actress and you're on set in Paris or Italy—somewhere extra magical—you're going to think back to this moment and laugh."

I sighed. "Wouldn't that be a dream?"

"It's going to happen—I'm sure of it." She placed small black straws in each of the glasses before I lifted the tray into the air. "Let me know if you're running late tomorrow, and I'll cover for you."

I caught her hand on the bar top, giving her fingers a squeeze, and then I delivered the final round of drinks, cashing out for the night. With my tips tucked securely in my apron, I changed into my old clothes and rushed out the back door.

The train station was only a few short blocks away, and I slid my pass through the reader before waiting on the platform for the orange line to arrive. Once I got on and found a seat in the corner, I pulled out my notes I'd taken during class and began to study. Even though the ride was short, school had taught me that every minute of my day had to count.

Arriving at my stop, I put my notebook away and quickly walked to our place. At the front of our building, I hopscotched around the broken steps, carefully opening the door so the shattered glass wouldn't come falling out on me. Knowing at this hour there was probably someone sleeping in the elevator, I climbed the stairs to the sixth floor, the light in the hallway flickering as I quietly stuck my key in the lock.

As I got inside, the lamp in the living room was on, and Gran was reading on the couch.

"Hi," I said loud enough for her to hear.

She glanced up from the paperback, her smile causing the wrinkles to bunch on the sides of her face. "How was your day, dollface?"

"Long but good." I left my bag on the counter and sat next to her, snuggling into her arm. "I thought you'd be sleeping." The scent of baby powder instantly filled my nose, the smell even stronger as her hand surrounded my cheek.

"I couldn't get comfortable. You know these old bones like to ache a bit extra at night." She set her book on the table, preferring to read than watch one of the four channels we got on our rabbit-eared TV. "You're home earlier than usual."

"It was a slow night at the bar." I circled my hands around the frailness of her upper arm, pulling it closer to me. "Did you eat?"

"I heated up some soup."

"Was it enough? Are you still hungry?"

"It was plenty for me, dollface." Her thumb rubbed back and forth across the corner of my mouth. "How was school today?"

"Theater class went great, but I have an elective that's much harder than I thought it would be. Luckily, I found a good study group that I think is going to help a lot."

After leaving Dylan's apartment, I'd tried not to let my brain return there—to thoughts of Ashe and his handsomeness, the surprise I'd felt when I learned they were roommates. I certainly didn't need to recount the minutes I'd spent in his bedroom, getting to know more about the sexy man instead of being present in the study session. But while I'd sat on their couch, I couldn't stop thinking about his light-blue eyes, the color of an early morning sky. The way his black hair made the angles of his face more defined, his cheeks deliciously scruffy, a gaze so strong that my feet felt cemented to his floor.

My life wasn't full of coincidences, and I certainly hadn't experienced any luck. I worked for everything I had, and I would for the rest of my life. That was something I'd accepted the moment I was born. Where some women would watch Ashe walk through that apartment door and think it was a sign, I'd considered it a warning.

And each second I'd spent talking to him confirmed that.

She gently patted my skin. "Are you able to go to bed, or do you still have some studying to do?"

I would be up until the early hours of the morning. Maintaining a high GPA was the only way I could keep my partial scholarship. If I lost that due to grades, I couldn't afford to go to this school. Community college wasn't going to give me the exposure I needed, and it wouldn't gain me access to BU's theater, which was so well-known and highly valued in the community.

"I have lots of work to do, Gran."

"If I know you, you haven't stopped long enough to eat today." She kissed the top of my head. "Go put something in your stomach."

13

I lifted her hand off my face and held the back of it against my mouth. Her skin was so soft and spotted, like the Swiss cheese I melted over her toast for lunch.

"Let me know if you need anything," I said before I got up and went into the kitchen, opening the cupboard that housed most of our food.

Choosing one of the cans, I emptied the ravioli into a bowl and heated it in the microwave. While waiting for it to warm, I checked the fridge to see if I could find something to pair with the pasta.

Up until a few years ago, Gran had done the grocery shopping. Now that her arthritis was more advanced, walking the three blocks to the store had become too much for her. Now, she often went several months without leaving our apartment. Every other week, I would go to the market instead, picking up enough food to hold us over, making sure to get the things she loved the most.

I took out a slice of white bread and dropped it into the bowl along with a spoon, and then I grabbed my bag from the counter. While I was adjusting the heavy strap, I noticed Gran had covered herself in a second blanket.

"How about some tea?" I asked her.

She looked up from her book. Despite all the love in her stare, I could see the stress. The worry. The toll both had taken, worsening each day.

Around the time she had stopped shopping, she'd also had to quit her job. Her fingers were too bent and frozen, making it impossible for her to work at all, so she couldn't continue being a seamstress. She could barely hold a coffee cup.

Supporting the two of us was a financial burden she didn't want to put on me.

But I gave her no choice.

"Not tonight, dollface." She set the book in her lap, even

that small action so clearly causing her pain. "You know I always hate this time of the month—when it's so close to the first."

"We'll be okay, Gran. You know I won't let anything happen to us."

There was so much emotion in her eyes, but she would never let it fall. "I hate that this is on you."

"I don't."

"You should be having a ball at your age, not having a care in the world rather than drowning in all these bills."

"Gran," I said, walking over to the couch, "the life we share together is the only thing that matters to me." I leaned down and kissed her cheek. "And what we have is perfect."

"My beautiful Pearl." Her voice was so soft, but each word was emphasized, and I felt the meaning behind every one. "Now, go eat before your food turns cold."

I gave her a smile and went into my room.

The space had once been a small den, but she had converted it once I moved in with her. She'd had a handyman build a partition that served as a door, and she'd hung shelves above the desk that she had bought me at a garage sale. Those shelves housed the books she had given to me over the years —*To Kill a Mockingbird, The Great Gatsby, Jane Eyre, Little Women, Anna Karenina.* Since we didn't live in a neighborhood where it was safe enough to play outside, I'd spent my younger years reading those classics, memorizing the lines. Gran would sew me a costume, and I'd pretend the couch was my stage and the rest of our apartment an audience. I'd act out each of the scenes, and she'd applaud at the end of every act.

I hadn't taken private acting lessons, like most of the other students in my major, but they couldn't recite Ophelia's monologue by heart and convince an entire theater of how much she loved Hamlet.

I could.

I kicked off my shoes and crawled on top of my twin-size bed, taking out the textbook for *Sexuality and Social Life*. While I soaked a piece of bread into the tin-flavored sauce, I began to read the chapter.

But each time I skimmed a new sentence, something lodged deeper into my mind.

A set of eyes.

Ones that were the color of the sky that I would see out my window in the morning.

THREE

BEFORE

ASHE

"Let's go get wasted," Dylan said from the couch, his feet crossed over the coffee table, a plate of pizza resting on his chest.

"Now?" Sitting at the table on the other side of the room, I bit into my slice of pepperoni. "It's only Tuesday."

"So?"

I flipped the page of my *Epidemiology* textbook. "So ... I have an exam in the morning that I'm really not ready for."

He took the last bite of the crust. "And you think the next couple of hours are going to make a difference? You either know that shit or you don't. And you do—you've been studying nonstop. Besides, you can wake up in the morning and cram for a few hours before the exam."

I finished mine as well and grabbed one more from the box. "You mean, when I'm hungover as hell and running on no sleep?"

He took a swig of his beer and smirked. "Isn't that how we do most of our studying?"

I shook my head and bit off the tip, a pool of pepperoni

grease falling onto my tongue. "How about we negotiate and agree to only have a few drinks and make it home before midnight?"

He got up from the couch, briefly pretending my shoulder was a punching bag before he got himself another slice. "You can aim for a couple drinks and an early night." He sat in the seat next to mine. "But we both know that's not going to happen. Moderation isn't something either of us is good at."

He was right.

Hell, tonight would turn into full-on debauchery, like most of the evenings we went out. I'd wake with a raging headache and barrel my way to class, trying to keep down the greasy breakfast I'd inhaled. That was what college was supposed to be about. That was, unless you were a premed major with a course load that was kicking your ass, like me.

"Have I sold you on tomorrow's hangover, or are you going to be a little pussy tonight?"

I took a drink of my beer and picked up the rest of the slice. "If I fail this exam, you're fucking dead."

He got up from his seat, chuckling. "We're leaving in thirty. Make sure you're ready."

I licked the sauce off my fingers. "You don't have any exams this week?"

He shrugged, grabbing another bottle of beer from the fridge. "Nothing I can't finesse my way through. You know this degree is just a technicality, so when I open my own private airline one day, they can call me a fool, but they can't call me an uneducated one."

"Make sure you keep a position open for me. I'm probably going to need it."

"Fuck that," he drawled. "You're going to be an incredible surgeon, and if anything ever happens to me, you're going to be the one who saves me." He smiled and pointed at the bathroom. "Now, fucking move it. You're down to twenty-five minutes."

We'd had these dreams since we were kids, and Dylan had been pushing me toward mine ever since. I was just as hard on him even if he didn't care as much about his degree.

College was better because we could do it together.

I tossed my paper plate in the trash and held my beer as I walked down the hallway. "Hey," I said to him from the doorway of the bathroom.

He was headed into his room and stopped to look at me. "Yeah?"

"You're buying tonight, and don't try to finesse your way out of it."

Laughter was his only response.

FOUR

AFTER

ASHE

The police headquarters was located about halfway between Back Bay and Mission Hill. It was a massive, rectangular building, the entrance shaped like the top of an octagon, the wide body covered in square panes of glass that were mirrored and tinted, making it impossible for anyone to see in.

Even at night.

A reprieve for someone who liked to come into the office in the early hours of the morning.

Like myself.

I swiped my badge at the front and took the elevator to the third floor, wandering down the dark hallway until I arrived at my desk. Files overflowed from the bins that ran along the side; empty coffee cups and sticky notes littered the back. I cleared a path large enough to fit my bag and unloaded the file of the most recent case I'd been assigned.

Lisa Mitchell, forty-seven, found shot between her shoulder blades in the bedroom of her three-million-dollar home on the 600 block of Boylston Street. Her photo was attached to the top of the folder, and I stared at her face, waiting for the missing piece of this puzzle to come to me.

For the last several days, I had been reviewing the details of her case and the results forensics had found so far.

Mitchell's housekeeper, the only person with a key and front-door code, had found her early in the morning when she arrived at work. She had called the police, and I had been one of the first on the scene.

Never married, owner of a large marketing company, Mitchell had been a prominent member of Boston's elite society—a social circle larger than most with connections that ran deep. Her social media accounts were full of countries she had traveled to, celebrities she had shaken hands with, and dinners that had been over five hundred a plate.

"Lisa, what the fuck happened to you?" I said, running my hand through my hair.

The sound of heels clicking on the floor filled my ears. I glanced up just as the captain approached.

"Morning," I said to her.

"Detective Flynn, what brings you in at this hour?"

Dressed in a pressed black suit and red lipstick, she was more put together than most at four o'clock in the morning.

"Couldn't sleep."

"Because of"—she looked at the file on my desk —"Mitchell's case or something else?"

It took me a moment to answer, "Life keeps me awake, Captain."

"You're one of a very large club." She took a seat in one of the chairs, her eyes telling me she understood. "How's the case going? Any leads?"

I gathered the notes I'd taken, hitting against the folder to make the edges even. "There are several people in her inner circle I still need to interview, and I'm waiting on forensics to finish a few outstanding reports."

"Voice mails? E-mails? Any luck on those?"

"They still have to be retrieved. She had a password on her cell and computer." I took a drink of my coffee. "It's moving, just not as fast as I'd like."

She held out her hand. "Let me take a look."

I closed the folder, ensuring none of the evidence fell out, and gave it to her.

I followed her eyes as she read my initial report before flipping through the photographs I'd confiscated from Mitchell's house.

"Who's this?" The picture the captain was pointing to was the person Mitchell had been photographed with the most.

"That's Barbara Simpson, wife and homemaker to one of Boston's most prominent attorneys and Mitchell's best friend, according to my research."

"Interview her. Immediately."

I grabbed a pen and held it against a pad of paper, ready to write. "What gives you that hunch?"

She unclipped the photos and spread them across my desk. "What's the common trait in each of these pictures?"

I had found them framed in Mitchell's home—one on her living room mantel, another on her dresser, the third in her office. As I studied them, I noted something in particular. Something I hadn't noticed before. "Simpson is staring at Mitchell instead of facing the camera."

"Exactly." I glanced up as the captain added, "Unless it's immediate family, women don't look at each other that way. My guess is that Simpson is trying to gauge Mitchell's reaction to the person who's taking the picture." She pointed at the photograph in the middle, where Simpson's eyes were slightly squinted. "My guess is that Simpson's husband is the photographer in each of these shots."

"Mitchell was having an affair with him."

"If I didn't have two kids about to enter college, I would bet my salary on that."

"That photo"—I nodded toward the one her finger was still on—"was taken at an event two weeks ago that Simpson attended with her husband." On the paper, I wrote a note to find out where the event had been held and to check their camera feeds. I set the pen down and took in Simpson's appearance again—the hardness of her lips, the stiffness in her shoulders. The glare in her eyes. "That's the face of a vindictive woman, scheming her next move."

"Congratulations, Detective. You might have just solved this case." She smiled. "In record time, I might add."

FIVE

BEFORE

PEARL

Tuesdays weren't any busier than Mondays, but with Erin behind the bar, I had once again been assigned the front of the house, so my section was the first to fill up. And it had been nonstop from the moment I arrived at work—only a few minutes late today, but Frank hadn't been there to scold me.

I had come in with a goal in mind, knowing my earnings needed to total six hundred by the end of the week or I wouldn't have enough for rent. Gran's disability check only dented what I owed each month, and the bar made up the large difference. As for tonight, I hoped to have at least a few hundred in my apron before I was cut. To earn a little extra, I'd prepaid for some cheap shots that I kept on my tray, offering them to my tables as an add-on or to anyone who passed by, like the couple on their way to the restroom.

I moved into their path and held out one of the shots. "Sex on a Barstool?"

"Hell yes," the man said, opening his wallet. "She'll take one." He set a twenty in my hand. "And two for me, please."

I gave him the small glasses, and then I was on my way to

my section when I heard my name come from somewhere behind me. An almost-faint sound as it faded into the loud music but in a voice I couldn't forget.

I turned around, searching the faces until I found his.

Ashe.

A baseball hat covered his hair and sat low over his forehead, causing a shadow to hover above his eyes. Still, there was no mistaking who he was, and his tall, athletic build was coming straight for me.

"Hi," I said, hearing the shock in my voice.

He stopped only inches away, his cologne surrounding me like it had when I ran into him in the hallway—a scent that was a combination of sandalwood and green apple. "Hey, Pearl."

His smile was so powerful that I was surprised a director hadn't convinced him to go the theater route.

"Want a shot?" I teased.

He took the small tumbler from my hand. "What is it?"

The concoction didn't have an official name. Erin had just poured a few juices together and topped it with a splash of vodka.

"Let's call it An Easy Lay," I said, laughing.

His grin widened, and he swallowed the mixture. "You've been in my bedroom; we both know there's nothing easy about you."

As his words registered, a heat moved across my face.

Rather than responding, I watched him take out his wallet and place a twenty next to the empty glass.

When I tried to give him change, he wouldn't take it, and he said, "I didn't know you worked here."

I thanked him for the extremely large tip and then replied, "For almost two years."

"Dylan and I come here all the time. Why haven't I seen you?"

"I'm sure you have; you just didn't notice me."

Even with the area so dark around his eyes, I felt his stare all the way inside me.

"I would have noticed ... you're impossible to miss."

I was sure he could see my reaction by the color my face was turning.

Not knowing what to say, I asked, "What brings you in tonight?"

"Dylan." He took a sip from the glass he'd been carrying. "He wanted to get drunk and wasn't going to take no for an answer." He adjusted the top of his hat, lifting it enough to show me that beautiful blue stare before tightening it over his head again. "Can I buy you a drink, or is there no drinking while you're on the clock?"

"That's really nice of you to offer, but I don't drink."

"Ever?" When I shook my head, he added, "How do you have the patience to work here?"

"The tips make it worth it." I held the edge of the tray against the bottom of my chest. Even though I hadn't felt his gaze move to that area, I felt so exposed when I was around him. "A lot of the servers spend all of their money here. I don't have to worry about that, not like if I worked at a grocery store."

His lids narrowed as his tongue slowly licked across his bottom lip. "You're intriguing. More so each time I talk to you."

The same was true about him.

But so was something else.

"Ashe, you're a dangerous distraction."

He laughed, a deep, honest noise that made him even more attractive. "That's an interesting choice of words."

"If you knew me, you wouldn't think so."

"That's all I've been trying to do. But every time you're within my grasp, you run from me."

I held the tray even tighter, the plastic rim digging painfully into my ribs. "I'm afraid tonight isn't going to be any different."

His lips parted, their fullness almost taunting me, causing me to imagine what they would feel like to kiss.

That certainly wasn't what I needed.

And that was why I stuck with men who weren't tempted to ever call again, whom I wouldn't ever grow feelings for.

Because feelings were the very last thing I needed.

I forced myself to take a step back and another.

"Where are you running to now, Pearl?"

I chewed the corner of my mouth, a heaviness lodging deeper into my chest the more I separated us. "I have to get back to work." My thumb had been holding his cash, so it wouldn't fall onto the floor. I waved the twenty in the air. "Thanks again," I said, and I turned around.

When I reached the bar, I was out of breath. Not from the short distance I'd walked or the speed I'd used. All the air in my lungs was gone because of him. His eyes, his presence, the sensations he caused each time I was around him.

"Are you all right?" Erin asked, lining up several shot glasses to make me another round. "You look like you were just ravished against a wall."

I reached up, flattening the top of my hair and then pressing my cold hand against my warm cheek. "I feel like I was."

My fingers returned to the bar top, clinging to the edge. I could feel Ashe's stare, the intensity like a fire burning me from the inside. It was strong enough that I glanced over my shoulder, searching for him in the space we had just been standing in.

But the spot was empty, Ashe no longer there.

That should have made me relieved.

Except it didn't.

SIX

BEFORE

ASHE

"She works here," I said to Dylan as I returned to the back of the bar, where we'd been sitting.

He turned toward me as I took the seat next to him. "Who?"

"Pearl, the girl from your study group."

"She does?" He glanced around the space, as though she were standing close by. "Where is she? Let's buy her a drink."

"One, she's working. And two, she doesn't drink."

He dropped his arms against the small table, moving in closer. "Who doesn't drink their way through college?"

I laughed. "She's the only one I know." I paused to really think about it. "It's admirable."

Dylan and I had come from a town of partiers, so we'd gotten a good taste of that life before coming to college. Our first two years in the dorms were mayhem. We had calmed down a little since moving off campus and my classes had gotten tougher, but we were both turning twenty-one this year, and there would be no need for fake IDs. I could only imagine what those birthdays were going to look like.

CHAPTER 6

"When are you taking her out?"

I lifted my glass off the table, hauling in a long sip through the straw. "I can't get her to talk to me long enough to ask."

"That's not like you, man."

I stared at the ice bobbing over the top of the vodka. "She's different, Dylan." I glanced up to see his eyes urging me to say more. "I don't know how to describe her; she's not like anyone I've dated before."

"Can you pin her down and get her number?"

A waitress came to the table, delivering another round. I downed the rest of what was in my glass, and we handed her the empties.

"She runs before I get even close to asking," I finally answered.

He leaned in further, his elbow almost touching mine, fingers gripping his cocktail as though I were about to reach for it. "Here's what I've learned about women like Pearl: when they're fast on their feet, they want to be chased."

"You really think so?"

He nodded. "She wants to make sure you're worth it." He clinked his drink against mine. "It's a good thing you are."

SEVEN

BEFORE

PEARL

Since the bar had gotten busier around midnight, Frank didn't end up cutting me, and I stayed past last call. We were fortunate to have a cleaning crew come in after hours, so the only closing duty I had was to make sure all the glasses were picked up from my section. That only took a few minutes to finish once the bar was cleared out, and then I was heading for the back room to get my things.

Too tired to change into my regular clothes, I just zipped my coat over my tank top and hoped the fishnets kept me warm enough in the cold. I carried my bag through the empty bar and hurried out the front entrance.

There were several people standing outside, the sidewalk almost as busy as the front of the bar had been, and within a few steps, I heard someone yell my name, followed by, "Come over here."

It was Dylan, standing off to the side with Ashe and a guy I didn't know.

As Dylan waved for me to come closer, I could tell from his voice and the movement of his hand how many drinks he'd had.

CHAPTER 7

I'd had that ability from a young age, even able to detect if drugs had been mixed into the booze.

A human breathalyzer, I liked to call it.

"Hey, gentlemen," I said as I went over to them. My feet hurt from wearing these boots all night, and the wind was whipping past my legs, causing me to shiver.

Dylan and Ashe separated, and I stood in between them. Ashe immediately introduced me to his other friend.

"How did I not know you worked here?" Dylan asked.

I laughed. "I don't know. I haven't been hiding."

Dylan draped his arm around my shoulders, a gesture that was only friendly. "We're practically family at this point. I think that calls for a discount on all future shots."

"Family, huh?" I continued to chuckle. "Like you're my brother from a different mother?"

"I was thinking, more like a sister-in-law." He took a step back, lifting his arm off me, and Ashe caught him to help keep him steady.

"I think our friend here has had plenty of shots," Ashe said.

And so had Ashe, but he wasn't nearly as drunk as Dylan. He wasn't slurring, and his feet were much steadier on the ground.

For some reason, that pleased me.

"Next time you guys come in, I'm sure I can arrange something," I told Dylan. "But that depends on one thing ..."

Dylan shifted his weight, and I knew it wasn't on purpose. "Talk to me, Goose."

I smiled. "How about you put together a few more study groups? It's going to be a long semester, and this class is out of my wheelhouse, but it's far too late to drop it and pick up another elective."

"Done—with one exception."

"A counteroffer?" I crossed my arms over my chest, hoping that would add more warmth. "I'm listening."

"You go out with my boy Ashe."

I should have known.

I'd fallen right into that one.

My head leaned back, the air slapping against my open neck, and I slowly turned to Ashe. His grin was warm. His eyes were a heat that moved through me as fast as a shower would cover my skin.

A few more study sessions would help me tremendously, but spending time alone with him would get me in serious trouble.

I felt all three sets of eyes on me while I focused on Dylan's and answered, "I don't date."

"You don't drink," Dylan replied, his brows furrowed to the point of a wrinkle. "And you don't date. What do you do, Pearl?"

"I study." As I took a breath, there was a quiver in the back of my throat—a reminder that I was nothing like the students I went to school with.

High school had been much of the same. I'd accepted that a long time ago, but moments like this made it hard—moments when the differences were voiced and I had to acknowledge them.

I turned my stare to Ashe, the disappointment so present in his eyes. "And that's what I have to go do now. Good night, guys."

I rushed down the sidewalk, feeling his gaze on me with every step until I turned at the cross street, where the freezing air found its way back to my skin.

EIGHT

AFTER

ASHE

A few hours after my conversation with the captain, her words still fresh in my head, I stood in Lisa Mitchell's living room, scanning the remaining photos on her mantel. In each of the shots, along with the ones I'd already looked at in her bedroom and office, she was facing the camera, and so were the other people she posed with. None of the other women were staring at her, like the ones she had of her and Simpson.

After a bit more digging, I learned that she and Simpson had met over ten years ago at a charity event. It appeared that the women had traveled together multiple times and worn matching pajamas when celebrating a friend's bachelorette party. Simpson had even shared photos of Mitchell on Facebook when it was her birthday, and Mitchell had done the same with Simpson. And during their entire friendship, Simpson had been married. Keith, an estate attorney, ran in similar circles as Mitchell and attended the same college—although a few years apart—and only three streets separated their brownstones.

But something nagged at me, and it was the lack of

evidence. A side-eye glare in a couple of photos and a hunch from the captain weren't enough.

I needed proof.

There was only one place I was going to find that in this house.

I rushed back up the stairs to Mitchell's bedroom and entered her massive walk-in closet. Standing in the doorway, I observed the four walls of clothing. An area in the corner housed all her furs. The large island built into the center had clear drawers, showing her rows of jewelry and watches.

She had been a successful woman. Her business was one of the highest-earning marketing companies in New England, and the initial reports I'd pulled showed she didn't have much debt.

Money clearly wasn't an issue. She already had status.

The only thing missing—from what I could tell—had been love.

Is love what got Lisa Mitchell murdered?

She had attended a fundraiser the night she was killed. *The Boston Globe* had been present and snapped a photograph of her in a long gold gown, a black fur coat over it. Both were on hangers, dangling on a hook on the right side of the closet, waiting for the housekeeper to get them cleaned. When Mitchell had been shot, she had been wearing a silk negligee and robe, telling me that she'd had time to come home and change.

I slipped on a pair of exam gloves and ran my hands over the dress. I could feel the silky material through the nitrile, making it easy to check for pockets or any foreign objects. When I detected nothing out of the ordinary, I moved the dress and began the same process on the coat. This was much heavier than the gown, the hairs of the fur so smooth. I found nothing on the outside and unzipped the jacket, locating a breast pocket. My hand dropped to the bottom, where I felt a light brush of a sharp corner. Had I not extended my fingers all the way down, I wouldn't have found it.

I slowly pulled out the tiny, wrinkled piece of paper, unfolding each side.

You look stunning tonight.
My limo is parked out back. Meet me in ten.

I reached into the pocket of my suit and pulled out an evidence bag, dropping the note inside, before I took out my phone and called the forensic analyst who was assigned to this case.

"Harvey," he answered.

"It's Flynn. Any updates on the cell phone and laptop for the Mitchell case? I'm going to need access to her voice mails and e-mails as soon as possible."

"Hey, Flynn. We should have that by this afternoon."

"That's just what I wanted to hear." I held the clear bag on the palm of my hand, viewing each of the letters, the black ink that had been used to write it. "I'll be by in about thirty minutes with a new piece of evidence. I'm going to need you to pull fingerprints and a handwriting analysis, and I need a rush on both."

"I'll do the best I can, buddy."

I was shoving my phone back into my jacket just as it started to ring. I checked the screen to see who was calling and held it against my face. "Flynn."

"Where are you?" my police sergeant asked.

I started making my way down the stairs to the first floor. "Mitchell's house, collecting more evidence. Why? What's up?"

"A woman was found dead in the elevator of a residential

building on Commonwealth Avenue, just north of Allston Street."

"Name?"

"Jane Doe. Around thirty years of age, auburn hair, lean build. No wallet was found, and neither were any identifying marks. We don't know if she was working or visiting, but we know she wasn't a resident. The team arrived about twenty minutes ago. I need you to head over now."

"I'm on my way."

I returned the phone to my pocket as I went out through Mitchell's front door, getting into the driver's seat of the department's vehicle that I'd parked out front. I still needed to collect a sample of Keith Simpson's handwriting and drop off the evidence bag to Harvey.

But first, I needed to put my eyes on Jane Doe.

NINE

ASHE

W*hen they're fast on their feet, they want to be chased.* Dylan's words hadn't left my head. And even though Pearl had claimed she didn't date, I believed she just hadn't found someone worth being with.

I was determined to be that person.

But first, I had to spend more time with her. My initial plan had been to see her at the study group Dylan had set up, but they had decided to meet at the library instead. When Dylan and I had gone to the bar on Wednesday, the bartender had told me Pearl was off for the evening. It only took a few smiles to charm her into telling me that Pearl was in a play and it was opening night.

The internet had given me the rest of the information I needed.

Pearl was starring in BU's rendition of *Rent*, and I was able to score a ticket to one of the shows. I even paid extra for a better view.

I knew nothing about the play or how large her role was, nor did I expect the auditorium to be packed, but there wasn't an opening to be found. I located my seat at the end of a long row, only three back from the stage, and the lights dimmed immediately. Within the first scene, Pearl was standing almost in front of me, dressed in the sexiest outfit, similar to what she had worn to the bar—tights with large holes and a dress that hugged every one of her curves, barely covering her tits. She was wearing much more makeup than normal, her hair wild around her head.

The scene was a strip club, and she was pretending to inject heroin into her arm, showing the high from the drug before she climbed on the pole.

I couldn't take my eyes off her; she was fucking breathtaking.

And she was so natural up there that I couldn't tell that she was acting. She had become the character she was playing, and I was a fly on the wall, watching the chaos of her story unfold, a life she was fighting so hard for.

I never once glanced at my watch, nor did my hands ever release the armrests. Every time she went backstage, I found myself anticipating her return, counting the seconds until my eyes found her again. Within a few scenes, I learned she had the lead role, and not a single actor she shared the stage with could even compare to her talent.

Pearl had been born a star.

In the little time we'd spent together, I had known she had a beautiful voice, a quiet presence that absorbed all of my attention. But not during any of our encounters had I expected anything like what I was witnessing now. And when the lights turned off at the end of the final act, the curtain opening to show the full cast onstage, taking their bow, I was disappointed it was over.

Pearl was standing in the middle, and the long line of actors parted, all of them facing her, applauding. The whole audience then got on their feet, clapping and shouting for her.

Including myself.

She gave a long-drawn-out bow, her smile sparkling, her hand on her heart, showing her appreciation before the stage cleared. As everyone ushered out of the auditorium, I found one of the stagehands, and he told me the actors exited through the back, so I made my way outside and around the large brick building. Two guys were walking out when I arrived, and I recognized them from the play.

"Excellent job tonight," I told them.

"Thank you," one responded, and the other nodded.

I waited by the bottom of the stairs, watching the door open every few seconds, scanning the faces that came out. I only had to wait a couple of minutes before I caught sight of her, rushing down the steps, her arms in the air as she reached the bottom, like she was getting ready to run.

Knowing she hadn't seen me, I gently clasped my fingers around her elbow and said, "Hey."

She instantly halted, a look of surprise filling her eyes. "Ashe. Hi." Clouds of white filled the cold air, showing how hard she was breathing. "What are you doing here?"

"I came to see your play. Pearl"—I paused, the awe still so present in my chest—"you were phenomenal."

"You ..." Her voice trailed off for a moment. "You just saw me onstage?"

"I was in the third row. I thought for sure that you had seen me a few times. At least, it'd felt like your eyes were on me."

She led us over to the side, clearing the path for the other actors who were trying to leave. "The stage lights are too bright," she said. "There's a wicked glare, and it's hard to see the audience." As she stared at me, her mouth stayed open, as though she was thinking about what to say. "Are you into theater? I'm just trying to understand why you came tonight."

She had tied her hair back, and a few pieces had loosened, the wind causing them to stick to her lipstick. I wanted so badly to pull them away, but I shoved my hands into my pockets instead.

"This is the first play I've ever been to. Well, aside from the ones we were forced to watch in school."

"And you came to mine?"

I want to be close to you.

That was the thought in my head along with a desire to pull her body against mine and ravish that gorgeous mouth.

Her lips teased me every time she licked them.

But if I did anything like that, Pearl would wiggle away. I knew that even though I knew nothing about her.

"I wanted to watch you perform."

She stayed silent, shaking her head, like she was trying to stop my confession from sinking in.

"I'm certainly no expert," I continued, "but what you did on that stage didn't look like a performance. It looked like you had transformed into that character. I've seen enough movies to know many people are cast because of their looks and they hold no talent at all. That's not you. My God, Pearl, you have something I've never seen before."

"Wow ... I don't even know what to say." Her chest was rising and falling so fast. "Ashe, thank you. So, so much." She was humble—I heard it in her voice, saw it in her eyes. That response wasn't from someone who had stumbled upon this major to get an easy degree. It was from someone who had worked their ass off, and tonight showed that. "And thank you for coming to support the cast and our department and—"

"I came for you."

The streetlamps showed her cheeks were turning flushed, and I had a feeling it wasn't due to the cold.

"I really appreciate that." She took in my eyes, and when it seemed like they became too much, she glanced to the road. "I'm sorry ... I have to go."

I had known she was going to run—that had become her pattern—so I had come prepared. "Let me buy you a coffee."

"I can't."

"Are you headed to the bar? I'll walk with you."

She sighed before she replied, "I wish I were going to work."

"I don't think I've ever heard anyone say that before."

When she spread her lips, it wasn't a smile, more like a sign that she was in agreement.

I put my hand on her shoulder, drawing her attention back to me. "Fifteen minutes, Pearl. That's all I'm asking for." Once her eyes were on mine, they didn't move, and I could feel her wavering. "You shouldn't go home and study after the performance you just had. You deserve to celebrate ... with me."

She took her time in answering. "Why do I get the feeling you're not going to stop until I say yes?" Only then did her lips finally tug into a smile.

I laughed, feeling accomplished as hell, and moved my hand to her lower back. "Come on. I know the perfect place."

TEN

BEFORE

PEARL

A she had watched my performance. As we walked to get coffee, I tried to wrap my head around that.

Aside from Gran, he was the only other person who had ever come to see me onstage. A man who had appeared in my life, completely out of nowhere, and now, every time I was around him, my chest tingled. My hands wanted to link with his just to feel the warmth of his skin.

But each time, I stopped myself, not letting myself go there. *There*, I had learned, would be the end of everything I had built. I just had to get through the next two years of school, and then I would be packing up our apartment and getting Gran out of here.

As Ashe held the door open to an all-night diner and I walked in from out of the cold, I was going against every rule I had set.

Fifteen minutes, I promised myself, *and then I'm out of here.*

Things were over between us before they even had a chance to start.

A waitress saw us come in and pointed to the large dining room. "Sit anywhere. I'll be over with menus in a minute."

I led us to a booth and slid most of the way in while Ashe took a seat across from me.

"This place has the best pie," he said, eyeing the counter, where there was a display case, several pieces sitting on plates inside. "Are you a fan?"

"Of pie?" I shrugged. "Sure."

"What's your favorite kind?"

I crossed my legs under the table, my hands resting on top of them, fingers clinging together. "I've only ever had pumpkin."

I thought of the pie Gran used to make for the holidays every year before her hands hurt too badly to bake. That dessert would be our treat for the whole week, and we'd split a piece each night. My stomach would feel so full from the thick creaminess that when it was time to go to bed, I would almost instantly fall asleep.

Ashe rested his arms on the table, and even though we were separated by a few feet of Formica, it felt as though our bodies were touching. "What? Only pumpkin?"

"I'm not much of an experimenter when it comes to food."

Conversation.

It could be my worst enemy at times, like now, as he opened boxes he didn't even realize were closed. Ones I'd moved into the attic of my brain, taped multiple times with several inches of dust resting on top. Where most attics were full of clothes and keepsakes, mine overflowed with memories.

Moments that I didn't care to revisit with him—or anyone.

"We need to change that," he said right before the waitress came to our table, placing menus in front of us.

"Just coffee for me, thank you," I said, handing back the

large, laminated sheet, not needing to be tempted by any of the descriptions when I'd spent money on the food I had at home.

"Same," Ashe replied, "and a slice of every flavor of pie you have."

"We have six kinds," the waitress said.

He smiled at me. "Then, we'll take six pieces." When the waitress left, he said, "You're going to be an experimenter tonight."

I took in the light blue of his eyes, wondering how difficult it was going to be to avoid him in the future if he continued pulling stunts like he had tonight. "You're too much."

"I want to see your expression when you try them. I assure you, there are much better flavors than pumpkin."

"But that's such a classic."

"I'm not saying it isn't good. I'm just saying there's better." He spread his arms out a little farther, making it feel like he was now on top of me. "I want to know more about you, Pearl. I've seen the girl onstage, who poured her heart out. I know you're a theater major and you share an elective with Dylan, you don't drink and you work in a bar, and you study for fun." He smiled, and it was the most beautiful sight. "But where are you from? Why did you choose BU? Why theater?"

My hands began to heat as I rubbed my linked fingers together. "I'm from Boston; I've lived in different sections of the city my whole life." I took a breath. "BU has one of the best theater programs in the area, and acting is all I've ever wanted to do."

The waitress delivered the coffee, and I watched Ashe mix cream and sugar into his, whereas I left mine black.

I held the cup, staring at the dark drink. "Painters empty their emotions onto a canvas. Writers craft words. I take on personalities that are so far from my own."

His lids squinted, as though he was processing what I'd just said. "Why are you always running?"

"Time works against me."

"Has it always been that way?"

I sighed, my brain gazing at all the boxes, the years before I had moved in with Gran. "Yes."

The waitress returned to our table, her tray covered in small plates. "Blueberry," she said, setting down the first one. "Apple, strawberry, peach, peanut butter, and cherry. You didn't ask for ice cream, but I brought some anyway—on the house." She placed a soup bowl between us that was filled with scoops of vanilla. "Have fun."

I laughed as she walked away, gazing at the buffet he had ordered. "My God, Ashe."

He picked up his spoon. "Let's start with the blueberry."

He faced the point of the slice toward me.

I cut off a small piece. "*Mmm.*" As I chewed, the tartness of the fruit slowly unraveled, the sweetness coming in next. "I like it."

"Now, with ice cream." He took a spoonful and added it to his second bite.

I did the same, the vanilla cutting some of the sweetness of the blueberry, making it taste even better. "Wow."

"You've really only ever had pumpkin? I thought apple was a staple in most people's homes."

"It probably is," I said, moving to the next plate. "Just not in mine." This one happened to be the apple, and I chewed the large chunk, the buttery crust exploding with a rich cinnamon flavor, like the topping I sprinkled on Gran's oatmeal. "This one is excellent too."

"Agreed." He wiped his mouth with a napkin. "Do you live in the dorms, or do you have a place off campus?"

I swallowed the apple and went in for more. "Off campus."

"In which part of the city?"

While thinking of a way to dance around his question, I moved on to the cherry. The minute it hit my tongue, I responded, "Not for me."

"It's not a flavor I really like either, but I wanted you to try it."

He moved that one off to the side. I hated to see any food wasted, but it was too sweet to take another bite.

I dug my spoon into the edge of the peanut butter, and as soon as it dissolved in my mouth, I couldn't stop myself from moaning.

"Sounds like you have a favorite."

I nodded, covering my lips with the back of my hand. "This is amazing. Rich but perfect."

The strawberry and peach were also good, but neither was as tasty and delicious as the peanut butter, so that was what I returned to. I took some ice cream with me and loved that bite even more. As I chewed, I felt his eyes on me, and I was sure he was waiting for a response to his previous question.

I set down my spoon, needing a break from the sweetness, and took a drink of my coffee. When I finally glanced at him, I took a few seconds before I said, "I live in Roxbury. It's where I grew up—well, mostly grew up." The corner of a box was eyeing me, and I shoved it away. "I live with my grandmother. She has crippling arthritis that's made her disabled, so I take care of her. We take care of each other actually."

"That wasn't easy for you to say."

I was shocked by his observation. But that only lasted a moment before I came to the realization that he saw things most people didn't, and I shouldn't have been surprised at all.

"To be honest, I just want to run right now."

"Why?"

I held the air in my diaphragm, hoping that would stop my

heart from beating so fast. "Because I'm not normally in situations where I have to answer questions like this. Aside from Erin, the bartender at work, I don't talk to many people." I focused on the swirls in the pie crust, his eyes just too much for me. "Ashe, I run to class, usually late from taking care of Gran in the morning. I run to study groups, always behind from speaking to my professors after class. I run to theater practice and then to work, consistently late and needing every tip I can get because I support us. I then run home to check on Gran, and I study all night. I wake up and do it all over again."

"You're remarkable."

"No." I shook my head. My intentions had not been to goad him into a compliment I certainly didn't deserve. I just wanted him to understand, although I wasn't sure why. "I'm just like anyone else who's trying to survive in this world with a lot of responsibilities on my shoulders."

"You're nothing like them, Pearl. You have more on your plate than any student I know, and look at everything you've managed to accomplish. Most would be drowning, but you're thriving."

When I looked at him, there wasn't pity in his eyes. Instead, there was the same expression as when he'd met me at the bottom of the stairs behind the theater. "Thank you ... I ..." I held his stare, the emotions bubbling in my chest. "I can't believe I just told you all that."

"I'm happy you did." He wrapped his hands around his mug. "Plus, it sounded like you needed to get that out."

I didn't discuss these things with anyone. I didn't write them down. I just released them while I was onstage, but I knew that wasn't enough. "You're probably right."

"I know I'm nothing more than a stranger, but I want you to know, you can talk to me. Whatever you need, I'm here."

I searched his eyes. "Why am I getting your attention?"

"I like you," he said without hesitation. "There's something about you that I can't seem to get enough of." He traced the edge of the pie with his spoon. "I attended your play just so I could hear more of your voice and see what you looked like when you were in your element." He paused, and I felt something move into my throat. "I get the feeling you didn't want to tell me about Roxbury and that you weren't raised in a privileged life, like the majority of the kids at our school. The more you get to know me—and I hope you will—you'll learn that I don't give a shit about where you live or how much you have. I only care about what's in that chest of yours—and I'm talking about your heart, nothing else. You're one of the most intriguing and fascinating people I've ever met, Pearl. I'll keep attending plays if I have to. I just don't want this to be the last time I see you."

I smiled.

I couldn't help it.

Beneath this gorgeous man was someone so kind and genuine.

And that terrified me the most because those were traits I didn't see often, and they were ones I didn't want to let go of even though I had to.

"I can tell you're fighting something right now. Be honest with me—what is it?"

His ability to read me always came in fast and hard, taking ahold of my heart and shaking it.

"You're asking for something that I've never given to anyone."

"More of you, you mean?"

I nodded and brought the coffee up to my mouth, swallowing the warm liquid, hoping it would calm me. "I don't want to portray that I'm completely innocent because I'm not. There have been guys; I just don't let anything last. I know you're going to ask why ..." I glanced down, the boxes now close enough that they were rubbing against my skin. "Before I came to live with Gran, I was with Vanessa. That's my mother." The boxes were threatening to open; I didn't want that, especially not tonight. "I saw what she went through with men." I tried inhaling, and it was becoming so hard. "I won't let that happen to me. I just want to get Gran out of Roxbury and into a nice place in either LA or New York and create a new life for us."

He reached across the table, his hand surrounding mine. He held me with a strength that didn't hurt, but one that made me stare into his eyes. "I'm nothing like them." His thumb circled around and locked between two of my fingers. "I don't want to distract you from your goals. I want to encourage you to reach them."

I felt the tightness move into my throat as I whispered, "That's what scares me the most."

ELEVEN

BEFORE

ASHE

I hadn't thought it was possible to find a woman as beautiful on the inside as she was on the outside.

But that was Pearl.

Purging her fears over six slices of pie.

As I took in each layer she'd revealed to me, I was inspired to show her more—more flavors for her to taste and more restaurants for her to sample different cuisines, finding new foods to fall in love with. And the whole time, in the back of my mind, I couldn't stop thinking about the restrictions she had set.

There was only one way to get past them.

"I want to meet her," I said.

She'd been staring at her coffee, her hand gripping the mug with my fingers on top of hers—a grip I had no intention of releasing.

She finally looked up. "Who?"

"Your grandmother."

She shook her head. "I'm extremely protective of her."

"You think I'd hurt her?"

"No, Ashe." She turned silent for a moment. "I just don't let anyone have access to her."

I rubbed my thumb over the tops of her knuckles. "Maybe that will change the more you learn to trust me."

Within a few seconds, she was pulling her hand away, lifting the spoon to finish the rest of the peanut butter slice. "You seem pretty confident you're going to break through my boundaries."

"I just know who I am, Pearl. I know what I can offer you. And I know you don't believe this yet, but I'm not like all the others."

"You're right; I don't believe it because no man—especially one as good-looking as you—is trustworthy."

I laughed.

Her stare started at my forehead, gradually lowering to my chin. "You're a lethal combination. If I were smart, I'd push myself out of this booth and flee for the door."

This time, I gripped her wrist, a part that felt so delicate as I rubbed the inside. "You never have to run when you're with me."

As she gazed down, she rested the spoon on the edge of the plate. "Thank you for coming tonight. Gran is the only person in my life who has ever shown up to anything ... aside from you."

"That's going to change." I grinned as I thought of Dylan sitting beside me during her next play. "You're now going to have a whole cheering section—as long as you're okay with that."

I watched her take several deep breaths.

"Honestly, I don't know what I'm okay with. This is a lot."

"We'll go as slow as you want."

"That's still very confident of you to say." She turned silent as she looked at the leftover pie, and then she drained the rest of her coffee before she added, "I really should go."

She'd given me more time and insight than I'd expected from her tonight, so I called over the waitress and asked for some boxes and two coffees to go. Before she left to grab my requests, I told her to hold on, and I glanced at Pearl.

"What's Gran's favorite flavor of pie?"

She shrugged. "I don't know if she's had any besides pumpkin."

"We'll also take a slice of peanut butter to go."

Pearl waited for the waitress to leave before she said, "You're too much."

"This is just who I am—you'll see." I pointed at the half-eaten plates. "You should bring home all the leftovers too."

"You're sure?"

"Positive."

The waitress returned with several Styrofoam containers, and I helped Pearl pack it all up into the plastic bag the waitress had left for us when she brought our coffees and the check.

I handed the waitress my credit card as Pearl said, "Thank you." The warmest smile reached her eyes. "For dragging me out and forcing me to celebrate—something I don't normally do. And for taking me here and stuffing me full of dessert." She held the box that contained Gran's slice. "For this too. It means the most."

"You're welcome." I knew my grin matched hers. "You'll have to let me know if she likes it."

"I promise she will love it."

I signed the credit card slip, and we got up and went outside. Standing by the door, she looked in both directions of the street, as though she was getting her bearings.

"Can I walk you home?"

Her eyes returned to me. "No."

I had known it was a long shot, but it was still worth a try. "Then, I'll walk you to the train station."

She didn't respond; she just started moving in the direction of the orange line. After several steps, she broke the silence. "I did all the talking tonight; you didn't even get a chance to tell me more about yourself."

I chuckled. "There isn't really much to tell."

"I find that hard to believe. Answer these questions for me ..." She paused to take a drink of her coffee. "What's your thing —you know, aside from medicine? What's your ugliest scar, and when was the last time you cried?"

We approached a crosswalk, and I looked down at the top of her head. It reached the center of my chest, the perfect placement to bend my neck just slightly and kiss her.

But I kept my hands and my mouth to myself and replied, "Even your questions are interesting."

"I'm not the kind of girl who wants to know the obvious."

"I'm still learning what kind of girl you are, but I assure you, it's a type I've never met before." The signal changed, and we crossed the intersection. "I'm a lover of sports, and I played football in high school. I was an all-state wide receiver." When we got to an area where we could stop, I pulled up the leg of my jeans, showing her the scar on my knee. "Tore my meniscus and fractured my tibia during a game my senior year."

"Were you going to play football in college?"

"I was recruited by a few Division II schools, but none of them had premed, and that meant more to me than being a college athlete."

"Whoa." She adjusted her purse, balancing the bag of pies and coffee in her other hand. "That couldn't have been an easy choice."

"Giving up a full scholarship? No." I looked toward the end of the block, focusing on the street sign as I continued, "But what was much tougher was seeing my dad in the hospital. Three years ago, the doctors had found a tumor on his kidney. It was caught in time, but there were some major complications that followed his surgery, and things got pretty rough there for a couple of weeks."

I didn't have to tell her that was where the tears had come in; I was sure she could read that on my face.

"I'm so sorry, Ashe. How's he doing now?"

"All good." I took a drink from my coffee. "He plays tennis every day in the summer and hits up the gym in the winter. He's probably in the best shape of his life now."

Her eyes softened. "A wonderful epilogue." The only time I had seen that look was when she was talking about her grand-mother. "Siblings?"

"I have two older sisters."

"That explains everything."

I laughed at her tone. "What does that mean?"

"You're used to being around women; that's why you're sensitive to them."

"I thought you were going to say I was a mama's boy, and I was going to fight you on that one."

"No, I don't sense that at all. You seem extremely indepen-dent." She stopped as we approached another crosswalk. "Is anyone in your family a doctor? I'm curious where your passion for medicine comes in."

"Just me." The lights from the train station were up ahead —a sign that I was running out of time. "I was born with this desire to save people, getting in and finding the problem and fixing it. It's all I've ever wanted."

"And you're making it happen."

"I have to survive premed first, and I'll admit, it's kicking my ass." The light changed, and we began walking again.

"MCATs will be next, and that score, along with my grades, will determine which med school accepts me."

"What's your top pick?"

"Johns Hopkins. It's a pipe dream, but, man, I'd love to go there. Harvard and UPenn are on my short list as well."

"There's no doubt in my mind that you'll be attending one of the three."

I slowed my pace. "You certainly have a lot of confidence in me."

She glanced at me, gazing through her lashes. "You don't stop fighting until you get what you want. Tonight is proof of that." Now that we'd arrived, she turned around, putting her back to the entrance. "I appreciate you walking me here."

"When can I see you again?"

"I don't know ..." She broke our eye contact, telling me how hard this was for her.

When they're fast on their feet, they want to be chased.

"You can trust me," I said, repeating the words I'd said earlier, and I opened the top of her school bag, finding a pen clipped to the side. I grabbed it, and since I didn't have a piece of paper, I held it against my palm. "What's your number?"

She was reluctant—that much was obvious—her stare moving from my face to my hand and back. Eventually, she rattled off each digit, adding, "Sunday is my only night off. Otherwise, I'm usually out the door by eight in the morning, and I don't get back until after work. Keep that in mind before you call."

"I'll find you. I'm not worried." I slipped the pen back in her bag, and my hand moved to her waist, gently grazing it as I leaned in closer to press my lips against her cheek. Her skin was so fucking soft; the scent of cinnamon was extremely strong, and I remembered it from the whiff I'd gotten in the hallway. I kept my mouth on her for a second longer and pulled back. "Get home safely."

Her cheeks were now a deep red, and she turned once again, giving me her back to hurry down the steps of the underground station.

I watched until she disappeared around the corner, her feet practically running.

TWELVE

AFTER

ASHE

I followed the police sergeant's instructions, heading toward Commonwealth Avenue, and I was more than a block away when I saw the police lights flashing up ahead. The building, like the others on this street, was higher end with a doorman that required a full check-in process before anyone entered the elevator, where Jane Doe had been found.

The lobby was taped off. Officers were swarming the area, and onlookers and several news reporters with cameramen were trying to catch a glimpse of what was happening inside.

I flashed my badge at a group of officers who were standing guard and ducked below the tape, showing my identification once more to get through the lobby door. I immediately noticed the doorman off to the side, getting interviewed, several residents going through the same thing as they stood in different sections of the large, open space.

The door to the elevator was open, a forensic analyst inside. His collection bags were spread out on the floor, where he would make sure every inch of the interior was dusted for DNA.

"Flynn," I said to him as he knelt next to the sheet-covered body. I waited for him to look at me before I added, "I'm the lead detective on the case. Tell me everything you've found so far."

"The doorman discovered her about an hour ago and called 911. The elevator door had opened in the lobby, and her blood had come trickling out. The doorman said she's not a resident and that she hadn't come here during his shift, but he's only been on for a couple of hours. I'm sure there's a call into the employee who was on before him."

I stood in the entryway, making sure my feet didn't cross the threshold. "Any word on the cameras?"

"Rumor is, they haven't been working for twenty-four hours. The whole system is down, and a tech was supposed to come this morning to get it back online. I guess he hasn't shown yet."

"Coincidence or premeditated?"

"You know this business, Detective. A case could be made for both."

There was commotion behind me, and as I turned around, a set of reporters was getting too close to the glass door and being escorted away.

I faced the elevator again and said, "Talk to me about Jane Doe."

He pulled the sheet back, showing me her face and auburn hair, and I mentally scanned the department's database, not recognizing either.

When I nodded, he returned the sheet to where it had been and said, "Ms. Doe was shot in the clavicle. She didn't have a purse on her, and there's no major identifiable marks from what I can tell so far. We'll run her prints when I get to the station."

"Let me know the second you find anything."

I was just taking a step back when he said, "There is something you should know, Detective." He grabbed the middle of the covering and moved it over the side of her body.

What was revealed was a sight that I would see when I closed my eyes tonight. I never saw the cases that ended happily, the ones where justice was found. It was the horrific, gruesome ones that kept me up at night.

Like this one.

I ran my hand through my hair. "Fuck me."

"If I had to guess, she was about twenty weeks along."

THIRTEEN

BEFORE

PEARL

I sat in the corner of the train, the rattling of the undercarriage shaking me in my seat. The bag of leftover pies was on my lap, and I lifted the corner of one of the to-go containers, picking off a piece of the crust. It was as delicious as it had been moments ago when Ashe and I shared the slice at the diner. Buttery. Flaky. Nothing like the store-bought pumpkin pie I'd been buying for the last few holidays since Gran could no longer bake.

I took one more bite and shut the lid, holding the bag close to my body. As I chewed, only one thought was in my mind.

Ashe.

He was like a rainstorm that came through the city in the middle of winter, the precipitation and thunder so untimely for that season. I'd hidden from storms my entire life, never going outside to let the water fall on me.

Tonight had caught me by such a surprise, and even though I had wanted to run many times, I hadn't. I'd felt each drip, my hair getting soaked.

But I'd enjoyed myself.

I'd even smiled more than once.

One was even growing over my face now as I pressed my hand against the cheek he'd kissed, the spot still warm, as though his lips had just left.

Just as I was pulling my fingers away, "Ruggles Station," was announced through the loudspeaker.

Once the train stopped and the door opened, I rose from my seat and moved across the platform and out onto the sidewalk in front.

Unless it was the very early hours of the morning, this section of Roxbury was always busy. Groups were huddled in doorways, on the benches, and in some cases, even in the middle of the street. I'd spent half my life in this neighborhood, walking back and forth to the train and the grocery store, that so many of the groups knew my face. They knew I wasn't a prostitute or an addict trying to score. I was just a girl trying to get home after a long day. Aside from some whistling and catcalling, which happened almost every night, I was able to get to our building, unbothered.

I opened our apartment door only a few inches when I heard, "Hi, dollface," from the living room.

I set both bags and my coffee on the counter and took the seat next to Gran on the couch. "How was your day?" I asked, kissing her cheek.

"My day?" She grinned and reached for my face. "No, baby, how was yours? Tell me all about tonight's performance."

My hands wrapped around the top of her arm, her scent filling me as I rested against her shoulder. I didn't need the comfort—not tonight—but this spot certainly gave me that. I had fallen asleep in this exact position more times than I could count.

"It went great. Everyone, for the most part, made their cues, and the audience was so attentive and complimentary.

Wardrobe worked extra hard to assist us with each change, and the lighting and set crews were outstanding. It went smoother than the show you had seen on opening night."

With her hand still on me, she turned my chin, so I was gazing at her. "You look and sound happier tonight—happier than you have been in a long time." She rubbed my cheek, and I felt her bent fingers, her pain too intense to straighten them.

Instead of commenting, I asked, "Are you hungry, Gran?"

"No, dollface."

"Not even for something sweet?"

She continued to stare at me, her wrinkled lids hanging over her eyes. "You brought home dessert? That's not like you."

I went into the kitchen, lifting the bags of pies I had left on the counter, and opened each of the lids until I found the slice of peanut butter. I grabbed a spoon and brought it over to her.

"Look at how beautiful this is." She stared at it from her lap.

"How about some tea to go with it?"

"I would love that."

Since the microwave had died a few days ago and I still didn't have the cash to replace it, I went into the kitchen and filled up a small saucepan with water from the sink and put it on the stove to boil. I took it off just when the bubbles began to form and filled a mug, dropping a tea bag inside. I picked up the leftover slice of peach and my coffee and joined her on the couch.

"Where did you get all of this?" she asked.

"A friend took me out to celebrate after the show." I pointed at the bag in the kitchen. "There are more leftovers in there, but that slice"—I nodded toward her lap—"is the only full piece." I smiled, the peach crumbling over my tongue. I covered my mouth as I continued, "They asked what kind you would like. My guess was peanut butter, so they bought this one just for you."

"What a wonderful treat." She dipped in her spoon, her hand shaking as she raised it to her mouth. Small crumbs fell off the sides of the metal as she surrounded the pie with her lips. Her eyes closed as she chewed, taking her time to savor the small bite. "Oh, it's heavenly." She took in several more spoonfuls before she voiced, "Dollface, would this friend happen to be a man?"

"Yes."

The excitement in her expression was undeniable. "Honey ..."

I shook my head. "Gran, it's nothing—"

"Don't you downplay it." Her hand went to my knee. "The minute you walked into this house, I saw something was different about you. I know you're afraid, baby, but don't be."

I stared at the sliver of peach, the tightness in my chest taking over. "I don't want to be like her."

"You're nothing like her, and you won't ever be."

Vanessa was Gran's only child, the father a man who was never spoken about—the same way my father had never been identified. Maybe they didn't know whom those men were; maybe they were too ashamed to admit whom they were. Whatever their reasoning was, I hadn't pushed either of the women for an answer. And even though Vanessa was Gran's daughter, I never hid my feelings, and she didn't with me—a pact we had made when I moved in.

"But, Gran, all I ever saw was men controlling her. From the moment she had me at sixteen and every day that followed, it never stopped. Even now, while she's behind bars, they send her money and smuggle drugs in for her."

She took the straw out of her water and set it into her tea, taking a short sip. "Dollface, finding someone to enjoy things with is not going to lead you down the same path. I know you don't want to be like your mother, but you also don't want to be my age and be alone, like me."

I set the pie on the table, unable to take another bite. "I can't afford the distraction." I glanced at her, and the emotion in her eyes caused this to hurt even worse. "I have so many goals for us, places I want to take you. I won't accomplish any of that if I'm tied down."

"Baby, love doesn't shackle you; it makes you fly. And if I know you, you wouldn't spend time with someone who would lock you in a cage. You'd be with a man who would fasten stronger wings to your back and point you in the direction of the sun."

Many of her words were the same ones Ashe had said. Still, right now, his were only syllables. He needed to prove they were true before I trusted him.

"There's a chance he could be a good one, Gran."

She emptied another bite into her mouth, her eyes closing once again as she enjoyed it. "If he was thoughtful enough to buy this for me, then I would say he's off to a good start."

FOURTEEN

AFTER

ASHE

"Congrats, my man," Dylan said, holding out his tumbler of whiskey, clinking it against mine. "You worked your ass off on this case. Having the murderer in custody must feel good as hell."

Dylan had been after me for weeks to go on a guys' trip, but I'd been in the thick of the Mitchell case, and I couldn't get out of town.

Once the handwriting on that note had proven to be Keith Simpson's and his DNA had been found inside Mitchell's body the night she died, things had begun to get interesting. The problem was that Barbara Simpson had an alibi for the hours following the charity event, and it took some time to crack the truth. What helped was the traffic camera on the cross street of Mitchell's townhouse, putting Simpson there at the time of Mitchell's murder, along with the polygraph we conducted on the gentleman who had claimed to be with Simpson late that evening, which showed he had lied. Simpson had hired one of the best criminal defense attorneys in the state, but the evidence I'd gathered and turned over to the district attorney was more than sufficient.

Simpson was going to jail; it was just a matter of how much time she would spend in there.

"I just hope the commonwealth will put her away for life," I replied. "That woman is one evil bitch, and the more evidence I found, the worse of a friend she'd proven to be."

"Aren't I one lucky motherfucker to have the best one?"

"I'll cheers to that."

We banged glasses again while Dylan said, "But, fuck, getting you out of town is as hard as dragging my fiancée away." He sighed. "You're drowning in cases; Alix is married to an ambulance. Who would have ever thought I would be the more flexible one?"

Dylan had been a serial dater until he met Alix in a restaurant one evening while he was sharing a meal with another woman. From that moment, she had become his world and the best thing that had ever happened to him. As a paramedic for Boston, she worked as much as me. That was the problem with our jobs—depending on how ugly things got, our shifts often became blurred, and hours turned into days.

"Drag her onto the plane like you did to me this morning. That's one way to get her to call in."

He laughed as he looked at me. "You think I haven't tried that? I was successful the first few times, but she's starting to outsmart me."

"God, I like that girl."

We chuckled, and I glanced behind my seat. There was a screen built into the wall that showed the distance we'd traveled and how many more miles we had until we reached our destination. We were only thirty minutes in and had a long way to go. If I kept up this drinking, I wasn't going to remember the landing.

CHAPTER 14

Fuck it.

I emptied my glass, and before I even set it down, Dylan's flight attendant appeared to fill it back up.

I was just starting to see double when I said, "Where are we going again?"

"Miami." He extended his legs across the small built-in ottoman in front of him. "I need some heat. I've had enough of winter."

"Did I pack shorts?"

Last night, Dylan and I had stopped at one of our favorite restaurants for dinner, followed by a bar—or three. That was when things had started to get fuzzy, and now that we were flying south, I couldn't recall if I'd gone back to my place to grab clothes.

"If you didn't, we'll buy you some when we get there."

With my hand wrapped around the glass, I reclined the seat, extending my legs in the same position as Dylan's. "Damn it, I needed this getaway."

"You've been putting in so many hours. I haven't seen you in fucking forever."

I turned my head toward him. "And you haven't been?"

"The king of deflecting."

I laughed, the whiskey aiding with that. "Every time I call, you're at the office or in the air. We both have our reasoning even if they're different."

I shifted once more to look out the window, seeing the clouds floating underneath us. We were so close that it felt like I could reach out and touch one.

There had been moments, not too long ago, when I would have tried.

"You want to tell me what's on your mind?"

I faced my best friend, holding the booze close to my lips. "Same shit, different day."

He nodded.
Because he knew.

FIFTEEN

BEFORE

ASHE

Only a day had passed since I'd watched Pearl's play, and instead of giving her a call, I decided to do something even better. That afternoon, I waited outside her classroom, the same spot where she had crashed into me. I made sure to arrive a few minutes before her class ended in case they were let out early. But as she had told me at the diner, she always stayed after to speak to the professor, and today was no different. A large crowd of students hurried out first, and she was the last one to leave.

"Hey, Pearl," I said as she came through the door, her attention focused on her notebook.

She looked up at the sound of her name, a smile filling her face once she realized it was me. "Hi."

I stepped closer to her, instantly smelling the cinnamon, remembering how perfect that scent had been when I kissed her cheek. "I take it, you got home safely?"

She nodded. "And Gran loved the peanut butter pie." Her hands lifted to the strap of her bag, gripping it between both palms. "She ate the entire thing. I couldn't believe it. She normally eats like a bird."

"That makes me happy to hear."

"She's very appreciative, and she wants me to thank you."

I read her eyes as I asked, "You told her about me?"

Her fingers suddenly tightened, knuckles turning white. "I mentioned you, yes."

I rested my hand on her shoulder, trying to loosen her up. "That's all you're going to tell me?" I shook her a little and winked. "Come on, Pearl ..."

She started to laugh, and it hit me that she wasn't uncomfortable; she was just in unfamiliar territory. She couldn't act her way through this scene, her emotions making her slightly fidgety. Along with bringing me up to Gran, I would take that as a good sign.

"You don't have to answer that," I said, lowering my hand to her waist, my placement gentle. "Answer this instead: what are you doing right now?"

She looked at her watch, buying herself a few seconds and giving me time to check her out. With her jacket unzipped, her shirt hugged her perfectly sized tits, and the style of her jeans revealed her long, lean legs. I would do anything to turn her around to see the tightness of her ass, but I kept my hand where it was.

Her eyes returned to mine as she said, "I'm headed to the library to study for a bit before I have to report to the auditorium."

"You have another show tonight?"

"Every day this week, and on Monday, we start rehearsals for the next play."

As she spoke, I started to plan my next move. "How much time before you have to be at the auditorium?"

"About three hours."

"Are you hungry?"

She nodded toward her bag. "I have some crackers in there that I'm going to eat."

With how long her days were, I wasn't surprised she had brought food, but crackers wouldn't do.

I slung my arm over her shoulders, leaving it there while I walked her toward the stairwell. "What are your thoughts on cake?"

The sound of her laugh was so honest and raw but light at the same time. "Gran used to make me one for my birthday. Vanilla with vanilla icing. But that stopped years ago, and I don't know if I've had cake since."

"Vanilla is your favorite?" I opened the door, and we entered the stairwell.

"I know what you're up to, Ashe." She grinned. "Would you let me get away with saying studying is my favorite and that's what I need to be doing right now?"

I smiled. "No."

"I figured." She paused for a moment. "You know, I think vanilla might be the only flavor I've had."

"What?" I tightened my arm, pulling her a little closer as I whispered, "I'm about to change your whole world."

We got to the first step, and even though she was glancing straight ahead, the emotion was clear on her face. "I think you already have."

"I'm so full; I feel like I could explode," Pearl groaned.

There were four half-eaten slices of cake in front of her. This time, chocolate, peanut butter, vanilla raspberry, and lemon blueberry were the flavors I had ordered, following a meal of grilled cheese and tomato soup. Every time she stepped

71

on that stage tonight and felt the fullness in her stomach, I wanted her to think of me.

"And I'm pretty sure I could take the longest nap ever." She yawned.

I checked my watch. She still had two hours before she had to be at the auditorium.

"I can make that happen. You know I'm right off campus. We can go to my place, and then I'll walk you back to school." I watched her process my suggestion. "I'm not going to try anything, Pearl. I've told you, you can trust me."

"That's not what I'm worried about." She set down her fork, chewing her lip, like it was more dessert. "I'm afraid that I'll keep enjoying every second I spend with you."

"That sounds like a good problem to have."

"Not to someone who's anti-relationships." She took a breath and held it in. "I'm also afraid that before I know it, I'll be making you a priority, and everything I've built will crumble away."

When I went to comment, she reached across the table, putting her hand on my forearm to stop me. I couldn't help but note that this was the first time she had touched me.

"But when I mentioned all of my fears to Gran, she told me to give you a chance. She would never say that unless she truly believed it." She looked down at the chunk of lemon icing on her fork. "Sounds silly, but I think I needed to hear her say that before I ruined something that has the potential to be one of the most beautiful things that's ever happened to me."

I wanted to pull her against me and wrap my arms around her, but she was on the other side of the table, so I squeezed her fingers instead. "I won't let you lose sight of your dreams, I promise you."

"You'd better not."

I lifted my fork, dunking it into the peanut butter frosting, and I reached across the table, wiping it on the tip of her nose.

"Ashe!" She laughed.

That was the only sound I ever wanted to hear.

"Let's get out of here. Are you ready?"

She scraped it off with her finger and stuck the sugary bite into her mouth. "Yes."

SIXTEEN

BEFORE

PEARL

The last time I had been at Ashe's apartment, I'd noticed hints of details. A sports-related something on the wall and a worn couch that was extremely comfy. Now, as I entered again, I made sure to memorize each piece that made up his home. The wall art, I learned, were signed jerseys that were framed, same with the helmets that were in glass boxes above the TV. The couch was navy and corduroy, pillows in the corners, dented from where heads had been lying.

He took me into the kitchen, dropping off the leftover cake, and I noticed the dishes in the sink and the open silverware drawer. The pantry door was ajar, the shelves full of bagged chips and boxes of macaroni and cheese. There was a basket of dirty clothes on the side of the living room and a pizza box sitting on top of the trash bin.

And all of it looked so perfect to me.

"Are you hungry?"

I laughed, pushing my back against the counter. "You're kidding, right?" I played with the container of cake, the movement sending me a whiff of the sweetness inside. "I don't think I'll be hungry for days."

He grabbed a glass from the cupboard next to me and brushed his fingers across my chin—a quiet, subtle move but one that sent goose bumps down my back. Then, he filled the glass with water, offering me some, which I declined, before he took a long drink.

How do you have this effect on me so quickly?

Why is it so hard to breathe when your eyes are on me?

Questions filled my brain.

So did his kindness, gentleness, sincerity—all unlike anything I'd ever felt. They were qualities that came so natural to him, like he wasn't trying at all—this was just who he was.

"Are you ready for a nap?" When I nodded, he added, "You know the way," and he pointed at his door but didn't move. "I'll take the couch."

I briefly remembered his big, wonderful bed that had lots of pillows, unlike mine at home. "No, Ashe ..." I tried to breathe again and couldn't as I said, "I want you to join me."

"You're sure about that?" He stood close, his hand coming to my face again, holding me steady.

I wondered if he could feel me trembling, if he could hear my heart pounding, if he could smell the sweat that was starting to bead over my skin.

Once he received my answer, his fingers found mine, and he led me to his bed. As I sat on his cozy mattress, it took me a moment to realize I hadn't voiced that answer. He had just seen it in me and known.

I'd watched that happen in movies. I'd read about it in books. I'd acted it out onstage.

But it was never something I had experienced, and I'd never thought I would.

Yet here was a glimpse.

And I wanted more.

I took off my shoes and jacket, and I rested my head on the pillow. As Ashe crawled onto the other side, he pulled the blanket over us.

"Wow, this is comfy," I groaned, every part of me sinking into fluff.

I sensed his eyes on me as I wiggled, testing to see if each spot felt the same. It did, and it was heavenly. I wasn't sure I'd ever want to leave.

"You're adorable."

I turned to my side to look at him, tucking the pillow under my cheek.

"That smile ..." He held the other part of my face, his thumb tracing my bottom lip. "It's beautiful to see." His fingers stayed there for a moment more, and then he reached for his nightstand. "What time should I set the alarm for?"

I did some quick math in my head and responded, and he turned toward me again.

"What are you up to tonight?"

His handsomeness pressed into the pillow in almost the same position as me. "I have a paper due in the morning, so that's my fun for the night. I wish I could come watch you, but I know the tickets are sold out."

"How do you know that?"

I felt his stare turn even deeper, followed by a grin that I couldn't get enough of.

"Because I tried to buy one."

"But you've already seen the play."

"I wanted to watch you again." He paused, and my throat tightened. "One time wasn't enough."

I shook my head over the pillow, staring into his baby-blue eyes, emotion rippling in my chest. This was the start of something powerful—I could feel it in my bones. "What if I could get you a ticket?"

"I would be there in a second."

Last time, I hadn't known he was in the audience.

This time would be entirely different, and I wondered if I'd be able to feel him in the air.

"But you have a paper to write—"

His fingers strengthened on my face. "I'd drop you off at the auditorium, come back, get a good dent in it, and finish it before class if I have to."

"You're sure? I feel like a giant contradiction right now because I'm doing what I made you promise not to do."

"Please get me a ticket, Pearl." His eyes intensified. "I want nothing more than to see you perform again."

I waited for my throat to open, the air not moving as freely anymore, and I replied, "They always reserve a few extra seats for the cast's families. I'll leave the ticket at Will Call, just give them your name."

"I'm really looking forward to it. And ..." He swiped across my top lip with the pad of his finger. A slow, steady move that made me feel the warmth of his skin. "If Gran can't be there, then at least I will be."

His words hit me hard.

I swallowed each one, feeling them in my chest before they simmered through the rest of my body.

He stretched up to my hairline, his palm now on my cheek, his eyes pulling me so close that I felt as though I were on top of him.

"Ashe ..."

Inches only separated our lips, but I swore I could taste them.

"I'm doing everything I can to keep my distance, and I'm failing."

So sensitive, so concerned with what I needed.

But if he was reading me—and I knew he was—then he would know that wasn't what I wanted in this moment.

Maybe, in this instance, he needed my voice to tell him.

"I don't want distance. I want your closeness."

His thumb paused in the center of my lips, and his eyes dipped, staring at them. Heat from his body filtered directly into mine.

"Once I kiss you, Pearl ... I don't know if I'll be able to stop."

SEVENTEEN

BEFORE

ASHE

"Ashe ... kiss me," Pearl whispered from the pillow next to mine.

I knew she wasn't fragile and that my lips wouldn't be the first to press against hers. But even though the desire to rip off her clothes and give her an orgasm was pulsing through me, I wanted to take my time. Pearl deserved to be savored, to receive equal attention to each of her curves, for my mouth to make her feel as good as my body could.

And I would do all of that.

It just wasn't going to happen today.

I surrounded her face with both of my hands and leaned in closer, holding her stare until our lids finally shut. When I couldn't hold off a second longer, I filled my lungs to capacity and closed the space between us, gently kissing her. I tasted the sweetness of the cake, the lemon and blueberry. The hint of cinnamon was there, too, wafting from her skin—a scent I now only associated with her.

The pressure of my mouth caused her lips to part, and I turned my face, fitting us together like a puzzle, our tongues quietly touching. The sound of her exhale told me her body was as worked up as mine, that she wanted to feel more than my hands clinging to her face. So did her response when I pressed my chest to hers and scissored our legs, tangling us into a knot.

While my tongue slid over hers, my hand dipped to her neck, her softness taking ahold of me, and I slowly crawled to her side. I stayed there, brushing my thumb back and forth until the bottom of her shirt lifted and I hit skin.

Her breath hitched as my fingers moved beneath the thin material.

If I had thought her neck was the smoothest I'd ever touched, her skin felt like velvet down here. And each inch I swiped, her breathing changed, and her kiss deepened.

I rose higher until I felt the wire under her bra, my thumb tracing the lace.

Every one of her exhales ended in a moan, especially when I skimmed across her nipple. The hardness formed a peak, and I grazed over it, cupping her tit in my palm.

I'd seen hints of her body in her work outfit, but I hadn't expected her to feel so perfect in my hands. How each bit of her that I felt caused my dick to throb, growing harder to the point where I thought it would burst through my jeans.

Her breaths were vibrating through me, the taste of her on my tongue and the feel of her pressed against me becoming too much to bear.

With all the strength I had left, I pulled back, pressing my nose to hers. I panted while my lungs screamed, my body aching for more. I gripped her waist, holding her steady, waiting for this sensation to calm down.

When I leaned back a little more, I saw the same fight in her. The same breathlessness. The same need, churning like a thunderstorm.

CHAPTER 17

Pearl ...

In that moment, I knew I'd done the right thing.

Diving my face between her legs wasn't going to get her to trust me. She needed to know I was different. That I was here for a reason that had nothing to do with her body.

My actions were the only thing that would show her that.

I pulled her shirt down until it was in line with her jeans, and I flipped her around, hauling her back against my chest, wrapping my arm around her. I tucked my face into her neck, and I took in her scent as I held our bodies together.

"Sleep well, Pearl."

"You ... too."

It took her several minutes to relax, but the tightness eventually left her, and the moment her breathing changed, I knew she was asleep.

My alarm wasn't going off for an hour, and for the next sixty minutes, I had no intention of letting her go.

EIGHTEEN

KERRY

The blindfold took my vision away. Something rough and ball-like had been shoved into my mouth, stopping me from screaming. My hands were tightly tied behind my back, the rope burning my skin.

All I wanted was to see.

Yell.

Use my hands to rip and claw.

And fight.

But I had been plucked off the street and thrown inside a vehicle.

The feel of the road, normally something that soothed me, felt like needles stabbing beneath my nails. Each bump made it even harder to breathe. Tears dripped, soaking my cheeks, as anxiety gnawed at the rest of my body.

Who is this man?

Why did he abduct me?

Where the fuck is he taking me?

And how the hell do I get out of here?

One minute, I had been walking to grab a snack from the

twenty-four-hour bodega down the street. The next thing I knew, something was placed over my mouth, stopping me from shouting, and I was being lifted into the air and tossed inside the back of a van.

That was when he had taken my sight away and shackled me.

When my senses were suddenly on overdrive.

Fear was eating at me, as though I'd never fed it any food before.

I kicked what I thought was the door, wishing for it to open, but it didn't budge. I kicked again, wiggling to the other side to try that wall, and turned more to attempt again. Something had to open. To pop. For a burst of light or air to rush through.

But nothing.

Just the steady hum of the road.

I didn't know how far we had gone—seconds felt like years —but there was slowness.

And then a stop.

I sucked in a breath as the engine turned off. A car door quietly opened and shut. Feet softly shuffled across what sounded like pavement. Keys jingled as they hit together, and finally, there was the swish of air I'd been waiting for.

But it had come because of him, not from me.

My body tightened as I waited for what was going to happen next.

"Kerry ..." His voice was like a cough, a hundred packs of cigarettes burning the back of his throat.

I'd never heard him before tonight, but I still tried to place him, digging through my memory. For a time. A place.

"My sweet, beautiful Kerry ..."

Tears soaked in through my lips, my mouth now filled and salty. Even my fingernails were quivering, as though they were loose in my fingers.

A sob came shuddering through me, escaping whatever he had placed in my mouth, and something hard and relentless slapped my face. When it happened a second time, I realized it was his hand. Skin on skin. A movement that created even more agony.

My cheek felt like it had been lit on fire.

Right before another sob had the chance to form, he was gripping my face, his fingers like clamps, holding me as though I were corn on the cob, pressing so hard that my teeth ached.

"Never speak unless I give you permission. Understood?" When I went to make a sound, he pushed even harder on my cheeks. "Asking you a question is not permission. Nod your head, Kerry."

He was even taking away my voice.

I didn't know what I was agreeing to, but I didn't want to get slapped again. I didn't want to be hurt in any other way. I just wanted him to let me go, and maybe this was the first step to make that happen.

I nodded.

"I'm going to carry you out of this van, and if you make a sound, I'm going to knock out every single one of those pretty teeth. I won't repeat myself. Nod your head if you understand."

Why do his threats sound so permanent?

Where the hell is he carrying me to?

I was holding back the sobs, but they were ravaging the inside of my body.

And I was holding back the urge to fight because my feet could only get me so far, and I needed my eyes and hands to get past him.

I nodded.

"Now, it's time to go to your new home."

NINETEEN

PEARL

A t the sound of the phone, I backed up from the stovetop, and without looking, I reached for the wall where it hung, holding the receiver to my ear. "Hello?"

"Hey, it's Ashe."

"Hi." I twirled the long plastic cord between my fingers, keeping an eye on the pot to make sure Gran's oatmeal didn't bubble over.

"How'd you sleep?"

I brushed the center of my lips, the feel of him still there even though it had been hours since he'd dropped me off at the train station following my performance. "Pretty great, you?"

"I was up all night, finishing my paper."

"Ashe—"

"I wouldn't change a thing." I could hear him smiling. "I know I told you this after your play, but, Pearl, you were incredible."

His words caused my cheeks to turn hot, the same way they had when he handed me a bouquet of flowers outside the auditorium. When I'd gotten home, I'd cut the stems to make them fit in a glass and placed them on the counter. And when I had gone to bed, I could still see his grinning face in the audience as the lights onstage dimmed, no longer blinding me, as he stood, clapping, while I took my final bow.

No one had ever bought me flowers before. The bunch of blues and purples and pinks were some of the most beautiful I'd ever seen. I hadn't known what to say when he gave them to me. I was still at a loss for words as I stared at them now.

"Thank you." I quickly looked in on Gran and saw her reading on the couch. "And for the flowers too—again. They're stunning. Ashe, I love them."

"You're welcome." He paused, and I stretched the cord to the stovetop to give Gran's breakfast a final stir. "I know things are crazy for you while you wrap up the play, but I want to see you. Tell me when you can make that happen."

I poured the oatmeal into a bowl, the steam telling me it was too hot to give to Gran. "How about Sunday night?"

"Does that mean I can have you until Monday morning?"

The moments we'd spent in his bed had been replaying in my mind. How difficult it had been to keep my hands off him, how different he had felt compared to the other men I'd kissed. Even his lips were more intimate.

"Yes," I answered, pushing myself into the corner of the counter.

"What about Gran?"

I turned, looking at her again through the cutout above the sink.

I'd left her before—she didn't require around-the-clock care —but I had just worried the whole time I was gone. The thought of her falling in the middle of the night, the idea of her being lonely—my heart couldn't handle either.

"I think she'll be okay, but we'll see."

"I understand, Pearl, and I support whatever you need to do."

That was something I liked the most about him—he really did understand, and he was always so concerned and thoughtful when it came to her.

My voice was only above a whisper when I said, "I really appreciate that."

"I'll see you Sunday night, then?"

I rinsed out the pot and added water to boil for her tea. "Yes, you will."

"How about I pick you up at your place?"

I dropped a tea bag into an empty cup, my hand freezing around the base of it. That was one thing I just wasn't ready for yet. "I'll meet you at your apartment, okay?"

"You got it."

We said good-bye and hung up, and I brought the oatmeal into the living room, setting it on the table in front of Gran. "Your tea is almost ready, just a few more minutes."

She picked up the spoon, trying to find a comfortable grip, changing it several times before she settled. "Thank you, doll-face. How's Ashe?"

I laughed. I couldn't hide a thing from her.

She patted the spot next to her, and I took a seat, watching her move the bowl onto her lap.

"He's doing fine," I answered. "He was calling to see if I had time to get together."

"And?"

There was a clean napkin on the table, and I lifted the oatmeal and placed the napkin underneath it, so if any spilled, it wouldn't burn her. "I'm seeing him Sunday night."

"I'm proud of you, baby." Her hand moved on top of mine, tapping my fingers. "I know this has been a bit difficult for you, but you're doing the right thing." She smiled, the lines around her mouth deepening. "And those flowers are just beautiful."

"Aren't they?" I grinned.

"You deserve to be courted, and that Ashe is doing a fine job."

I didn't disagree.

"Be right back," I said, hurrying into the kitchen to finish her tea. I plopped a straw into the mug before I brought it out to her. "Careful, Gran. This is really hot." I placed it on the table.

As I sat, her hand cupped my cheek. "You keep me fighting, dollface. Every day I spend on this earth is because of you." Her baby-powder scent strengthened the longer she touched me, only adding to the sentiment in my chest. "Maybe one day, when your children are grown, you'll be able to see all the things you've done for me and realize how amazing you are."

I turned my face, kissing her palm. "I wouldn't have it any other way, Gran."

Emotion moved into her eyes. "Get off to school. I don't want you to be late."

"Can I get you anything before I leave?"

"I have everything I need right here."

I released her fingers and stood. "I'll be back after the play tonight."

"I'll be fine," she said as I rushed into the hallway to grab my bag from my room. "Just like I'll be on Sunday when you stay at Ashe's."

Her hearing wasn't perfect, so I was surprised she'd been able to piece together what Ashe and I had spoken about.

"Gran ..." I said when I returned to the living room, wearing my jacket, my bag hanging from my shoulder.

"Don't you *Gran* me, missy." She took a bite of her breakfast, the look on her face emphasizing her words. "I want you to go out and have fun and not worry about me."

"That's impossible. I'll always worry about you."

"Pearl"—she set the spoon into the bowl—"one day, you're going to be old, like me, and you won't be able to get these years back. I won't let you live with regret, do you hear me? So, go out and have fun and enjoy yourself and laugh. Go run those feet around the city and kiss in the rain and hopscotch over the puddles—things I can't do anymore. Be a kid—that's all I'm asking—and don't miss out on life because of me."

"I'm not missing anything because of you." I walked back over, sitting so I could be close to her. "You make everything better, Gran."

Her hand returned to my leg. "Promise me."

I clasped my fingers over hers, her skin always so cold. "Promise."

She puckered her lips together—an expression she used to call her kissy face when I was younger.

I leaned in and smooched her cheek. "I'll see you tonight."

"I love you, baby."

TWENTY

KERRY

Where are you taking me?
Those were the words I wanted to scream when his vile hands reached inside the van, clamping my hips and pulling me. Once my butt hit the end, he picked me up. My stomach dropped as it felt like he tossed me over his shoulder.

But I couldn't shout.

Or see.

Or protect myself with my hands—they were still roped behind my back.

My hearing was the only sense that wasn't restricted, and I took in every noise until he placed something over my bent body.

Heavy, scratchy.

Like a wool blanket.

And it shut off the night air and the subtle sounds, and I could only hear the louder ones.

Tears continued to stream from my eyes as I hung upside down, the blood rushing to my head only making it worse.

I hit the back of his thigh after each step, the ache in my stomach bubbling.

The anxiety building.

The desire to kick him with my feet was so strong, but I had to force myself not to.

I counted the steps. On the ninth was the sound of a creaky door opening and shutting. I searched for a smell, and there was none—at least, not under the blanket. Eleven more steps, and he stopped.

My nostrils flared to take in as much air as I could hold.

While I balanced over his shoulder, he moved something with his arms. Wheels scraped against the floor. A padlock loosened.

A second one.

And a third.

We were suddenly descending a flight of stairs, the cold of a basement coming under the blanket, followed by a musky scent.

Fourteen steps, and then the grittiness of shoes pressed against cement.

There was no warning. My breath just left my body as I flew through the air. I couldn't yell, couldn't cry out, couldn't gasp—fear was holding those expressions hostage. My shoulder slammed into something semi-soft as I landed, my hip and thigh hitting next.

A mildewy scent filled my nose.

Tense as a rock, sucking in through my gagged mouth, I rolled until I was on my knees.

The moment they were bearing my weight, he pulled off the blindfold.

Air hit me in a whole different way, my eyes burning, watering.

Blinking.

An overwhelming feeling took hold of me as I finally put a face to that scratchy voice, one I was positive I'd never seen before.

"When I can trust you, I'll take off the gag and handcuffs."

Trust me?

I guessed he was in his early fifties, well over six feet tall, with gold wire-rimmed glasses, lenses cloudy from dirt. His head was shaved, his double chin wiggling with each word he spoke.

Hatred and anger and confusion and misery—they all combined and boiled.

Why?

How long are you going to keep me?

What are you going to do with me?

I wanted to scream every question.

"You have a long way to go before you earn my trust, Kerry."

But I'd done nothing wrong.

My heart pounded so hard that my chest was lifting, my shoulders rising.

"See that up there?" He pointed to a camera in the corner of the ceiling, a red light steadily glowing in the center. "I'm always watching you. Be a good girl, Kerry."

I shook my head. I didn't understand.

"No?" He seethed. "You're not going to be a good girl?"

He had read my movements wrong; he thought I was disagreeing with him.

I quickly nodded, rectifying my previous response, pleading with him to show me some mercy.

He stared at me with dark, beady eyes. "Before I leave, I want to make something clear." He pushed his glasses high on his nose, his fingers short and hairy, nails bitten down to the quick. "I control you now. I decide when you eat and if you get rewarded. The only decisions you're allowed to make are when to use the bathroom"—he pointed at a bucket in the corner —"and when to be a good girl. If you comply, things will be much easier on you. But if you don't, I will make this a living hell"—he showed a sideways smile that was dripping with evilness—"where you'll be begging for me to kill you just to make it stop."

The tears were choking me.

Quivers shuddered through every part of my body.

He walked over to the wooden stairs along the left side of the small room and turned toward me when he reached the base. "Silence—that's what I expect from you. Do not utter a sound while you're in this room. Nod if you understand."

There was so much emotion in my eyes that he turned blurry.

But I nodded.

And a wave of nausea came up my throat.

He went up three of the steps and said over his shoulder, "Make yourself comfortable, Kerry. This is your new home ... where you'll be spending the rest of your life."

At the top of the stairs, there was a click from the door shutting, followed by the sound of padlocks.

One.

Two.

Three of them.

I immediately started convulsing in sobs, losing my balance and falling onto my side. I didn't try to stop and calm my feelings. I just held in the sounds and cried, forcing myself not to throw up through the gag.

"Where you'll be spending the rest of your life."

As those words repeated in my head, every syllable stabbed me.

Branded me.

Filled me with an unfathomable pain.

I'm going to die in here.

And with each tear that dripped, I lost a little more hope.

TWENTY-ONE

BEFORE

ASHE

The buzzing that came through the intercom in our apartment told me Pearl had arrived, so I slipped on my jacket and went over to the speaker.

I held down the button and said, "Hey, I'll be right down."

Knowing the stairs were faster than the elevator, I rushed down the flights and was walking toward the glass door when I saw her standing on the steps out front. As she glanced down the sidewalk, I took in her profile, and it was as gorgeous as looking at her straight on.

Pearl's features weren't like a puzzle, where the different pieces created a stunning picture. Instead, each part of her was just as beautiful, making a face that was fucking breathtaking.

I took a few more seconds to appreciate the sight of her before I opened the door. Once I got outside, I gripped her waist, and she exhaled in a gasp the moment my mouth touched hers.

"You scared me."

I pulled away, feeling her shiver. "I didn't mean to."

"In a good way." Her teeth found her lip, tugging on it. "Sometimes, Ashe, you make it hard for me to breathe."

I leaned down for another kiss—this one deeper, where I tasted the cinnamon. "These past couple of days were a long time away from you."

We had spoken on the phone every morning, but that wasn't the same as holding her against my body, smelling her in the air, seeing her smile at my words.

"You have me now." Her hands circled around my neck. "What are you going to do with me?"

I rubbed my nose against hers, the thought of her naked on my bed flashing in my mind. But a lot was going to happen tonight before we made it back here. And once we did, I wasn't sure naked would even be on the agenda.

"Are you hungry?"

"The answer to that is almost always yes."

I slipped her fingers between mine and brought them up to my face, where I kissed her wrist. More cinnamon teased my nose as I led her down the sidewalk and to the cross street. I hailed the vacant taxi that was approaching, and we climbed into the backseat before I gave the driver an address.

"What kind of restaurant are we going to?"

I smiled. "One that's a surprise." I put my arm around her shoulders, pulling her next to me. With my lips pressed against her cheek, I watched her stare through the window, the expression on her face as though she were seeing the city for the first time.

Maybe that was the case.

But I wanted to believe it was the happiness she was feeling that was putting that look in her eyes.

As the driver maneuvered through the traffic, I checked my watch. Every detail about tonight mattered, each part needing to mesh in order for it to come together the way I wanted. The good thing was, we arrived on time, and confusion filled Pearl's eyes as we pulled up to the residential building.

I handed the driver enough cash to cover the fare and tip, and I led Pearl to the entrance. A friend of Dylan's was waiting by the door for us. I thanked him as he opened it, and I brought her to the elevator, pushing one of the buttons once we were inside.

"Who was that guy, and where are we going?"

I squeezed her fingers. "That was a family friend Dylan's. As for the rest, you're going to find out soon."

Once we reached the highest floor, I took her down the hallway and into a stairwell, climbing a short flight. At the top was a locked door that I'd propped open when I was here earlier, and fortunately, no one had closed it while I was gone.

"What is this ..." Her voice drifted off as I took her onto the roof and she realized what she was looking at. Her free hand flew over her mouth, her eyes wide and a little watery. "Oh my God, Ashe." She slowly took in the entire space, her stare eventually returning to me. "I don't even know what to say."

I held her waist, pulling her in front of me. "Rumor is, you're turning twenty-one in a few days, and since you have to work on your birthday and I knew you wouldn't want to go out and get wasted, I planned this."

She shook her head in disbelief. "How did you know when my birthday was?"

I grinned. "I asked Erin the last time I was at the bar." I turned her once more to face Boston's skyline just as the sun was setting through the high-rises.

Dylan and I had come here a few months ago for a party, and it was one of the coolest spots I'd ever been to in the city with a view that couldn't be beat. When I'd started planning Pearl's birthday, I had known this was where I had to bring her.

In the center of the roof, I'd set up a table covered in

candles, and rose petals were sprinkled on the floor and around the rim of the balcony. A small stereo in the corner played music. A cooler off to the side held tonight's dinner. And the backdrop was Boston—every dip of architecture, every rise, every noise it had to offer.

"Ashe ..."

I held our linked fingers against her stomach. "I'm truly speechless."

"Happy birthday, Pearl. I hope this is one you'll never forget."

"Never." Her voice softened. "Ever."

The sun lowered below the buildings, leaving the most colorful sky behind.

I slowly faced her toward me again, gripping her cheeks to kiss her. "Do you want to eat?" When she nodded, I helped her into her seat at the table and then reached into the cooler. "I got us some sparkling apple cider. I hope that's okay?"

Her eyes were even smiling. "It's perfect."

I opened the bottle, took out two champagne glasses, and began to fill them. "As for dinner, cooking isn't my specialty, so I grabbed something I thought you would like." I placed the first to-go box on the table. "There's this restaurant in China-town my parents have been taking me to since I was a kid. The food is going to blow your mind." I set down several more cartons in the center. "I didn't know what you'd want, so I guessed."

"I love it."

I laughed; she was so cute. "You haven't even tried it yet."

"I don't have to. I'm just in love with all of this." She put her hand on my arm. "No one has ever done anything like this for me." She took one of the petals off the table and held it to her nose. "I'm overwhelmingly blown away."

"That makes me happy to hear." I handed her a set of chopsticks and opened the cartons, pointing to each one as I described them. "There's chicken in here, beef over here, and pork in this one." I set two more containers down, lifting the plastic lids. "Here are two different kinds of rice because you can never have enough fried rice, in my opinion."

I dropped spoons into all of the dishes and began to serve myself, signaling for her to do the same. She took a little from each, adding a large pile of rice on the side.

"Here are some extra sauces." I placed a handful of the small, plastic sleeves onto the table. "There's duck sauce and soy and hot mustard—whatever you like."

She watched me open the corners with my teeth, pouring all three kinds onto my plate, and she did the same, eventually taking a bite of the beef.

"Wow. This is something else."

I filled my mouth with some rice. "Oh, man, I know. When Dylan and I were kids, our parents would take us there once a month. Both our families would pack into Dylan's mom's caravan, and we'd drive there together. Dylan and I would eat so many bowls of crispy noodles that we were sure they would start charging us for them, but they never did." I added another heaping spoonful of rice to my plate. "Now, whenever one of us goes home, my parents always bring us there."

She took in a mouthful of pork lo mein. "Tell me more."

I added another packet of hot mustard to the rice and mixed it into the chicken. "Dylan and I were rowdy when we were younger, always getting in trouble. We didn't cause harm or anything like that, just reckless, fearless kids constantly looking for an adventure." I laughed as I thought of some of the shit we used to get into. "I remember this one time in the middle of winter, we'd just gotten a huge dumping of snow. We added some slush to our snowballs, making them icy, and we were playing dodgeball with the cars driving down the street."

"You're kidding."

"I told you, reckless. Anyway, it was Dylan's turn; he wound up and threw too high, and it hit the windshield. The glass didn't break, but the driver slammed on his brakes and came running after us. We were stupid enough to do it in front of my house, and while we took off, he rang my doorbell and ratted us out to my mom." I shook my head. "Man, we never did that again."

"Your parents were pissed?"

I laughed. "Little bit. I think we were grounded for months over that one."

"Tell me about one of the hard times."

Her interesting questions constantly made me think.

"My grandfather died the spring of my sophomore year, my grandmother three months later. They'd lived about an hour away in Brockton, and I had been really close to them. Dylan and I would spend a lot of our weekends there. When they passed away, I couldn't sleep. I couldn't even close my eyes." I wiped my mouth with my napkin, staring at my plate. "During those nights, I'd sneak out and go to Dylan's. We'd watch a movie, and eventually, hours later, I'd fall asleep. But he would wait until he knew I was sleeping, and then he'd go to bed— never before me, not even once."

"He's important to you."

"He's my brother. There isn't anything I wouldn't do for him."

Her smile told me she understood. "He's lucky to have you."

"No." I picked up the chopsticks and attacked the beef. "I'm lucky as fuck to have him."

After struggling with the chopsticks, she used one of the spoons to scoop up some rice. "I often wonder what it would be like to have a sibling. It's such a foreign feeling that I can't even imagine it." She swallowed and took a drink. "You come from such a big family, whereas it's just Gran and me. It's a strange comparison."

"Not strange at all." I popped a piece of broccoli into my mouth. "Sometimes, having only one person in your life can feel like a million. Gran is your mother, father, and siblings, all in one. I suspect she's more than enough."

She stared at me, not eating while I spoke. "You're right."

"Listen, when I was growing up, my sisters and I fought like hell, and that's all we ever did. Family dinners were loud, and they took forever. There were three women in my house, so I never won a single argument." I laughed. "Don't yearn for the way I grew up because if life suddenly changed and you were stuck in a family of five, I guarantee you'd want to switch back."

"You're probably right." She set down her spoon and put her hands on her stomach. "I'm so stuffed. I don't think I can eat another bite."

"You have to save room for dessert."

Her eyes widened. "There's more?"

She looked like a kid who had just realized there was more than one present for her under the tree.

"It's at my apartment. This'll give you some time to digest before I fill you with cake."

She wrapped her hand around the glass of cider and sipped it. "This is magical."

"No ..." I stood from my chair and held out my hand. Once she grabbed it, I brought her over to the edge of the balcony. "*This* is magical."

"I've never seen Boston this way before."

Even though I was standing behind her, holding her body against me, I positioned my neck in a way where I could see her profile. Like I'd done in the taxi, I was experiencing the city through her eyes, a view far more mesmerizing than the one in front of us.

I gently wrapped my arms over her chest, the back of her head resting against me. "How do you normally see it?"

She was silent for several seconds, but a change of tone eventually broke through. "Where I live, there's someone homeless every few feet. Drug dealers on the corners. Violence in the streets, screaming behind closed doors, gang signs spray-painted on every surface. When I take the train to school, I rush inside a building and then hurry to work." She paused. "I never stop to notice the beauty." She looked over her shoulder at me. "Not until today."

She kissed me, taking her time.

"Thank you for bringing me here and for giving me the best birthday I've ever had." Her eyes opened as she whispered against my mouth, "And for making me stop running."

TWENTY-TWO

BEFORE

PEARL

"Happy birthday, Pearl," Ashe said as he placed a cake on the table. There were two chocolate tiers and twenty-one candles lit along the top, my name written in sparkly icing with flowers frosted around it. "Make a wish."

I stared at the small fires, a thought coming into my mind. There was only one thing I'd ever wished for year after year.

I hope I'm able to move Gran out of here and give her a better life.

I sucked in as much air as I could hold and tried to blow out every candle, but a few were so stubborn that it took another breath to put those out.

Just as I finished, he took my face into his hands and kissed me. "I can't wait to taste the peanut butter on your lips."

His smile caused a flutter in my chest, and so did the feel of him on my cheeks.

"That's the flavor you got?"

"It's your favorite."

Details.

Ashe paid more attention than anyone I'd ever met, making it one of the sexiest, most endearing qualities about him.

I wrapped my arms around his shoulders and kissed him. "From every bit of my heart, I thank you."

"Don't feel like you have to keep saying that." His voice was so tender. "You've shown your appreciation since the moment you arrived at my apartment tonight."

That felt like days ago.

Because never had I expected this evening to turn into this.

But maybe I should have.

From the very beginning, Ashe had shown me how wonderful he was. And each day, he'd continued to prove that he was the type of man who would decorate a rooftop with flowers and candles, play music, and feed me Chinese. At this point, I truly believed he would do anything to make sure I had a memory to hold on to forever.

"I don't think I've shown you enough," I whispered.

"Trust me, you have."

Trust.

That word hit me hard, rolling all the way to my stomach, heating and bubbling like the oatmeal I'd made Gran for breakfast. It was a word that had held no value for most of my life, every promise made to me broken until I'd moved in with Gran. She was the only person who made me believe in trust.

Ashe wasn't far behind.

He grabbed a long knife from the drawer and handed it to me. "Do you want to do the honors?"

I smiled. "I'll let you make the mess."

He laughed, carefully sticking the blade into the center of the cake and dragging it to the edge, repeating the motion until there were several slices. He used the flat side of the knife to lift the large pieces and plate them. Once we each had one, he took out some vanilla ice cream and spooned that on the side.

"As kids, we always had ice cream with our cake," he said, sitting next to me at the table. "My mom used to buy us strawberry. I think that was her way of trying to get us to eat more fruit." He took a bite. "But I think vanilla tastes best with this."

I dipped my spoon into the creaminess and added some of the cake, making sure a frosted flower made it in as well. All of the flavors mixed together in my mouth, and I moaned, "You're not wrong."

"You like it?"

"Love." My eyes closed. "Really, really love."

When I opened my lids again, he was grinning, and he reached across the small space, rubbing his fingers over my cheek. "God, you're beautiful."

My face warmed under his hand. "Are you going to cut a piece for Dylan?"

I hadn't asked if he was here when we first arrived. I just assumed he was in his room.

"He's gone for the night. But I assure you, he'll dig in the second he gets back in the morning."

"Do you have eggs?" When he nodded, I added, "Good. Then, I'll make you guys breakfast, and we can have the cake for dessert."

He stared at me for several seconds. "You've decided to stay?"

Even though I'd stuck a few overnight things in my bag, I'd still debated while I was on the train to his apartment tonight. Once I opened the sleepover door, I wasn't sure I'd be able to close it, and something told me I'd be spending many more nights over here.

In my head, it seemed like an urge I should fight.

But in my heart, I knew I couldn't.

Waking up next to Ashe was what I wanted.

"Yes." I swallowed, the richness slowly sliding down my throat. "I'm not going to go home."

A smile spread across his delicious mouth before he closed the distance between us and kissed me.

"Peanut butter," he whispered, licking me off his bottom lip. "I knew it would taste so good on you, and I was right."

As I stared at his mouth, his voice echoing in my ears, a hunger began to pulse inside me. One that increased as I looked at the dessert he'd had made for me and the vase of flowers he had bought me. The fridge full of leftover Chinese and another bottle of sparkling apple cider he'd purchased as a backup.

His thoughtfulness was everywhere.

The feeling inside my chest was what caused me to rise from my chair and move over to him, slowly taking a seat on his lap. As he gripped my waist, I hugged his neck, my arms eventually resting on his shoulders.

"One of"—I kissed his cheek—"the best"—my lips moved over his nose—"nights of"—I went across to his other cheek —"my life." I pulled back when I reached the base of his neck.

"It's not over, Pearl."

Goose bumps covered my skin.

He reached behind me and returned with a flower, holding it to my nose. As I inhaled the soft rose scent, our eyes locked.

"We're just getting started."

I suddenly felt like those candles before I'd blown them out —my limbs lit, my body dripping with heat. My skin turned incredibly sensitive, every movement of his fingers causing tingles to explode. When he leaned his mouth closer, he lowered the flower, the soft petals brushing across my lips.

A wave of pleasure shot through me, and it happened immediately again as he ran the rose down my neck and over my throat, stopping at the collar of my shirt.

"Ashe." I quivered.

He scanned my eyes back and forth, desire bursting from his stare. "Unless you tell me to stop ... I'm about to carry you to my bed."

TWENTY-THREE

BEFORE

ASHE

There were times when Pearl didn't need to speak—I could see the answer right in her eyes. That happened now as I told her I was going to carry her to my bed unless she stopped me. Desire was pooling in her stare, her breathing labored, her body responding to every shift of my fingers.

That was more than enough to tell me what she wanted.

The problem was that it would take me too long to bring her into my bedroom.

I needed to touch her now.

While she balanced on my lap, I found the bottom of her shirt and peeled it over her head. Underneath, she wore a black bra, her perfectly round tits tucked into the lace. I loved the way she had reacted to the flower, so as I kissed her neck, I trailed the rose behind me, letting her feel the heat from my mouth and the softness from the petals.

I moved my plate of cake out of the way and leaned her against the table, dragging the rose to the center of her tits and over the tops of them. When the bra became too restrictive, I unclasped the back, removing it from her shoulders, letting it fall to the floor.

"Gorgeous," I whispered, eventually meeting her eyes. "I can't believe you're mine."

Her breathing rapidly increased, and I traced the flower around her nipple, my mouth closing in on the peak, blowing on it after I sucked. Every inch I moved across produced a sound from her lips—a pleasure-filled gasp as I went quickly and a long-drawn-out exhale when I used my tongue.

I couldn't get enough.

I needed more of her taste, more of her body, more of her sounds, knowing they were from the way I was making her feel.

Her fingers crawled through my hair, pulling the strands as I flicked the end of her nipple. Her chest was rising and falling so fast, goose bumps covering her flushed skin. When I used my teeth, her back arched off the table as she breathed, "Ashe."

When our eyes connected, there was an intensity in hers, even more so when I said, "I want you. Now."

I held her against me and wrapped her legs around my waist, lifting her and carrying her through the kitchen and down the short hallway to my room. I placed the flower next to her on my bed and unbuttoned her jeans, pulling them off with her shoes. Only a pair of sexy black panties were left. I wanted full access to her body, and they would only tease me if I left them on, so I yanked those down as well.

As she lay naked, staring up at me, I started removing my clothes.

Her eyes took in each bit of skin I revealed, and when I got down to my boxers, I heard, "My God, you have a nice body."

I smiled, stripping off the remaining piece, and joined her on the bed. Beginning where I had left off, I ran the petals down her stomach, stopping at the top of her pussy.

"*Ahhh*," she breathed the second I grazed the rose across

her clit. Her legs widened, letting me in, as her hands clutched the blanket beneath her. "Ashe, this feels"—she took in a long inhale—"so good."

While I rubbed the flower across her inner thighs, my mouth moved to her clit, my nose buried in her delicious scent. I flattened my tongue and swiped the entire length, dropping the rose to give her my fingers. I circled one through her wetness before plunging it inside. I tilted my hand upward and licked her clit with hard, fast strokes.

I was surprised by how quickly her orgasm built, her moans telling me she was close. I reached up and pinched a nipple, her hips swaying with each pass of my tongue.

When I sensed her teetering on that edge, I grabbed the flower and held it between my teeth, using it to caress her clit in circles, the petals moving in horizontal and vertical patterns.

"Fuck!" she shouted, her hand tightening on my head, knees bending, toes pushing into the mattress.

As I watched her shudder, my dick throbbed—from the feel of her tightening around my finger, from her breathing, which was the only sound I could hear.

This was the sexiest sight I'd ever seen.

And it turned even hotter when she sighed, "Ashe."

It only took one syllable, and I knew the intensity that was flowing through her body.

From me.

That thought alone was enough to make me want to come.

She began to still, and I dropped the flower and grabbed a condom from my nightstand, kissing her while I rolled it over me. Once it was secure, she clung to my neck and lifted her back, welcoming me in.

I carefully pushed through her wetness, knowing she was probably extremely sensitive at the moment, and her tightness instantly took hold of me.

"Fuck, Pearl." My forehead pressed into hers. "You feel incredible." I tried to breathe. "You're so tight." My balls were tingling from the sensation of her. "And so fucking wet."

Her legs moved around me, her breathing now matching mine.

When I finally got all the way inside her, I pressed my lips to hers, and her moan vibrated across my mouth. With each thrust, she got wetter, she squeezed me tighter, and her back rose higher off the bed.

My body was on fire, especially as I started to move faster, stroking into her with more power. Her pussy was milking me, and while I increased my speed, moving in as deep as I could reach, I took her nipple into my mouth.

"Oh fuck." She quivered.

The peak of her tit already so hard, I traced the circle with my tongue, sucking the middle, grazing my teeth across the tip. I moved to the other side, giving them equal attention, and just as I pulled away, I lifted her in my arms. I turned us, sitting my ass on the bed, and leaned against the back wall. I straddled her over me, making my hands free to wander across her body.

"Fuck me, Pearl," I moaned just as her tits began to bounce in my face, her hips rocking over my cock.

She lifted as high as my crown and lowered to my base, doing that several times before she kept me fully inside and pumped me while she rotated in a circle.

I took one of her nipples into my mouth, my fingers moving to her clit, and she cried out, "*Yesss,*" the second I put pressure on both.

While she rode me, I took in this beautiful girl. Her lips were parted, her neck tilted back so her throat was exposed, pleasure spreading across her magnificent face. She was a stunning combination of dips and curves with long, dark hair that feathered across her soft, glowing skin.

ASHE

A fucking vision unlike I'd ever seen.

When she was onstage, she was confident and brilliant and alluring. Naked, in my bed, a whole different kind of beauty radiated from her, making her ravishing.

Her neck straightened, her lips hovering just above mine as she continued to bob over me. I felt her start to tighten again, and because I was learning her body already, I knew she was getting close.

So was I.

"Faster," I growled, keeping one hand on her clit, the other guiding her up and down.

I arched my hips, giving her the fullness of my shaft, and her sounds told me she was climbing. I took over the movements, pounding into her with more power, the momentum increasing between us.

When I felt the surge begin, my fingers bit down on her hips, and I hissed, "Pearl, I'm there."

She kissed me and moaned, "Come with me."

As her pussy pulsed around my dick, a wave of sensations moved through my abdomen, into my lower stomach, and through my shaft until I exploded. "Pearl ..." I gripped her with the hardest strength. "Fuck."

"*Mmm*, yes." She was bucking against me, clutching me from the inside. Her wetness thickened, her sounds peaking until we reached the same calmness, our breathing the only movement that was left.

Her lips, still near me, brushed against mine before she really pressed down to kiss me. "I never knew it could feel like that."

I took a moment to find my voice and leaned back to take in her eyes. "Sex?"

She nodded. "To experience that with someone you really care about, like I do for you."

"It's only going to get better."

She smiled, her cheeks flushed, small pieces of hair sticking to them. "It's hard to believe there's better than that." She ran her fingers across my lips, shaking her head as she stared at them.

I gripped her face, and right before I kissed her, I whispered, "There is ... it's called love."

TWENTY-FOUR

BEFORE

PEARL

I didn't have a hard time sleeping in Ashe's bed. In fact, the moment he wrapped his arms around me, the warmth of his body closing in, his exhales on my bare shoulder, my eyes closed. Seconds later, I was fast asleep. His pillows were like clouds, his blanket so cozy, his arms a type of heat I'd never known I wanted, but one I now couldn't imagine letting go.

My internal clock—the one I'd gained from taking care of Gran for so many years—caused me to rise before the sun. So, I stayed in bed and watched the city come to life through Ashe's bedroom window. He lived across the street from a section of brownstones that didn't hide the view—unlike the concrete high-rises that blocked every side of my apartment, the scenery outside our windows like a prison cell. But from here, I saw the sun teasing the thick clouds, the noises of the city telling me it was just starting to wake up.

Kenmore Square was so different than Roxbury.

Calmer even if it was busier.

Pedestrians were out for their morning jogs, and others

were dressed in suits to head into work early. Those weren't things I saw in my neighborhood.

Roxbury was the morning after a long bender, hugging the toilet as the ground wobbled beneath you. Kenmore Square was slowly waking up with a cup of coffee after a full eight hours of sleep.

We came from opposite worlds in almost every aspect.

And I was really enjoying his.

I checked Ashe's clock. His alarm would be going off in twenty minutes, so I carefully wiggled out of his grip and snuck out of bed. I slipped on one of his T-shirts and a pair of boxers that I'd grabbed from the floor, tiptoeing to the kitchen. My cake was boxed on the counter, and I cut three slices, sticking them on separate plates.

Inside the fridge, I took out a carton of eggs and a package of bacon and found a few fry pans in the cupboard. After spraying both bottoms, I cracked the eggs into one pan, scrambling them once they were all in. The bacon sizzled on the other side of the stove, and as they cooked, I made a pot of coffee.

"Please tell me you'll be moving in soon," Dylan said from behind me, catching me off guard. "I could really get used to this."

I turned around, laughing. "Not anytime soon, I'm afraid." I handed him a full mug. "But I'm happy to cook whenever I'm here." I set the pieces of cake on the table, nodding for him to take a seat. "How was your night?"

"Seeing that you're still here, probably not as good as yours."

I laughed again, returning to the eggs to stir them. "Ashe made it super special. It's a birthday I'll certainly never forget."

"That's my boy." He grinned as I glanced at him over my shoulder. "I know it's not here yet, but happy birthday, Pearl."

"Thank you." I poured some coffee for myself and for Ashe and set those mugs on the table, adding the creamer from the fridge and some sugar that I'd found next to the salt. "How are you feeling about our exam on Friday?" I flipped the bacon, the grease splashing onto the sides of the pan.

"I'm thinking one more study session with the group might do us some good. Can you meet this week?"

As I divided the bacon and eggs onto the three plates, I ran my schedule through my head. Now that the play was over and we were at the beginning stages of our next performance, I would have a lot more time. But that also meant I'd be spending almost every evening at the bar. The thought of that was a bit of a relief since I didn't have nearly enough cash to cover rent.

My responsibilities had paused when I arrived here last night, but the real world was slamming into me again, a crack of thunder between my ears each time a new bill or an upcoming test or assignment popped into my head.

"I'll figure out a way to swing it," I told him, watching Ashe walk in.

"Holy shit," he said as he stopped in the center of the kitchen. "It smells so fucking good in here."

With him dressed in only a pair of gray sweatpants, I was glad I had taken the food off the stove, or it would have burned because I couldn't take my eyes off him. His chest and stomach were all muscle with the lightest dusting of hair—a space that I wanted to cover with kisses. Even though I had touched him last night and up until I got out of his bed, seeing him in the light gave me a whole new appreciation.

Ashe wasn't just nurturing and kind.

He was handsome.

And sexy as hell.

He took the plates out of my hands and brought them to the

table, returning to give me his mouth. A subtle whiff of his leftover cologne made my chest tingle, and the taste of his toothpaste numbed my tongue.

"Good morning, beautiful."

Now that my fingers were free, they went to his stomach, his abs tightening as I ran across them. "*Mmm*, morning."

"I hated that you were gone when I woke up, but seeing how hot you look in my clothes"—his eyes dipped to my chest and then to my legs—"you're forgiven."

"I hope you don't mind; they were just easy to slip on—"

"I wouldn't want you in anything else."

I smiled, my teeth immediately going to my lip as a moment passed between us that told me if Dylan wasn't sitting at the table, I would probably be spread across it.

Naked.

"Go take a seat before all the food gets cold," I said.

"I have a better plan."

I giggled and steered him toward his chair.

When the three of us were seated, the boys exchanged a few words about Dylan's night, sounding like he had spent it with mutual friends.

Within a few bites, Dylan had stopped talking and was staring at me, gnawing on his bacon. "Pearl, this is fucking awesome."

"It's excellent," Ashe agreed, reaching for my thigh under the table. "You didn't have to do all this."

"But we're glad you did," Dylan replied.

We all laughed, and I lifted my black coffee, holding it to my lips.

"I'm happy you like it." I set down the mug and picked up my fork to dig into the cake. "But admittedly, I'm most excited about the dessert."

"Cake for breakfast," Dylan said with eggs in his mouth. "I like this trend."

"Wait until you try it," I told him. The rich peanut butter exploded on my tongue, my mouth watering from the richness. "It's the best thing ever."

"Well, shit, I'm sold," Dylan said, dropping his bacon to dig into the cake. "Damn, you weren't kidding." He moaned as he took another bite.

My eyes flitted between the two men, and I laughed to myself as I watched them.

This was certainly much different than sitting at the coffee table with Gran, where we shared all of our meals. She was the only person I'd eaten with in a very long time. But these guys made me feel so comfortable, and I hadn't realized how much I would enjoy staying here.

"But these eggs," Ashe said, shoving in another mouthful, "they're so tasty and light."

"They're not peanut butter cake," I replied.

"They're better." He winked at me, his fingers leaving my leg to search for my hand. When he found it, he linked us, his thumb rubbing the back of my palm.

Dylan devoured both plates and set his fork down. "My hungover ass is going to bed." He set his dishes in the sink and came back to the table, stretching his arms above his head, yawning. "I'll figure out when everyone is free to study, and I'll let you know."

"Sounds good."

"Thanks again for breakfast," he said and disappeared down the hall.

Ashe was just finishing his last bite of cake when I asked, "Who gets the shower first?"

We had class at the same time, in about an hour, so I knew we had to get going, or we'd be late.

He licked the frosting off his fork and took all of our plates to the sink. When he returned to my side, he held out his hand for me to grab, staring at me through his thick lashes. "No reason to choose." He grinned, and a wetness started to pool between my legs. "Not when both of us can fit in there."

TWENTY-FIVE

AFTER

ASHE

I walked over to my desk with a large cup of coffee, removing the plastic lid the moment I sat down. The steam of the roast hit my face, and I took a long drink of the sweetened mixture. The coffee in our break room tasted like sludge. I'd spent eleven years in this department, and not a goddamn person here, including myself, could make a decent cup.

My desk was covered in paperwork and files, not a spot open to set down the cup. I didn't know how it'd accumulated so much since I'd left last night, but it seemed that every time I returned, there was always more.

More cases.

More forms to complete.

More witnesses to interview.

More bullshit to tackle, so the captain wouldn't be all over my ass.

A cycle with no finish line, making it impossible to ever get caught up.

I was taking more folders out of my bag when I heard, "Flynn," from behind me.

CHAPTER 25

I turned, seeing Rivera walking into the department—a detective I'd worked with since I'd started.

"What the hell dragged you in this early?"

He chuckled as he sat in the desk next to mine. "My wife kicked me out of bed. Said I was snoring. The couch is lumpy as a motherfucker, so I figured I'd come in and get some work done." He stretched out his feet, balancing them on the edge of his trash can. "Got a busy day today?"

I pointed at the mess. "You tell me."

He laughed, knowing I wouldn't get through much of it. Part of our job description was being chronically overdue in almost everything behind the scenes. As long as the files had enough for the district attorney and the sergeant who reviewed them, many of the little things could fall through the cracks.

"How about you meet me for lunch?" he said, taking a drink of his coffee. "It's been a few weeks; we need to catch up."

"I'm there as long as I don't get called into a case."

He checked his watch. "I've got to interview a woman out in Dorchester at around ten. Shouldn't take more than an hour or two. I'll text you when I'm done, and we can meet up."

"Anything good?"

He lifted a file into his hands, skimming the first few sheets inside. "Missing daughter. I talked to the mother at the forty-eight-hour mark, but we're approaching ninety-six hours, and not a goddamn thing has turned up. I need to go talk to the mother again and make sure she doesn't know anything." He shook his head. "These cases ... you know how I feel about them."

He showed me a photo of the girl, and I asked, "No other leads?"

"The twenty-year-old left her cell phone at home, no boyfriend, and the best friend hasn't heard from her. Mom is distraught with four other kids at home, and there's no dad in sight." His eyes were heavy, almost weighted down. "Another fucking picture to add to the others." He nodded toward the wall at the entrance of the department, where we hung print-outs of anyone who had gone missing in the borough.

I ground my teeth together. "Every one of those makes me hate Boston a little bit more."

He stood from his chair, stopping by mine, his hand landing on my shoulder. "Every city has monsters. Ours aren't any eviler than anywhere else. I'll see you later, Flynn."

TWENTY-SIX

KERRY

The gag was gone.

So were the ropes that had tied my hands behind my back.

I didn't know how long they had bound me. With no windows in the basement, I couldn't differentiate time, but I'd eaten twice since he had taken them off.

My stomach constantly grumbled, the pangs almost unbearable.

I'd never been much of a foodie, but now, it was all I thought about.

A greasy burger with cheese melting down the side.

Spaghetti with loads of meat in the sauce.

Pepperoni in double rows on a pizza.

Anything thick and heavy to fill me.

The first time he'd entered with food, he'd had a paper bowl of oatmeal, filled only halfway. There was no taste—he hadn't cooked it enough—and most of it had gelled into hard clumps.

I didn't care.

Instead of using the plastic spoon he had brought, I held the bowl to my mouth and swallowed. It felt like cement as it hit my stomach.

The ache started almost immediately.

I wrapped my arms around my tummy and rocked back and forth.

My mouth watered.

I hadn't wanted to get sick.

I had just wanted to feel full, so I could curl up in a ball on the thin, lumpy mattress and finally get some sleep.

But within a few minutes, I had been hovered over the bucket, losing every morsel along with the acid in my stomach.

A bucket that he still hadn't cleaned or swapped out for a new one.

Why?

That word burned the same way the bile had.

I couldn't shout it in the basement. I couldn't cry it from my lips.

I couldn't make a fucking sound because of his threats.

Silence or else ...

The good girl.

The girl I had to be, so he would feed me again.

This time, a small bowl of rice.

I didn't eat it as fast, chewing every grain until it turned to mush. That stayed in, and I was able to rest on the mattress and close my eyes.

And not obsess over my hunger.

But I was waiting.

Waiting for the sound of the three padlocks.

Waiting for what was going to happen next.

Once I heard the first come unlatched, I perked up, anticipating the police rushing down the stairs to save me. Or hoping he was going to reward me and let me out for being a good girl.

I wasn't going to be here for the rest of my life.

My mother would have called the police; they would have traced my trail.

Someone would find me.

They had to.

Because I couldn't keep existing like this.

And he wouldn't want to keep me—I had to be fed and taken care of.

Watched.

What good was I to him? What was my purpose?

Each time he came into the basement, I wanted to ask him. That had been three times so far, and I still wasn't any closer to finding answers.

But my back flew off the mattress as the scraping of the metal echoed again, the second lock now loose.

The third.

The latch—a small cutout square in the wall, which was also covered in metal, just wide enough for him to squeeze his body through—then opened.

I'd checked out the space during my many walks around the rectangular-shaped prison, about the size of the living room in our apartment.

I knew every corner. Every dent in the cement.

How the one lightbulb that hung from the ceiling flickered whenever he moved across the floor upstairs.

The next sound was a pair of thick-soled black boots hitting the first step.

It wasn't the police or a knight in shining armor.

It was him.

The wooden steps weren't sanded or painted, and I dreamed of the day he would come down in his bare feet, full of splinters, in so much pain that he wouldn't be able to chase me.

And I'd be able to run past him and escape.

That wasn't going to happen today.

As he descended, I envisioned what food he had with him that would fill my stomach.

But as he got to the bottom of the stairs, there was only a cloth bag hanging from his shoulder.

No oatmeal.

No rice.

Nothing.

My stomach protested, a grumble so hard that I felt it in my throat.

"It's time," he said, standing in front of my mattress, his voice scratchy but flat.

Time for what?

There was no emotion on his face. No energy in his tone.

It was like someone had vacuumed the decency out of this man, and what was left was a vile, heartless devil whose eyes made me want to scream.

There was something very wrong about them—about him.

The glasses only intensified his evilness.

"Ronald isn't going to wait anymore." He pushed the rims higher on his nose, his gobbler jiggling from the movement. "I've been a patient man, Kerry. My patience is up."

Ronald ... so that's his name.

The cloth bag dropped onto his forearm as he reached into his back pocket, producing a cell phone.

I wanted nothing more than to reach for it.

Dial 911, and I would be out of here.

"Don't even fantasize about it, Kerry."

He was inside my head.

His gaze piercing me.

"Eating and breathing are privileges. If I sew your lips shut, fill your nose with plugs, and cut off your arms, you won't be able to do either, so I suggest you get that thought far out of your head."

He smiled, showing straight white teeth. The front left one was slightly chipped, like he'd bitten wrong into a steak bone and never bothered to get it fixed.

As though he sensed me staring, he ran his tongue over it.

A slithering motion like a snake.

I shivered, the shaking reaching all the way to my fucking toes.

Tears followed. I couldn't stop them. I didn't have the power to hide them.

They just ran and dripped, and it made him smile harder.

Eventually, he looked at his phone and said, "Let me introduce you to the loves of my life."

Finally, a different sound.

An emotion.

A glow that I hadn't seen from him before.

He tilted the screen in my direction, showing a photo of a porcelain doll. She was in a white dress and had ivory skin, her hair pulled back into low pigtails.

"Clementine," he said. "She's just precious." He flipped to one just like her, but this time a blonde, wearing the same dress and style of hair. "Victoria. She's feisty."

Different pictures of dolls came onto the screen each time he swiped. He would say their name, and I would study their appearance, learning quickly that he didn't have a preference in sex, as there were just as many men as women. And each photo revealed different shades of skin, hair, body styles, weight, and height.

Some life-sized. Some so small that they would fit in my palm.

But every one of the girls had two things in common.

Pigtails and a simple, thick-strapped white dress that was frilly at the bottom and puffed at the waist.

"Kerry," he rasped, putting the phone away, "it's time to add you to my collection." He glanced up at the ceiling as though he were taking in the view. "I've built you this big, beautiful dollhouse. It's all yours, no other dolls to share it with." His eyes found me again just as I was tucking my knees to my chest, rocking over the mattress. "You're one of the special ones." He extended his arm, the bag dangling from his fingers until it dropped in front of me. "One of the lucky ones."

As the bag fell, the top opened.

A slight tilt of my neck showed me what was inside.

If there was anything in me, I would have thrown up. But I was empty. Not a single drip of water, except for tears, had passed through my mouth in what felt like days.

"Take it out."

Tremors shook my hands; my fingers didn't want to unclench.

But I knew better than to defy him.

I reached inside and pulled out a white dress, the straps thick, a size that would definitely fit me.

The smile had returned to his lips, the wrinkles in his cheeks as high as his eyes. "This is the last dress you'll ever put on."

Noises would only get me in trouble, but I was filled with them.

Cries.

Screams.

I slapped my hand over my mouth, so none would escape.

"You're learning." He eyed my hand. "That makes Ronald very happy."

He took a few steps back and sat on the floor. He was so tall and uncoordinated, and he came down like a tree, his height making him look so awkward on the ground.

"Get changed." He folded his legs, rubbing his hands together like they were cold. "Don't keep me waiting."

Every question I'd had suddenly slapped across my face.

Why I was here.

What he was going to do with me.

What my life was going to be like in this basement.

The truth was like a bullet that missed my heart, hitting a spot that made me suffer, feel every bit of the agony and pain.

Something from inside the bag was pulling at my attention.

I leaned forward again to get a better look.

Two elastics.

For my hair.

"I'm ready to play, Kerry."

TWENTY-SEVEN

BEFORE

ASHE

"You're making it extremely difficult to study," Pearl said as she gazed at me over the top of her textbook.

Since we had known we wouldn't get anything done at my apartment, we'd agreed to meet at the library. A place where we could spend time together and still concentrate on our work, but where I couldn't lay her across my kitchen table and strip off her clothes.

Except from the moment she had walked in, wearing jeans that hugged her gorgeous legs and a tight white tank that showed the tops of her perfect tits, I couldn't stop thinking about what I wanted to do to her.

"Yeah? Well, I've read the same paragraph six times," I admitted.

She chewed the end of her pencil. "You have an exam tomorrow that's going to be painfully difficult if you don't know the material."

"So is sitting this far away from you."

She laid the book flat and reached across the space between us, the warmth of her hand landing on mine. "Is this better?"

"No."

She smiled, shaking her head. "You're insatiable."

"And you love that about me."

Her smile reached her blue eyes, a blush coming through her cheeks as she glanced down to start reading again. I tried doing the same, but the paragraph was a blur, the words not sinking in, the thought of spending one more second with *Organic Chemistry* fucking torturous.

It wasn't as though it had been days since I'd seen her. Dylan and I, along with a few friends, had gone to the bar while she was working on her birthday. We sat in her section. She'd kept the drinks coming, and I'd made sure the boys gave her a whopping tip at last call. And we'd napped at my place a few days ago, and this was our third study session at the library.

But it wasn't enough.

I needed more time alone with my girl.

"When can I get you to stay at my place again?"

She glanced up, still teasing her lips, but she paused to bite the eraser. "Tomorrow night, I'm all yours."

"I like the sound of that."

She leaned in closer, like she was about to tell me a secret. "I'll even make breakfast in the morning."

"Now, that's dangerous."

She laughed, a sound almost like a wind chime, one that I wanted to hear every day. "I'm glad you liked what I made, but bacon and eggs are super easy. I fear you're giving me a little too much credit."

"The last time I made scrambled eggs, they still had half the shells."

Her eyes went wide as she tried to hold in her giggle. "Then, I'd say I'm practically a chef."

I was quiet for a moment, watching this wonderful girl across from me. "Tell me something, Pearl ..." I'd certainly learned a lot more about her—foods she hadn't tried, places she wanted to visit, her intricate relationship with Gran. There was still so much to discover, many questions that hadn't been answered and this was one. "If you could do anything on a day off, what would it be?"

The sweater she wore over the tank top was hanging at her sides, and she crossed it over her chest. "I would travel, but that really isn't possible with Gran, and I definitely don't have the funds."

"What's your next choice?"

Even though she was looking at me, her mind was suddenly in a different place—I could tell from her expression, the way she was zoning out, like she was digging through her thoughts. "I would go sledding."

"Really?"

She nodded. "I've only been once." Her voice quieted, the pain building in her eyes. "It's one of the only good memories I have of Vanessa."

I didn't know anyone who called their mother by her first name. Whatever Pearl's reasoning was, it had to be dark.

I crossed my arms on top of my textbook and said, "Tell me about it."

She took several breaths, holding the sweater tightly across her as she started, "I was young—around five, maybe six. We were living with her boyfriend at the time in some run-down slum." She paused, and I could sense her going back there and that it was a place she didn't like to revisit.

"He'd stolen a set of tires the night before—he was going to pawn them for drugs—and I was on the floor, playing with one. I shouldn't have been—it was big and heavy and could have hurt me—but there was nothing else that was safe to play with. And it was late. I should have been asleep hours before, but it had just begun to snow, and it was the first snowfall of the new year."

I glanced at the window behind her head; the flakes coming down outside were sticking to the glass. I was sure she noticed the same thing happening behind me.

"Vanessa was on a happy drug that night instead of the heroin that made her nod out, and she was dancing around, holding her hair up like it was a cape, telling us she wanted to fly." She scratched the table with her thumbnail, as though there were something on it that she was trying to chip away. "She told her boyfriend to grab the tire, and he carried it outside. I remember it being so cold and windy, and the snowflakes immediately soaked through our clothes."

Her hand stilled, and she looked past me—my eyes maybe too much.

"We ended up at some hill. At the top, she sat on the tire and held me on her lap, and we went down." She smirked, but even that was full of pain. "It was such a steep drop, and I screamed and laughed. At the bottom, the rubber skipped on the snow, and we tumbled out." When her eyes found mine again, tears were ready to drip. "But it was fun. So much fun. And that was something I never had with her." She wiped the bottoms of her lids, sighing. "In that moment, she wasn't yelling at me for not taking care of her, she wasn't shoving a needle in her arm, she wasn't dragging me from one guy's apartment to the next. She was being a mom, and I felt that joy even if it was short-lived."

"How many times did you go down that hill?"

"Twice." She blinked, keeping her eyes closed as she whispered, "And the second time was even better."

My heart was fucking broken.

But I wouldn't show her that. I wouldn't even hint at it because Pearl would never want me to feel bad for her.

What I could do instead was fix it.

I reached across the table, holding out my hand for her to grab. "You want fun?"

She clasped her fingers in mine, the sweater falling to her sides, showing me her chest again. "Yes, and if it's an escape, that's even better."

I smiled, feeling my bottom lip under my teeth as an idea came into my head. "Done ... and it's going to start right now."

TWENTY-EIGHT

BEFORE

PEARL

A she stood from his chair and came around to my side of the table, clasping my fingers again and helping me to my feet. We'd come to the library to study, and we had so much work to do, but his expression told me nothing would be getting done today.

"Should we grab our things?" I asked as he weaved us through one of the large, tall stacks.

"They'll be there when we get back."

I stayed behind him, our hands locked, finding myself almost jogging to keep up. With Ashe's legs so much longer than mine, I had to take two steps to his one.

In the back corner of the room, we entered a stairwell and went up two flights and through another door, where he led me down several aisles. I was so lost and had no sense of direction; I couldn't imagine where he was taking me.

We were halfway down one of the stacks when he slowed and turned around, his hands finding their way to my face. I couldn't stop smiling as he kissed me, panting a bit as we tried to catch our breath. When his hands moved down my sides and around to my ass, I knew exactly what he had in mind, my body instantly responding. I melted from his touch, his attention causing my skin to hum. Soft moans falling from my lips after each exhale.

He couldn't wait for our date tomorrow night.

He needed to have me now.

That thought alone was enough for me to get completely lost in.

His mouth moved to my neck, kissing the spots that weren't covered by my sweater, even pushing it aside so he could feast on more. His hand rose to my breast, pinching my nipple through my bra, the pleasure so sharp that my back arched.

"Ashe ..." I tugged on the short strands of his hair, winded against his mouth. "Oh God." I shuddered as he began unbuttoning my jeans, the pads of his fingers reaching under the top of my panties. "What if someone sees us?"

"They won't."

"You know that for sure?"

He backed me up until I was pressed against the rows of books, and I grasped one of the wooden shelves, squeezing it as his finger dipped inside me.

"I promise," he growled, his sound vibrating through my chest. "This is where I usually study, and I'm always the only one here."

"*Fuuuck.*"

I pushed his hand so it went further into my pants, and I spread my thighs to give him more room. My neck leaned back as he kissed across my throat.

While his thumb skimmed my clit, I fumbled with the button on his jeans, lowering the zipper and diving into his boxers. I surrounded his hardness with my palm, lifting and lowering it over his shaft.

"I need you," he moaned. "Right fucking now."

He was using his foot to pull down my jeans, and I slipped out of a boot to free up one of my legs. That was when he picked me up and straddled me across his waist, holding me against the bookshelf.

His lips were devouring mine when he said, "Can you reach my wallet? There's a condom in there."

"I'm on birth control."

He pulled away to look into my eyes. "Are you sure you're okay with this?"

"Yes."

Within a second, his mouth returned to my lips, and he moved my panties to the side to position himself. His grip shifted to my ass, and he slowly plunged inside me.

"Oh fuck, that feels good," I breathed, the fullness taking ahold of my body.

The sensation of skin was entirely new—I'd only ever felt latex before.

"Damn it, Pearl," he breathed as his speed increased, the power he was using causing my shoulders to bang into the hard-covers. "You're so fucking wet."

Holding on to the shelf with all the strength I had, I couldn't focus on anything aside from the way he was making me feel. My orgasm was building, my breath gasping from my lungs, a tingling moving through me.

"Oh God," I sighed.

I wrapped my arms around him, hugging his chest to mine, taking the pounding he was giving me, my wetness guiding him in.

"Kiss me, Pearl."

My face had fallen into his neck, but I pulled it out to give him what he wanted. His mouth, as talented as the rest of him, owned me the moment his tongue slid in.

A sensation burst from between my legs, his dominance causing those pulses to increase.

"*Mmm*," I groaned as his speed turned even faster, and in this position, I could do nothing but take it. Each plunge felt better, even when he gave it to me harder. "Just"—I breathed, my body heading toward the peak—"like ... that."

He bit down on my lip. "I can feel you getting close."

His nipping set off another set of tingles, and I urged myself upward, meeting him at each thrust. My clit was rubbing against the top of him, the friction driving me there even quicker.

"So close," I told him.

The intensity moved into my navel and then lowered, the sensitivity threatening to pound through me. His hips began to really rock, and his breathing deepened, telling me he was feeling just as good.

"Ashe ..." His name was the last sound I made before the orgasm clutched me, my body going to a place I couldn't return from.

Just when I thought it couldn't feel any better, he changed again to hard, deep, relentless thrusts, the quivering now rattling through me.

"Pearl ... fuck ... me."

His mouth slammed against mine, and I felt each buck of his hips shoot another stream into my body.

We moaned together.

And clung to each other until his movements stopped.

The feral look in his stare turned softer as he pecked my mouth. "Damn," he exhaled. "That was ..."

"So fucking sexy."

He laughed, and the warmth of his breath heated my lips. "I want to have you on the stage."

I thought about his statement, clarifying, "The one I perform on?"

"Mmhmm."

As I gazed at him, I thought of the excuses I could come up with to gain access to the auditorium when no one would be there. "I think I can somehow make that happen."

He kissed me again. "In the meantime, I have more ideas."

"You mean, other places to have sex?"

"That ..." He rubbed his nose over mine, his touch so gentle. "And ways to make you smile."

TWENTY-NINE

AFTER

ASHE

Since the police had taped off half the street, I parked a block away from the crime scene. Several officers were huddled together on the sidewalk as I approached, everyone facing the alley, nestled between two commercial strips.

"What time was he found?" I said from behind the group, ducking under the yellow tape.

"Got a call about thirty minutes ago," one of the officers said as he turned toward me.

I recognized him from being a frequent at many of these scenes.

I checked my watch; it was a little past eight in the morning.

"The chef of the neighboring restaurant came in to prep for lunch and found him," Charlie, the officer, continued.

I stood with him by the mouth of the alley, analyzing the placement of the body. A few feet from the restaurant's dumpster, it would have been impossible for the chef to miss him.

"Victim's name?"

"No wallet," Charlie replied. "But he has plenty of tattoos

that can be run through the system to see if anything comes up."

"And his dental records?"

"No-go on those." I glanced at him as he added, "His teeth were yanked, gums so goddamn bloody that it must have happened close to the time of death."

I shook my head. "Fuck me."

"Whoever did this certainly didn't want to make it easy to identify the body." His hand went to my shoulder, shaking it. "Nothing like starting your week out with a John Doe."

"It's all right," I told him. "Challenges keep us from getting lazy."

Or from sleeping, but I didn't have to tell Charlie that.

I gave him a nod and stepped into the alley, staying to the side, always cognizant of altering any DNA in the area.

"How are things going?" I asked the forensic analyst.

Kneeling beside the body, he dropped several swabs into an evidence bag and looked up at me. "Should be wrapped up in another twenty or so, just a few more samples to collect."

"Anything preliminary?"

He lifted the sheet that covered the victim, showing me the wounds that punctured John Doe's chest. He happened to be shirtless—a detail I noted—making it much easier to determine the location of the entry points.

"Any of these bullets would have killed him." With his finger, he circled the air above the four holes that were spread around John's heart. "The need for four shots?" He looked at me. "Whoever it was really wanted to make sure the son of a bitch was dead."

I scanned the alley, looking at the numbered markers where the evidence was documented. "Any casings turn up?"

"Not a single one so far."

"Teeth extracted, shells taken from the crime scene—fuck."

He sprayed some type of solution onto the ground and then rubbed it with several swabs. "Definitely no novice here."

Wanting him to finish so we could get the body into the lab for testing, I handed him my card, and just as I was turning around, Rivera was walking toward me.

"I heard the call come through, and I was only a few blocks away, getting coffee," he said to me.

"Another early one for you. Wife kick you out again for snoring?"

He released a long and loud exhale. "She says I need to get some of those nose strips. Can you believe that bullshit? I'll tell you, man, I need a solid eight hours soon, or I'm going to crash." He held up his paper cup. "I can only pound so many of these." He pointed to the alley and asked, "Any leads?"

"No, and not much evidence either."

"Jesus, it's going to be one of those, huh?"

I followed him under the tape, waving at Charlie as we passed. "Afraid so." We walked across the sidewalk and toward the street where both of our cars were parked. "Do you have plans Saturday night?"

"Why do I feel like I do now?"

I laughed. "Dylan is going to be out of town, and he gave me his Celtics tickets."

"Box seats? Hell yes, you know my ass is in."

We reached my car, and I leaned my back against the driver's window. "I keep meaning to ask you, what happened with the case of the missing girl? Anything turn up?"

"Nah." He shook his head. "The mother gave us a list of all her daughter's friends, and not one of them had seen her that night or knew her whereabouts. Her younger sister, who shared a room with her, said she vaguely remembered hearing her leave in the middle of the night but didn't know what time and they'd said nothing to each other. We searched her phone and couldn't find a goddamn thing."

"She just vanished into thin air?"

He was quiet for a few seconds. "A fucking tragedy is what it is." With his eyes on me, he nodded toward his car. "Get in. I'll take you to breakfast." When I didn't immediately respond, he added, "Forensics has more testing to do, and you can't conduct any interviews. Most of the places around here aren't even open yet."

"You have a point."

"Not my first rodeo, cowboy." He shadowboxed my shoulder. "Get your ass in my car."

THIRTY

KERRY

There was a doll sitting on one of the stairs.
He had placed her there after.
After he played.
After he violated my body.
I hadn't thought my life in this basement could get worse.
I had been wrong.
So fucking wrong.
Worse was what happened when I put on the wide-strapped white dress. When he touched me. When he dropped his jeans and forced himself inside me.
I wasn't allowed to cry.
Scream.
Fight him.
Because there was a punishment far worse than the one he was giving me.
He had promised me that.
Now, sometime later, I could still sense his deathly black eyes looking at me and feel his disgusting hands.

I just wanted to scrub him away, but there was no water down here.

No soap.

Just a bucket full of my pee.

The doll, sitting on her perch like a fucking bird, wouldn't stop staring at me.

She had red hair made of yarn, a white dress identical to the one I'd worn earlier. Rosy cheeks with a stream of freckles across them.

Her shoestrings were big loops of black thread.

When the tears had finally stopped, when I had no emotion left, that was when I'd seen her.

I hadn't been able to stop staring at her since.

Sitting on the bare mattress—the asshole not even kind enough to give me a sheet or blanket—I held my knees to my chest and rocked over the thin bed.

She was taunting me.

His love, his pet, his toy—she was here to make me even more miserable.

I went over to the stairs and grabbed her fabric arm, dragging her to my bed. I tossed her down, and once I sat, I began hitting her with my fists.

I wanted to hurt her.

I wanted her to feel my pain.

I wanted her to take some of it away.

And inside my head, I was screaming all the things I couldn't say out loud.

How fucking dare you do this to me!

Why did I deserve this?

Why are you putting me through this?

Why are you hurting me? Wasn't kidnapping me, taking me away from my home and my family, enough?

You have to stop. I can't bear another fucking moment.

When I ran out of energy, when I had no more breath left in my lungs, I tossed her into the far corner of the basement.

She fell onto her side, facing me.

Dark, beady eyes, just like his, gazed in my direction, haunting me.

Reminding me of the abuse.

Torture that I knew was going to happen again.

Because I was now his doll, locked in his fucking dollhouse.

Available to play with whenever he had the urge.

To rub his greasy, gnarly bald head all over my chest. To make me clean his filthy glasses with my tongue.

All just foreplay.

A buildup to when he lifted the bottom of my frilly dress.

To when things became unbearable.

Dear God, help me.

The tears were back.

Stinging.

Burning my skin as they dripped.

A knot clogged my throat.

A tightness gnawed my chest.

Both strangling me to the point where I couldn't take a breath.

I couldn't suck in any air.

I couldn't stop my heart from pounding.

I couldn't stop the shaking that was taking over my body.

I didn't know what was happening to me, why I wasn't able to breathe, why these tremors were rattling me like I'd been thrown in the washing machine.

But it all kept getting worse.

I clasped my hands around my neck, begging for whatever this was to let go. But it felt like someone had placed a plastic bag over my head. There was nothing to inhale, nothing to see.

Just hopelessness.

Thoughts of his face, his hands, those horrible fucking eyes were filling my head.

I slapped the bed, mentally trying to fight them away, and a wave of nausea moved through me.

I couldn't make it to the bucket.

I couldn't even get onto my knees.

My mouth opened, and bile shot out of my lips, hitting the ground beside the bed.

With each heave, I hoped to purge him out of me, to rid myself of the memories etched into my brain.

To forget the way he had made me bleed.

And to only remember the happier times—the love from my family, the hug of my mother's arms.

When there was nothing left to vomit, I glanced up and saw the doll's eyes.

They hurt.

Everything hurt.

I wiped my mouth with my arm and pushed myself onto my knees.

Air slowly started to come back in, and my hands fell onto the cold, rough floor.

I crawled.

A nail snapped and broke along the way. The skin on my knees split open, the tiny grains from the cement filling the cuts.

But I didn't stop until I reached the doll, hauling her against my chest.

Her soft yarn hair tickled my chin as my arms circled her back, and I buried my face in her neck.

I didn't mean to hurt you.

It won't happen again.

I'm so fucking sorry.

Please forgive me.

Please ...

I wanted her to hug me back, to wrap her cotton-filled arms around me and squeeze.

To tell me everything was going to be all right.

To cradle the back of my head and rub my hair, like I was doing to her now and how my mom had done to me when I was younger.

But there was none of that, just her presence and the feel of her against me.

I would take it.

Because having her here—even if she was his—meant I wouldn't have to endure this alone.

THIRTY-ONE

BEFORE

ASHE

"Three," everyone screamed from inside the bar, holding their glasses high in the air. "Two," they continued the countdown. "One," they finished before shouting, "Happy New Year!"

I lowered my beer, and instead of taking a drink, I squeezed Pearl's waist and kissed her. She wrapped her arms around my neck, her lips parting to let in my tongue. I pulled her against my chest and set down the bottle, so I could lift her into my arms.

When I'd found out she had to work New Year's Eve, there wasn't a question as to where the guys and I were going to hang out this evening. She had reserved a table for the four of us in her section, and after last call, she would be coming back to my place to spend the night.

And tomorrow morning, while we cuddled in my bed, I was going to ask her if I could meet Gran.

Almost four months had passed since she had run into me in the hallway. She didn't need to hide anything from me anymore. She could trust me. Nothing would change the way I felt about my girl, and I wasn't going anywhere.

I would keep saying those words until she believed them. Until they lived in her heart.

Where she lived in mine.

I brushed my lips across her mouth and whispered, "Happy New Year, Pearl."

Her legs squeezed my waist, her arms balancing on my shoulders. "Happy New Year."

I stared into her eyes, still in awe that she was mine. "God, I'm so fucking crazy for you."

"*Mmm*," she moaned, a smile covering her gorgeous face as she pulled her lips away. "My year starts with you." Her grin grew even wider. "That couldn't make me happier."

I gripped her ass, feeling how perfect it was. "I'm never letting you go."

"You'd better not."

"This year is going to be all about fun." I rubbed my nose over hers. "Are you ready for that?"

"Yes." She tightened her hold on me, hugging me with all her strength. "The only time I've ever been able to close my eyes and feel safe is when I've been with Gran." Her legs locked, feet resting against my lower back, as she cupped my neck with her palm. "And now, Ashe, I feel that with you."

I rubbed my thumb over her chin, staring into her eyes, accepting the best gift she could have ever given me.

THIRTY-TWO

BEFORE

PEARL

As I cuddled into Ashe's chest, the smell of New Year's was still on his skin. Remnants of the beer I'd served him and the smoke from the bar. A holiday I'd always dreaded working even though the money was amazing because it was so crowded that I could barely get around and everyone was incredibly sloppy and only getting drunker as the evening went on.

Yesterday had been different.

Ashe was the silver lining.

The sweetest, gentlest man coming in with his friends, just so he could spend the whole night with me. When the bar began the countdown, he'd searched the crowd until he found me, joining our lips as the clock hit midnight.

I couldn't have asked for a better shift.

Or a better way to start the year.

And as I stared up at his face, I truly didn't know how I'd gotten so lucky.

I was just grateful I had taken off my shoes and stopped

running, or I would have missed something extremely beautiful.

He stirred as I brushed my fingers over his scruff, his eyes slowly coming awake.

"*Mmm*," he groaned so softly. "Morning." He rubbed his hand over my naked back, massaging between my shoulder blades. "How did you sleep?"

"Perfect."

He kissed my forehead, leaving his lips there for an extra few seconds. "I'm glad."

"Are you hungover?"

I'd served him enough beer last night to guess he probably had a little bit of a headache even though his eyes were clear and he wasn't wincing.

"Not too bad."

He put his hand in my hair, brushing through the strands, and I rested my face against his chest, the movement so relaxing.

"What are your plans today?"

"Since Frank wouldn't put me on the schedule for tonight and I don't have any homework, I have nothing on the agenda. I do need to go home soon and check on Gran."

"I'll come with you." My body stiffened, and I imagined he'd felt it because he added, "Pearl ..."

He'd offered to come with me many times before. I'd turned him down or avoided an answer each time. But as I glanced up from his chest, his hand went to my cheek.

"Don't hide her from me. She's the person you love most in this world; share her with me."

"Ashe ..." My voice was so soft. "It's not her I'm hiding." I sat up, crossing my legs in front of me.

His hand went to my knee, and he rolled onto his side to face me. "Talk to me."

CHAPTER 32

I glanced out the window, at the adorable-looking strip that was across from us, housing a cute coffee shop that we went to all the time and a restaurant that he'd taken me to a few weeks back. On the ends were brownstones that were probably worth several million.

"Where I live looks nothing like this."

"So?"

As I gazed at him, he seemed unaffected by my brief description. I needed him to understand.

"So, it makes me uncomfortable—the thought of showing you my neighborhood when I compare it to yours."

He cupped my cheek, his fingers rubbing a small section of scalp behind my ear. "I want to see every part of you, Pearl. Even the parts that make you uncomfortable. And believe it or not, I would be so proud if you showed me your home."

I was staring into his eyes, searching for answers. "I don't understand."

"You work at the bar almost every day of the week, you go to college full-time, you're the lead actress for the school plays, you support your grandmother, you put food on the table, you pay all of the bills." He placed his fingers on my heart. "You do all of this without anyone's help; every bit of it is on you. And yet, you still make Dean's List every semester." He kept his palm there but extended his fingers to my shoulder. "Most kids, like myself, wouldn't be capable of even half that. We've been given everything we have, and we haven't worked a day in our lives. So, instead of worrying what I'm going to think, you should be proud to show me everything you've worked your ass off for."

I looked around at the matching furniture in his room and the expensive signed jerseys he had framed on the wall and the fluffy comforter that matched his pillowcases.

"You're right," I said softly. "It might not be the best, but it's ours."

There was no judgment in his eyes, just admiration. "And I will love it."

I knew this was the next step in our relationship; it just wasn't an easy one. I had no experience, no knowledge on how to tackle this vulnerability, how to continue to reveal all the different sides of me when each came with new, uncharted emotions.

But I would learn because holding back wasn't fair to him.

Just as he began to rub my muscle, loosening me up, my eyes closed.

I took in a deep breath and said, "Okay." My lids opened, and I stared into his eyes. "I'll take you home."

THIRTY-THREE

BEFORE

ASHE

I'd never been to Roxbury. The farthest I'd ever taken the orange line was to the Mass Ave. stop to visit friends at Northeastern. But I'd heard things about that area; it was impossible not to when it was known as one of the roughest, gang-ridden sections of the city.

When stepping off the train with Pearl, I had images in my head of what I expected it to look like, and the reality met every expectation. There was graffiti almost everywhere, trash littered the sidewalks, a drug deal took place on a bench as we walked by.

Pearl acted as though she didn't notice, and I assumed she had become immune to it all. I was sure if I'd spent most of my life here, I would have been as well.

While my hand was holding hers, she used her other one to point to a building across from us. "I lived there with Vanessa. I was probably around nine at the time. We only lasted a few months, and then we moved there." She was nodding toward the next high-rise, both almost identical. "At some point in my life, I've lived in most of the buildings in this area."

"You mostly stayed in Roxbury?"

"With Vanessa, I lived in Dorchester for a bit and Jamaica Plain, but she seemed to like Roxbury the best. I don't know; maybe the drugs were better here." She paused. "Gran has had the same place for as long as I can remember. She liked it because it's so close to the train station, and she used to take the orange line to work. She was a seamstress for a small shop in the Back Bay until arthritis made it impossible for her to sew."

None of the areas she'd mentioned were any safer than Roxbury.

I lifted her hand and held it against my lips, kissing the backs of her knuckles. "When did you move in with Gran?"

"When I was twelve." She looked straight ahead. "Vanessa overdosed one night, and one of the junkies who lived with us carried her to the clinic. Before he took her, I was shaking her. Her lips were blue, mouth foaming." She sighed. "It was fucking awful." She finally glanced at me. "The next morning, when she got discharged, she came home and didn't have anything to shoot up. She took me to her dealer's house and didn't have enough cash for her usual, so he fronted her, but he wanted something for collateral." She bit her lip, breathing heavy. "She left me there."

"Tell me you're kidding."

"For four days." She glanced down, and I saw the pain in her profile. "She had known she was going to use me as collateral—that had been her plan all along."

I squeezed her fingers, giving her every bit of strength I had.

"I always protected her, always took care of her, always made excuses for her. But once she finally came and got me, I went to Gran's, and I never looked back."

"I understand now." I kept her fingers against my mouth, still kissing them. "I wouldn't call her my mother either."

Her eyes softened, and within a few seconds, she whispered, "Ashe ... we're home."

Her building didn't look different than any of the others, except the front steps were shattered with massive gaps between the breaks. Instead of grass, the property was surrounded by dirt, the snowfall that had just melted making it muddy. She took me around the back, where the lock had been broken and was dangling out of the door.

Instead of the elevator, we rushed up the stairs and down a hallway, Pearl opening the third to last door on the left. The paint was flaking off, but at one point, it looked to have been teal.

"Gran," she said once she stepped inside, "I'm home, and I've brought Ashe with me."

"Dollface," I heard as I closed the door behind me. "Happy New Year."

Pearl walked straight past the kitchen and into the living room, where Gran was sitting on a couch against the wall. Pearl sat next to her, kissing Gran's cheek, and I watched Gran's fingers hold Pearl's face.

"Gran," Pearl began as I entered the room, "this is Ashe."

She couldn't have weighed more than a hundred pounds with gray hair and heavily wrinkled skin, eyes that were warm and endearing, like Pearl's had become.

"The hands are fragile," Gran said as she held one out to me. "You're the size of a football player, so just don't go and tackle them."

"He's gentle, Gran."

I let her fingers fall on my palm, and I surrounded them. "It's such a pleasure to meet you. Should I call you Gran?"

"Gran or Esther—either is fine." She pulled her hand back and patted Pearl's lap. "Switch here with my Pearl. I want to take a good look at you."

Since there were no other seats in the room, Pearl moved to the floor while I took her place, immediately feeling Gran's gaze on me.

"He's very handsome, dollface."

I quickly glanced at Pearl as she said, "I know." Her cheeks flushed a little. "I'm very lucky, Gran."

She patted my knee so softly that I barely felt it. "Thank you for taking such good care of my baby. She's extremely special to me, as I imagine she is to you."

I nodded, feeling myself take a deep breath. "I care about her a lot."

"I can tell." She looked at Pearl and said, "Dollface, would you mind fixing me some tea? The wind has been coming through these windows all morning, and I can't get rid of this chill."

"Of course. I'll also turn up the heat." She rose from the floor. "Can I grab you anything?"

Gran's hand rested on my shoulder. "She makes the best tea."

"Then, I'll take one too."

Pearl grinned. "Coming right up."

When it was just the two of us—I figured that was what Gran had wanted—she said to me, "Pearl has never brought a gentleman home before. From the moment she returned with those slices of pie, I knew you were special to her."

I took a quick look at the kitchen, making sure she wasn't watching us through the small window. "I've been enamored with her since we met."

She didn't move her hand when she replied, "My Pearl has spent her whole life fighting. She was determined to be the first in her family to graduate high school and now college." When she breathed, I saw the love for her granddaughter and the emotion that followed. "I know she can be cautious and closed off, even challenging at times, but once you break through, she has a filling like that wonderful peanut butter pie." She stared into my eyes, reading them in a whole new way. "Thank you for being patient with her."

I exhaled, "I would have waited forever."

Her hand moved to my face, as though she were reading Braille on my cheek. "She found a good one; I can feel it in my bones."

"What are you two talking about?" Pearl inquired as she came back in, handing me a steaming mug, placing one with a straw on the table in front of Gran.

"Ashe was just telling me about your New Year's." She left my eyes to look at Pearl. "I hope you didn't work yourself too hard and you got some good rest last night."

Pearl knelt in front of her. "It went perfectly. All of it." She put her hand on my jeans, pulling the loose material. "I'm going to give Ashe a quick tour, and then I'll make you some breakfast. Oatmeal today or cold cereal?"

Gran looked at me again. "Do you see how good she is to me?"

"The best," I replied, holding out my hand to help Pearl stand.

When I expected her to pull away, she clasped her fingers with mine. Gran's eyes told me she had noticed, and her expression reinforced that she approved.

"It was an honor to meet you, Esther."

"You too, young man."

I followed Pearl into the short hallway, where there were two doors across from each other and an accordion-style partition at the end.

"Bathroom," she said, pointing to the one on the right and then switched to the left, adding, "Gran's room." She slid the accordion door open. "And this is my room."

There was a mattress on the floor and a small desk on the side. A few pictures hung on the walls above a dresser, which must have held all her clothes since there was no closet. I went over to the photos to check them out. One was of her on the stage, dressed in character, and I guessed it was from high school. The other few were taken even before that, where she was standing in different poses with Gran.

"Man, you were adorable."

Old books were lined across her shelves, and I picked one up, reading the inside inscription of *The Outsiders*.

One of my favorites, dollface.
I hope you get lost in the words.
—Gran

Small, cozy, and full of the most important moments.

I set it back down and looked at her. "It's the perfect bedroom." I surrounded her face with my hands, gently kissing her. "Gran is pretty incredible." Her eyes lit up as I continued, "I see so much of her in you."

"How so?"

I tilted her face up, holding her steady. "When I looked into her eyes, I thought I was staring into yours." I pressed my lips to hers again. "You might be protective on the outside and slow to let anyone in, but what's inside is so unique, so loving, so much like her."

She was quiet for several seconds before placing her hands on top of mine, holding me against her face. "Thank you for pushing me to come here." Her eyes closed, and she let out a long breath. "I'm so happy I finally showed you this part of my world."

I rested my arms on her shoulders, pulling her closer to me. "No oatmeal or cereal for today. I'd like to go down to the store that we passed on the way here and grab some bacon and eggs and some pancake mix. Would Gran like that?"

"She would love that." A smile grew across her gorgeous face. "But does that mean you're going to help me cook?"

I laughed. "I'm going to hang out with Gran on the couch and get every naughty story from your past, so I can tease you relentlessly."

As she stared at me, her smile changed to one that was more emotional, and she eventually fell against my chest, where she wrapped her arms around and hugged me.

She didn't need to say anything.

I could feel every word in her grip.

THIRTY-FOUR

KERRY

I could barely call it a bed.

Thin, stuffed with what felt like wood chips, with still no covering or sheet, and hardly any cushion from the cement underneath.

That wasn't the only thing that sucked down here.

There was no heat, no natural light.

Just stairs, cement, the bucket, and my doll—Beverly was what I'd named her.

Despite all the hell, I was a good girl.

I'd try my hardest to be.

When he put me in the wide-strapped white dress, I would hold in my tears. They were dripping on the inside but not on the outside.

Like the screams that shook me from within.

Like the words I wanted to call him.

Like the spit I wanted to shoot into his eyes.

He'd reward me for being good.

He'd bring me a book.

I'd read it over and over.

And when I was good again, he would replace it with a new one.

Except, once in a while, it was one he'd already given me.

Those were the times I wanted to be extra bad.

I didn't dare.

When he handed me a paperback, it was always worn. Some would have a missing page or two. Corners would be dog-eared.

I wondered by whom.

If that person had things to do—ironing and cooking and running errands—and would set down the book, returning to it much later.

I was sure they weren't put in a white dress.

Positive they weren't being held in a fucking basement.

There were times when Ronald was feeling even more generous, and he would bring down a bag that didn't have a white dress, but clean clothes for me to change into.

A bucket filled with water and some soap.

On those days, I would bathe.

I would dunk my head into the bucket after I washed my body and lather my greasy locks, urging the dirtiness to come free.

Waiting to feel a sense of relief other than constant grime and pain.

But that never came.

Clean no longer existed.

I could change, wash, soak, and I would still feel soiled.

And he would still take my picture despite how disgusting I was.

When I was dressed in white, he would make me pose.

Smile.

Turn my head as though I were a centerfold.

I didn't know how many he took.

I didn't know what he did with them.

I knew nothing ... like how much time had passed.

But I could guess.

When my nails grew long enough to bite, I assumed it had been a week.

When I got my period, a month.

That was what my life had turned into, nail-biting and periods.

And playdates that I tried to block out.

And no voice.

It had been so long that I forgot what it was like to speak.

When he actually allowed me to answer, I wasn't permitted to talk above a whisper.

I couldn't even tell him how badly the hunger was getting to me, how the lack of consistent meals was causing my body to shrink away.

I was light-headed.

I was positive I was seeing things that weren't there.

Beverly lifting her cotton-filled hand.

Beverly waving at me.

Beverly shouting, "STOP!"

She was in pain.

She needed me.

I pulled her into my arms, squeezing her, trying to give her all my comfort—the same way she had done to me many times.

You're okay.

We're going to get through this.

She was silent.

Still.

And then I heard, "FUCK!"

I squeezed her tighter.

My poor Beverly.

I would do anything to make her feel better.

I tried to stand, thinking a little pacing might help ease her, but my knees collapsed onto the cement.

I had no energy.

No stamina.

Everything was spinning.

I clung to her soft fabric, holding her against my chest, my face in her neck.

Talk to me.

Tell me what's wrong.

"I can't take this anymore!"

Oh, Beverly.

It's okay.

I patted her back, holding her even tighter, wishing I had the strength to move the few inches to the bed so I could lay her down.

But I couldn't.

I had to just stay right here.

I was so tired, and my eyes shut.

Until I heard another sound.

A high-pitched one.

Like a cry.

A scream.

A fighting word that came with spit.

"NO!"

Oh God, my poor Beverly ...

THIRTY-FIVE

AFTER

ASHE

I punched in the security code at the front door of Dylan's
Back Bay townhouse, smelling barbeque the moment I
walked in. He'd told me to come hungry. I'd been so busy at
work, so I'd missed lunch, making me ravenous by the time I
turned the corner into the main living space.

"Ashe, you tardy motherfucker," Dylan said from the couch
the second I entered. "It's about goddamn time your ass
showed up."

"Work," I blamed, my reason for being over thirty minutes
late.

I loosened my tie as I made my way toward him. I hadn't
even had time to go home and change, knowing that would tack
on another twenty-five minutes before I got here.

We pounded fists, and I continued on to the kitchen, where
Alix and Rose, her best friend, were drinking wine.

"I see he gives you plenty of shit too," Rose said as I
approached.

"He's just getting warmed up," I told her, kissing her cheek.
"There's a lot more where that came from."

I moved over to Alix, and she set down her glass to hug me. "You know he gets extra cranky when he hasn't seen you in a long time."

I smiled. "You mean, cranky isn't his normal demeanor?"

She laughed. "Good point." As she pulled away, she added, "It's so good to see you, Ashe. We've both missed you terribly."

"See, even my wife is giving you shit," Dylan said.

"I'm not your wife yet. I still have time to escape," she teased back.

On the kitchen island, between the two women, was an extra glass. I placed it in front of me and lifted the bottle of red wine they were sharing, pouring a few fingers' worth, and then I took it down like a shot. "Work has been ..." I shook my head, trying to find the right word.

"Hell, I know ... and I get it," Alix replied. "It hasn't been any prettier in my department."

Alix saw tragedy from an entirely different angle, but she still saw more than enough. And each day that passed in this city, the cases seemed to be coming in faster.

"I don't know how either of you does it," Rose replied. "The things you guys witness, I'd never be able to sleep again." She wiped the corner of her mouth, the wine matching her lipstick.

"This helps," Alix responded, holding up her wineglass. She glanced at me, an understanding in her eyes. "What can I get you to drink, Ashe?"

"Beer." I patted her shoulder and moved to the other side of the island. "But no need to get it for me. I'll help myself."

While I grabbed one of the bottles and screwed off the top, the ladies joined Dylan on the couch, giving Dylan's chef more room to spread the food out onto the island.

I said hello to him and took a seat at the end of the large sectional, next to Dylan.

As I was kicking my feet onto the ottoman, Alix asked me, "How's life been aside from work?"

"Honestly, life has been all work lately."

"I hate that fucking answer," Dylan replied.

Alix turned to him and said, "You don't have much room to talk, mister. You've been back and forth to London so many times that it's making me jet-lagged."

Dylan had opened an office there, and pre-Alix, he would have just lived in the UK until it was up and running. But he'd been traveling back and forth to be with her, and I knew that had to be a lot on both of them.

"What do you want to bet that if we dimmed the lights and covered us in blankets, the four of us would be asleep in seconds?" Rose joked. "A year's salary?"

I held up my beer. "I'm Team Rose on this one."

Dylan looked at me and said, "Jesus, I miss the college version of you. It's not even nine o'clock yet."

"That makes three against one." Alix yawned.

"You all need to snap out of this and buck up," Dylan barked.

Rose rested her head on Alix's shoulder. "Maybe this should turn into a *Sex and the City* night."

"You mean, fuzzy slippers and soft robes and kicking Dylan into the guest room so we can have the bed?"

"*Yasss*," Rose sang.

"There's not a goddamn chance of that happening," Dylan said, leaning forward to look at both girls. "You're going to put your big-girl panties on and go out to dinner and go dancing and have drinks, like you've been talking about for days. Meanwhile, Ashe and I are going to drown ourselves in Chef Mark's barbeque and some Macallan single malt and the NBA."

"Shit," I replied. "That does sound sexy."

"Your man might be right," Rose replied. "Cosmos and

dancing and those extra-greasy slices of pizza we always buy from the pushcarts outside the bar? It does sound pretty fabulous."

Alix shimmied her shoulders as though music had started playing. "*Ohhh*, the pizza."

Dylan kissed the top of Alix's head. "And then you can call in tomorrow, so we can lie in bed all day, hungover as fuck."

"Dylan—"

"Rose, have my back here."

"Alix, listen to your soon-to-be hubby. He's got a point."

"Agreed," I chimed in.

"We all know I'm probably not going to do that." Alix laughed.

"Rose, get her good and wasted for me."

Rose stood, holding out her hands for Alix to grab. "I'll happily accept that mission."

"Oh God, you two," Alix sighed, giving Dylan a kiss before she got to her feet. She then came over to me, and we kissed cheeks.

"Great to see you," I said to her. "You too, Rose."

The ladies waved and grabbed their jackets and purses from the kitchen and headed for the front door.

Dylan watched them leave and said, "Only a couple more months, and that woman will finally be my wife."

I turned toward him, swallowing the gulp of beer in my mouth. "Now, that's a wedding I can't wait to be in."

"Everyone I love under one roof while I marry the girl of my dreams, followed by the most kick-ass reception Boston has ever seen. Yeah, I can't wait either." He looked at the TV, but I could tell he wasn't focused on the game; he was inside his head. "And then we'll be spending a week in South Africa and another week at Mount Kilimanjaro—no work, just Alix and me and not even a goddamn cell phone to interrupt us."

"And a wedding band around your finger."

He was quiet for a few moments before he glanced at me. "It's wild, man; the moment I opened my company, a feeling came over me, and I knew it was what I was meant to do." He took a drink from his tumbler. "Marrying Alix is no different. She's the woman I'm supposed to spend the rest of my life with."

I knew that too. From the moment they'd met, there was never a question in my mind that those two were supposed to be together.

"I'm so fucking happy for you guys." I gripped his shoulder. "You know I love her like a sister."

"Wait until you hold your niece or nephew in your arms."

My back shot off the couch. "She's pregnant?"

"Not yet." He shook his head, grinning. "But if it's up to me, she will be very soon."

I continued squeezing him, keeping my grip tight. "Dylan Cole, changing diapers and getting spit up on. I'm ready to witness that."

"Seeing my baby pregnant and rubbing my hands all over her belly ..." He exhaled. "That's what I'm ready for first."

I took a few deep breaths. "I hear you."

He had looked away, but his eyes were back on mine, and they were different than before.

Instead of his mouth, they were doing all the talking.

And I knew exactly what they were saying.

THIRTY-SIX

BEFORE

ASHE

s I was double-parked outside her apartment building, Pearl rushed out the back door, bundled in a jacket, hat, and mittens—things I'd told her to wear for today.

"I didn't know you had a car," she said, climbing into the passenger seat.

"I don't." I waited for her to get settled before I pulled into traffic. "It's my mom's. I borrowed it for the day."

She was smiling as I glanced at her. "Are you going to tell me where we're going?"

"Surprising you will be much more fun."

She continued grinning as I turned down several streets on the way to the interstate.

Today had taken a bit of research, as the destination was somewhere I'd never been. But because it was so high on Pearl's fun list and seeing her smile was at the top of mine, I knew I had to make it happen. With some help from my parents, I'd found what I needed, and fortunately, it would only take about a half hour to get there.

I reached across the front seat, holding her hand in mine.

"I'm sorry I didn't make it to the bar last night, like I'd planned. Dylan really wanted to go, too, but that paper took me all night to finish, and it kicked my ass."

We'd had a month off for Christmas, where I'd gotten to spend almost every day with her, and now, we were back to the full swing of another semester. I missed that time off—when school hadn't dominated a majority of our life. If I wasn't attending class, I was preparing for one, or doing homework, or buried under mounds of studying. The amount of work was coming on thick, and the hours I spent with Pearl were thinning out.

"Don't worry about it." Her fingers weaved through mine. "It was slow, and I got cut early. I went home and studied for the test I had this morning."

I quickly glanced at her.

"And that's the only reason I didn't come over, knowing we wouldn't have gotten any homework done."

I was disappointed to hear I could have woken up next to her this morning, but she was right; we weren't our most productive when we were in each other's presence.

I lifted her fingers to my lips. "You're forgiven but only because I have you for the afternoon."

"And the night."

I looked at her again. "You don't have to work?"

Behind the happiness in her eyes was an even stronger emotion.

Worry.

Each shift she didn't go into the bar meant a month that would be financially tighter, a concern that she wouldn't make enough to cover everything she needed. She rarely spoke about it, but she didn't have to—I could see the stress.

I kissed her knuckles before setting her hand in my lap.

"Let's grab some food later and cook it at your place, so Gran can enjoy it too."

I felt her eyes on me.

"Are you sure you don't want to go out or eat dinner in your bed instead?"

I turned off the highway and came to a stop in front of the light. "Do you know what we're about to hit?"

"I'm hoping it's not something with this beautiful car."

Damn it, she's so cute.

"Our six-month anniversary."

She squeezed my fingers, her voice turning quiet as she replied, "I know."

"I think I've shown you in that time how much Gran means to me."

"You have." She adjusted the collar of her jacket, so it wasn't rubbing against her mouth. "I just ... I don't know."

The directions were written down and tucked into my pocket for reference, but I remembered I needed to take a right at this light. I waited until it was clear and turned.

"Talk to me, Pearl."

She took her time to respond, waiting until we stopped again. "Sometimes, you feel like a dream. Like this is all too good to be true."

Since the light was red, I released her hand and cupped her cheek, my fingers sliding under her hat. My stare held hers steady. "Don't you know I feel the same way?"

As she exhaled the air she'd been holding in, I gave her a kiss.

"I've never been this happy in my entire life," I whispered against her mouth.

When I turned toward the windshield, she kissed the inside of my hand. "Me too."

My foot returned to the gas, and I made a few more turns before entering what looked like an abandoned parking lot.

"You still have no idea where we are?" I pulled into a spot and shut off the car.

She searched the space around us—the trees that surrounded both sides of the large lot, the little view across that showed a few cozy neighborhoods. "Nope, I'm clueless."

"Good."

I nodded for her to get out and met her at the back of the car. When I lifted the trunk, she gazed at what was inside, her eyes then instantly meeting mine.

"You didn't?"

I took out the two sleds that I'd packed in, holding them like surfboards against the ground. "I did, and this is supposed to be the best hill in the area."

She jumped into my arms, legs circling my waist, hugging me. Each of her breaths hit my neck, the speed of them increasing with every second that passed. "I love you, Ashe."

The sleds fell from my hand as I wrapped my arms around her, my eyelids closing at the sound of her words. I held her so tightly—a hand gripping the back of her head, the other holding her against my chest.

I waited until her eyes were on me again before I said, "I love you."

I kissed her softly, so she could feel, not just hear, what was happening in my chest.

Our mouths stayed tangled, the coldness creating a thick white fog as we breathed each other out.

"And I love you for doing this for me," she sighed, now a few inches separating us.

I swayed her in my arms as though music were playing, her smile growing with each dip. "I told you it was going to be a year of fun. Are you ready?"

She clenched the tops of my shoulders, but I barely felt the squeeze through my jacket. "Yes."

I went to set her down, but she didn't move.

I laughed at more of her cuteness coming through. "Are you sure? Because you're going to have to let me go to make that happen."

"That's the problem, Ashe ..." The emotion in her face was taking ahold of me, clenching as tightly as her fingers. "Every time I'm with you, it gets harder and harder to do that."

THIRTY-SEVEN

BEFORE

PEARL

"Good morning," Ashe said as he pulled me against his chest, my face falling somewhere around his neck.

I stretched my leg over his, my eyes blinking from the spring sunlight that came through his window, yawning from the little sleep we'd gotten.

I had known coming here after work was going to make me even more tired than usual, but I'd wanted to spend every second I could with him.

Even if that meant hardly any sleep.

I nuzzled into the crook of his muscles. "Morning."

"I hope you don't have any plans today." I glanced up at his eyes, and his hand cupped my butt as he added, "Because I have no intention of letting you leave my bed." His hardness pressed against me, the tone of his voice changing.

"*Mmm*," I groaned, my hips meeting his. "I can give you a few hours, but then I have some errands to run to get everything ready for tonight."

"What's tonight?"

"Gran's birthday."

His hands were suddenly on my face. "Why didn't you tell me?"

I shrugged. "I don't do anything crazy to celebrate. I just make her favorite foods for dinner and banana pudding for dessert—she loves that for some reason—and I always swing by the used bookstore to grab her a couple of paperbacks."

He held my chin. "No."

"No?"

He rolled me onto my back, hovering over me. "I'm going to take you both out for dinner." When I didn't respond, he went on, "You're an excellent cook—I'm not trying to take that away from you. This is just something I'd like to do ... if you'll let me."

There was so much love in his eyes that I couldn't breathe.

I couldn't form any thoughts.

I couldn't even answer him.

"I realize I wasn't invited." He laughed. "Maybe I'm imposing. If I am, just tell me—"

"Not at all." I swallowed. "This is just one of those moments when it feels like a dream."

He pressed his nose to mine, rubbing our tips back and forth, his fingers on my ribs. "You're very much awake, and you haven't given me an answer."

When I'd met this man, the leaves had started to change colors and fall from their branches. With my hand in his, I'd watched the first snow fall. And now, clasped once again, spring was whistling from behind the window next to his bed. Each season, he had continued to surprise me. I wasn't sure if that was something I'd ever get used to—how his thoughtfulness and caring nature were a constant theme in our relationship. I'd certainly never seen that in all the years I'd lived with Vanessa.

But men like him really did exist.

I had proof.

"I would love that more than anything." I took a breath, the tightness in my chest another reminder of how real this was. "But I don't want you to pay—"

"I knew you were going to say that. I knew you were going to try and stop me, and there's no way I'm letting you."

"Ashe ..."

His hand moved to my cheek, his thumb swiping my bottom lip. "How much would you normally spend on dinner and books for Gran's birthday?"

Since I bought items I typically wouldn't—like steak and twice-baked potatoes with cheese and sour cream, fresh vegetables instead of canned, and the pudding—it exceeded my average food budget. I'd planned on getting her some white wine as well—now that I was old enough to buy it.

"Probably around fifty, maybe sixty."

"Take that money and go get her nails done instead. Wouldn't she love that? Someone to rub her hands and make her feel beautiful for the day?"

I didn't know if Gran had ever gotten a manicure. I couldn't remember a time that I'd ever seen them painted. I trimmed them for her, her hands no longer able to grip the small clippers. I even cut her hair, keeping it in a short bob that only required me to scissor straight across.

"Ashe ..." I shook my head, torn. It wasn't his responsibility to feed all of us on Gran's birthday.

"Please, Pearl." He kissed my lips. "This is something I really want to do." He framed my face with his palms. "You take Gran to the salon and give me the address, and that's where I'll pick you up and take you girls to dinner." He leaned in closer, his lips inches from mine. "I just need you to say yes."

There was a knot in the back of my throat. A burning as I tried to fight away the tears. "Yes."

He kissed me again, soft, like a whisper. "Tonight is going to be perfect, just you wait and see."

Less than twelve hours later, every word he had promised came true.

Gran sat with us at a small, square table, several candles lit between us in the middle, the dim lighting in the restaurant showing the flicker of fire across her face. One that had been grinning since I'd returned to our apartment this morning and told her I was taking her out. At the salon, she had gotten a cut and a blowout, a style much sleeker and more defined than I was capable of creating. Short light-pink nails sparkled from her hands, which had been massaged in lotion.

Ashe had chosen a steak house in his section of the city. Many of the cuts of meat I'd never even heard of before. I picked the one that had the smallest amount of ounces, Gran getting the same, and Ashe ordered several sides since they didn't come with our meals.

Gran sipped her white wine through a straw, looking so tiny in the big, round leather chair. "This is the nicest restaurant I've ever been to."

The same was true for me, of course, but I said nothing, not wanting to take this moment away from her.

She reached across the tablecloth, her eyes lit with love as she rested her fragile fingers on Ashe's arm. "I don't know how I'm ever going to thank you."

He curled his fingers around hers, smiling back. "Having you here with me on a day that's so special is more than enough."

I knew it had only been six months. I knew we had some heavy decisions to make next year after we graduated. I knew many things could happen before and after that. But the way he looked at the woman who was the only mother I'd ever had —with admiration and protectiveness in his eyes was something I would never forget.

"The only thing I wish for each year is for my dollface to be happy." She continued to gaze at Ashe. "You've made that wish come true."

She turned toward me, her smile even brighter, tears welling in her eyes. I couldn't remember the last time that had happened. Gran wasn't one to ever get weepy; she was the strongest woman I knew. "I love you more than anything in this world, baby."

Ashe's fingers were squeezing mine under the table.

A feeling filled me that I'd never felt before.

Never in my entire life.

Contentment.

"I love you," I whispered to both of them, my voice not able to go any louder or I was positive the tears would drip.

THIRTY-EIGHT

KERRY

I couldn't take my eyes off the plate.

It sat on the stairs, the smell reaching all the way over to my bed.

Where I was lying.

The dress was off and, "Good girl," was being growled in my ear.

I didn't listen to him.

I didn't feel his presence.

I was a pit of emptiness.

Filled by him but solely focused on the plate.

All I could smell was the meat.

Hearty, rich, savory, like pot roast. Small wisps of steam rose into the air. Bland-colored carrots, softened but still erect, stood from the center.

My stomach grumbled.

The side of my face was shoved into the dewy-smelling mattress, blocking half my vision.

I still stared, not blinking.

The potential of a full belly was the only thing keeping me from breaking.

The warmth.

Comfort.

Suddenly, the pain halted.

There was a chugging of air.

Like a train putting on its brakes.

His weight was then gone.

He released the back of my head, my face lifting from the mattress like a suction cup.

The sound of metal, a loud cough, feet moving across the gritty cement, and then, "Do you think you've earned yourself a meal?"

I pulled my bare legs against my chest, wrapping my arms around them.

The clothes I had taken off to dress in white were close by, but I wasn't allowed to put those on yet.

There were rules.

I dragged my eyes away from the plate, meeting his emotionless black pits.

He liked to play this game.

Make me question if I was deserving enough.

Make me fear if he was going to leave the food since there had been times when he took it with him.

I nodded.

"Use your voice, Kerry."

My throat stung as my lips parted, sucking in air and pushing it through my chest—a pathway that had been clogged from not speaking for so long.

It had been at least a period and two nail-bitings since I'd uttered anything above a whisper.

"Yes." My spit was thick, and I cleared my throat. "I've been the best."

He laughed.

His glasses fell halfway down his nose, his gobbler wiggling as though it were saying hello.

"You're so fucking greedy." He rolled up his sleeves, showing dark hair that curled. "You're nothing but a disappointment."

My body began to shake as he grabbed the wide-strapped white dress off the floor and walked over to the stairs.

I held my breath as he went up the first five and stood over the plate.

He glared down at it.

Then at me.

"Should I spill it on the floor and make you eat it that way?"

I shook my head.

Silently begging.

"Do better, Kerry."

How?

I didn't fight.

I didn't tell him no.

His lips stretched across his teeth. "Do fucking better."

He glanced back at the plate.

The tears were building, my hands clenching.

He began to bend, like he was going to lift it, but stopped.

His eyes were on me now.

Reading my body language.

As he laughed again, the noise vibrated through each of my muscles, burrowing into my chest, where it echoed long after he stopped.

"You pathetic doll."

He continued to climb, and at the top, the latch shut.

One, two, three locks clicked into place.

I didn't put my clothes back on.

I hurried over to the stairs instead, climbing until the plate was in my hands, before carefully returning to the bed.

He hadn't left me any utensils, so I used my fingers to scoop up the meat.

I moaned the quietest noise as it dropped onto my tongue.

The juices, the texture, the flavor—they were perfect.

I went slow, nibbling at a speed my stomach could handle.

When I was halfway done, I forced myself to take a break.

To set the rest aside, giving me something to look forward to in a little while.

I turned to Beverly, where she was resting on the other side of the room.

When I'd first heard the latch, that was where I'd placed her.

I didn't want her too close.

I didn't want her to watch.

She had been upset enough already.

I put on my clothes and went over to her.

I pushed my back against the wall and sat down, holding her in my arms.

Her face was against my chest.

Her hair was wild, so I tamed the yarn with my sticky fingers.

She was sad—I could feel it in her body.

She didn't like when the monster came down into our cave.

She didn't like when he played.

I needed to cheer her up. I needed to make her feel better.

It's going to be all right, I told her. *It's over ... he's gone for now.*

While I waited for her to respond, like the screaming and fighting words that had burst out of her not that long ago, I rested her face on my shoulder.

I began rocking my body, humming an almost-silent tune, tapping her back.

There was no specific beat, no words. Just a quiet, steady rhythm.

And when I needed to add some drums, I reached behind me with my other hand and knocked on the cement.

"*Hmmm*," I sang to her. "*Hmmm, hmmm, hmmm.*"

Knock.

Knock.

"*Hmmm. Hmmm, hmmm, hmmm.*"

Knock.

Knock.

Just as I took a breath, I heard something.

A sound I hadn't expected.

One that made me turn silent.

That made my whole body freeze.

This time, it hadn't come from Beverly.

I was sure of that—she was in my arms, making it impossible.

It had to have come from someone else.

I waited to see if it happened again.

A few seconds later, it did.

Soft, subtle but definitely clear.

Someone was knocking back.

THIRTY-NINE

AFTER

ASHE

"The city is going to be fucking torture today," Rivera said as we walked inside a coffee shop, waiting in the short line to place our order.

I gave the barista my credit card since it was my turn to buy and took a sip of the dark brew she'd handed to me in exchange for the payment. "Every year, it's the exact same," I said to him on our way out. "Drunk people stumbling everywhere, the Back Bay covered in glitter. Screaming, chanting. It's like Boston's version of fucking Mardi Gras."

"And a police nightmare."

I opened the door for us, and we stood on the sidewalk out front.

"When I was in college ..." My voice died out as my mind took me back there. A time when I'd thought I'd be wearing a white lab coat and scrubs to work. When medicine and Pearl and Dylan were the only things that mattered in my life.

The memories were unfolding faster than I could control them.

CHAPTER 39

"When you were in college ..." Rivera said, reminding me of where I'd left off.

"Right ..." I cleared my throat, staring at the ground, pushing those thoughts away. "Dylan and I would make Patriots' Day a tradition every year. We'd get shit-faced and watch the marathon." I shook my head, still remembering. "And now, being thirty-three and working in law enforcement, I have a much different view of the holiday."

"Ain't that the truth?" He banged his coffee against mine as if it were a beer. "What are you up to today?"

A guy walked by us, his face and chest painted like the Italian flag, arms high in the air, shouting to no one in particular.

I sighed. "I'm parking myself at my desk, finishing some paperwork for the DA. You?"

"I've got a few witnesses to interview for a homicide I was called to last week. I'm going to have to fight the traffic all day; it's going to be hell."

I took a drink. "Good luck. I don't envy you one bit."

He dodged three girls who passed us on the sidewalk, their arms hanging over each other's shoulders. They could barely walk, and it wasn't even nine in the morning yet.

"And I don't envy you," he replied. "You'll be calling me in an hour, bitching that people haven't stopped coming by your desk and you haven't gotten a goddamn thing done."

"Probably."

He laughed, taking a few steps back in the direction of his car. "I'll see you tomorrow."

"Bright and early when she kicks your ass out." When he flipped me off, I added, "Get a fucking nose strip already."

"Yeah, yeah. I see whose side you're on."

I continued chuckling as I made my way to the police station.

FORTY

BEFORE

PEARL

"Come with us," I said to Dylan, taking a seat next to him on the couch while Ashe stood in front of us, his suitcase and my duffel bag by his feet.

"Nah," Dylan sighed. With the TV remote in his hand, he flipped through the stations, like it was a challenge to see how fast he could press the button. "I'm feeling lazy as hell, and this couch is way too comfortable to get up."

"Come with us," Ashe declared, mirroring my words.

"I'm good. You guys have fun," Dylan shot back.

Yesterday had been our last day of finals, our junior year now wrapped and over with. Most of the students were heading home for the summer. For us, home wasn't a plane ride or a long drive away. That was why Ashe had wanted to get out of town for a few days—to unplug after all the work we'd put in and celebrate the start of a long break.

And both of us, more than anything, wanted Dylan to join us.

"Why are you being so hardheaded?" I asked, shaking his arm until his eyes landed on me. "You know I've never been to

Maine before, and it would be even more fun if I had both of you to show it to me." I glanced at Ashe, and he was smiling, encouraging me to continue. "I'm not taking no for an answer, so go pack a bag. Ashe will call the hotel and change our king room to two double beds—"

"Hell no," Dylan said, cutting me off. "That's where I draw the line. If I go, I want my own room. I've heard more than enough of you guys—we share a wall in this apartment; don't forget that. The last thing I want is you keeping my ass up while we're on vacation."

My skin blushed as I laughed. "Fair enough. We'll book you your own room." I glanced at Ashe again. "Quick, call the hotel before he tries to back out."

Ashe hurried into the kitchen, grabbing the cordless phone.

I faced Dylan. "You need to go pack."

He stretched out his limbs, yawning, ending in a more reclined position. "But I have such big plans here that I don't want to miss."

"Like what?"

He adjusted the pillow behind his head. "Sleeping and flying."

"We're only going to be gone for three nights. You'll have the rest of the summer to sleep and fly."

I pushed myself off the couch, halfway through the living room when I turned around and said, "If you're not going to pack, looks like I'll just have to do it for you."

"Jesus," he groaned. "You're as relentless as your boyfriend."

I laughed and continued to his bedroom, finding his suitcase in his closet and unzipping it on top of his bed. "How many pairs of shorts do you want to bring?"

"All right, all right!" he yelled, followed by the sound of him getting up from the couch. "I'm coming."

_____

"I'm going to admit something even though I really don't want to," Dylan said from the top of Cadillac Mountain. He nudged my arm, making sure I was listening. "I'm happy as hell you dragged me here."

I looked at him and smiled. "Told you."

We'd spent the majority of our vacation in Portland, but late last night, we'd decided we wanted to do some hiking, and the boys had suggested we come here in the morning. This mountain was supposedly the most beautiful in the state, and it had taken a bit of a drive to get here, the terrain tougher than I'd ever expected to climb. But as we sat together on the peak, I was so happy we'd come.

Never in my life had I seen a sight more stunning than this.

The view was endless, the colors of the sky changing now that we were up this high. Trails were carved into the distant mountains, trees sticking up from them, like tiny stick figures when I knew they were probably as tall as houses. The rock of each ridge was a deep purple with a blend of navy and brown.

And beneath us was the bluest water I had ever seen with small islands freckling several different spots of the sea.

This was my first true hike.

My first real vacation.

The highest I'd ever been in the air.

As I sat on the ledge, my legs dangling over the side, a sense of calm moved through me.

A sensation I certainly hadn't felt during the last month, trying to juggle the bar and studying for finals and wrapping our final play of the semester.

And spending time with the man I loved.

But that was all behind me. I had the next few months off from acting and homework and classes, and now, I could enjoy

Maine, where there was silence and warmth and Ashe's arm surrounding me.

I rested my face on his shoulder—a spot that had become a home I couldn't get enough of.

A home much different than the one I shared with Gran.

"Thank you," Dylan said softly from beside me. I looked at him just as he added, "I'm really glad I didn't miss this."

I put my hand on his arm, releasing it after I said, "Me too."

The last two days we'd spent time at the beach in Ogunquit, renting boogie boards to ride the waves, and at night, we had gone to the bars in the Old Port after long dinners by the wharf.

But this was my favorite moment.

Where the beauty took hold and made it hard to breathe. Where the quietness was the perfect soundtrack. Where my heart sped up every time I looked in Ashe's direction.

Like I was doing now.

He didn't have to tell me how gorgeous it was here or how much he loved me or how happy he was that Dylan had joined us.

I saw every one of those things in his eyes.

And I nodded, telling him I agreed with each one.

FORTY-ONE

AFTER

ASHE

R ivera had been right; I hadn't gotten a goddamn thing
done at the office aside from moving a pile of folders
from one side of my desk to the other. From the moment I
had stepped through the door, it had been a fucking
shitshow.

Holidays were like full moons; they made the residents of
our city even crazier than normal. Phones were ringing off the
hook, my desk line being one of them—witnesses suddenly
remembering things they'd originally forgotten, loved ones of
victims checking in for updates.

As I looked around the office, I wasn't the only one
distracted. Every detective in here was in the same situation,
and as we caught eyes, I could see the stress in theirs.

It had been a wasted day, and I never should have come in.

I either needed to stop answering the phone and get some
work done or get my ass home and take all the paperwork
with me.

Now that I'd finished talking to the DA's assistant, I placed
the receiver down. She had kindly reminded me that she

needed my notes no later than tomorrow morning, or the DA would skin me.

Needing to get started, I opened the file I'd been trying to get to since I'd had coffee with Rivera, and I picked up a pen and the notebook that I kept with me on crime scenes, where I jotted down all the details while they were still fresh in my head.

I was just in the middle of transferring the first few sections when a noise shot through the department.

One that was so fucking loud, so rattling, that it sounded like a crash of thunder had erupted through the ceiling, splitting the floor in half.

The pen dropped from my hand.

My fingers shook, my heart pounding inside my chest.

My stare lifted, looking across the unit to find the cause, but each face I came across had the same question as me.

An eerie silence took over—calls halting, all talking ceasing.

I gripped my desk, my stomach twisting into a fucking knot, as one call came through, and it went to the captain's desk. A glass wall separated her office from the main space. I watched her pick up the phone, the expression on her face as she listened, her lips moving in response.

She set down the receiver and walked out to speak to us, every detective staring at her.

Waiting.

Her face ghostly white.

Not a single one of us shifted in our chairs or cleared our throats.

I was positive none of us were even breathing.

Because we knew.

Our training told us exactly what that noise had been.

It was just a matter of where it had come from.

The captain stilled, balancing on her heels, hands clenched

in front of her. "There's been a bombing ..." She glanced around the space, swallowing before she delivered, "At Copley Square."

That was the location of the finish line.

Where thousands of people from our city and from all over the world had congregated, watching the runners pass through.

Within a second, every detective was on their feet, hands on our guns, running for the stairwell.

FORTY-TWO

KERRY

I'd been such a good girl.

In my head, I told myself I would always be one.

That I would follow his demands.

That I wouldn't fight back.

But even I could only take so much pain.

Until I broke.

And I was fucking shattered.

When his teeth gnawed into my shoulder, the bite so extreme that flashes of light shot through my eyes, and his nails gripped my thigh like cobra fangs, I screamed.

At the top of my lungs.

And then I shouted, "STOP!"

I pushed him away, hurling my body to the farthest cement wall.

His deathly eyes stared at me as my chest pounded, as the blood dripped down my arm. In the filmy, bile-colored light that hung from the ceiling, I could already see the bruises forming on my thigh.

Dark red drips fell off my hand onto the wide-strapped white dress.

I swore I saw steam coming from his mouth.

"You naughty fucking doll."

I shook my head, swallowing. "I can't," I gasped. "I just can't anymore."

I needed someone to hug me.

To make him stop hurting me.

To take me out of this basement.

"You're going to regret this." He wiped his mouth with his arm, the curly hairs scraping across his facial scruff, making the most dreadful sound. "You just really fucked up."

His belt rattled, echoing through the room. His breath came out in huffs.

"Have you ever been punished before, Kerry?"

"Isn't that what this is? Day after day of nothing but punishments?"

I knew I should have kept my mouth shut, but I was already in trouble.

It couldn't possibly get worse.

He laughed.

It was a cackle that dragged out, extending for several beats.

Like I was on a comedy stage, having delivered the funniest joke he'd ever heard.

The second he quieted, I used all the strength I had left to add, "Fuck you."

The pain trumped my conscience.

I was done.

I couldn't take another violation.

The isolation.

The abuse.

The threat that I'd be here for the rest of my life.

Hope was the sun rising each morning. But when you were

in a basement with no windows, there was only darkness with no end.

If he wasn't going to give me an end, then I was going to make one for myself.

"Kerry ..." He pushed his glasses high on his nose. "Oh, fucking Kerry." He rubbed his hands together, like he was washing them with soap. "You are one stupid doll."

His size didn't allow him to move fast, so each step added to the buildup.

I stared at his hands, waiting for what they were going to reach for first.

They came forward, and I tried to lean to the side, but there was nowhere to escape.

He grabbed me but not skin or muscle, like I'd anticipated. He gripped the wide straps of the white dress and pulled so hard that it ripped off me.

"You don't deserve to be taken care of like a good doll."

I sat, naked, on the floor, hugging my knees.

He held the dress to his face, smelling it. Rubbing the fabric across his rough bristles. "Do you know what happens with dolls I no longer want to play with?" He laughed again, a warning, as though I was about to find out.

But there couldn't be anything worse than what I'd already gone through.

I couldn't be hungrier than I was now.

I couldn't be more battered and bruised.

He took my clothes off the floor and carried them up the stairs, watching me the entire time until he disappeared at the top.

The latch clicked, and one, two, three padlocks followed.

And then the single light that hung in the ceiling turned off.

Filling the room with pitch darkness.

I shivered, running my hands over my arms, feeling the dampness from the blood.

The lack of light made the room feel even colder than normal.

The only things down here to warm me were the cot and Beverly.

With no glow, I couldn't see her, but I knew she wasn't far.

I pushed myself down the wall, the grit and sand scratching the skin on my butt. I moved slowly, reaching into the blackness, feeling for her cotton or yarn, clasping the second I touched one.

"Beverly," I cried. "Hold me." I set her arms on my shoulders, squeezing her against my chest.

She wasn't hugging me with the strength I needed.

She wasn't telling me it was going to be okay.

My shoulder was aching; my thigh was throbbing.

"Oh God, Beverly." I held the back of her head. "Tell me I'm going to be all right."

Tears were wetting her hair, my sobs sending tremors through her body.

"Beverly!"

I just needed her voice. I needed her to talk to me. I needed something other than nothing.

I pulled her off me and shook her in the air, trying to wake her up. "Bev—" I started, but a sound cut me off.

A voice.

One that was familiar.

Because I'd heard it once before.

I'd thought it was Beverly's, but there was no way it could have been hers; it had come from the other side of the wall.

I pressed my ear against the cement.

I listened.

And I heard, "I'm here," followed by, "Don't worry, Kerry. He'll forgive you."

FORTY-THREE

BEFORE

PEARL

As my eyes opened, my back slowly lifting off the floor, I could feel the audience staring at me. I could almost hear their long intake of breath, holding the air in their lungs, waiting to see if this final act was a retelling of *Romeo and Juliet* or if this was our own spin—an ending that wasn't going to result in my death.

It was a fair question.

Our director had certainly modernized the tale from the set design to the clothing. He'd made changes to the original script to keep the audience guessing.

I'd rehearsed this part hundreds of times onstage and in our apartment, even when I was at Ashe's.

The setting was Romeo's home, the floor of his bedroom, a bed behind me that we'd endlessly made love in. As I leaned up from the carpet, he was next to me, our arms still stretched toward each other, our fingers almost touching. From my position, the lack of movement in his chest told me he wasn't breathing. I pulled myself closer, placing my cheek there, listening.

No sound.

No rise and fall.

When my ear went to his nose and then his mouth, there was no intake of breath.

"No!" Tears streamed down my face, and I tasted them on my lips when I shouted, "*Nooo*," again. I pounded his chest with my fists, begging air to move through his lungs. Sobs came out in bursts, each quiver causing more gasps. "Please." I lifted his head, holding his face in my arms, kissing each part of it. "Please." I swallowed, the spit becoming too thick for my words to sound clear. "I need you."

I'd practiced ways to make the lines sound authentic, to make the emotion appear real. But all I had to do was think of Ashe, the way it would feel if he were taken from me, and the tears naturally fell, the idea of him suddenly being gone from my life causing tremors to shake my entire body.

I curled into the crook of his arm, resting my face on the spot where I always cuddled Ashe—the home I had built on my boyfriend's chest—and gripped his shirt in my palm. "No, Romeo!" I wailed. The sobs made my voice convulse, pain etched deep in my face. "I-I can't l-live without y-you."

I lifted his arm that was dead weight and draped it over my body. I needed the feel of him. The warmth. The sensation of still having him with me. "I d-don't want t-to be in a-a world w-without you in it-t," I whispered.

I glanced up his chest, the same way I always did to Ashe when we talked, and I pressed my lips to his.

One final taste.

One last good-bye.

"I love you."

I pulled my mouth away, the feel of him still so present, and I went over to the table, where there was a small vial of medication—the same cocktail that had killed my Romeo. Using the syringe that had taken his life, I stuck the tip into the medicine and filled the chamber.

A ritual I'd seen Vanessa do when I was only a kid.

I pulled the tourniquet from Romeo's arm, and holding the needle between my teeth, I tied it around the top of my bicep, tightening my fist. Tears dripped onto my arm as I pumped my fingers for a vein.

Now on the floor, my back resting against Romeo's side, I stared up at the sky. My eyes closed, my heart opening. It was a moment, like the one I'd taken before I blew out the candles on my peanut butter birthday cake.

A silent wish.

And when my lids opened again, I guided the fake needle into the crook of my elbow. My arm dropped, my breath becoming shallower each second.

I fell against Romeo, my head resting on his chest.

My back arched as my heart tried to beat, my lungs attempting to fill.

When they couldn't, the last bit of air exhaled out of me before my wheezing turned to quietness.

That only lasted a second before there was an eruption of applause from the audience.

The heavy red curtains closed. I pushed myself up from the stage, Romeo doing the same, and he quickly threw his arms around me.

"You fucking nailed it, Pearl."

"You too," I replied. "You were really incredible."

We hurried off the stage, watching the curtains open again as members of the cast rushed to the front to take their bows. The order was based on role, Romeo and I the last to go. The entire audience was already giving a standing ovation by the time we arrived. With the lights slightly dimmed, there was no glare, and I was able to make out their faces. Just a few rows back was Gran. She was on her feet, clapping, Ashe and Dylan on each side of her.

Real tears were in my eyes.

I curtsied in the center of the stage, the clapping getting louder, and I blew my family a kiss.

Romeo, now facing me, used both arms to point in my direction, showing his admiration and respect, and the audience's praise exploded even louder.

My heart was bursting, my hand pressed against it.

Thank you, I mouthed to him and then again to the audience before we joined hands and rushed backstage, celebrating with the crew and director.

Opening night had been a true success.

Once I grabbed my things and said good-bye to the cast, I hurried out the back door, where my family would be waiting.

Gran was sitting on the seat of her walker at the bottom of the stairs, Ashe and Dylan next to her.

"Oh, my dollface, you were spectacular."

I flung my arms around her, and she pulled me close, the scent of her baby powder filling my nose.

"You were a sight to be seen up there, a real showcase. I couldn't be prouder."

Gran's vision had been getting worse—a condition glasses couldn't fix—and I wasn't sure how much she could have actually seen from her seat. But my sound, the music—they were enough for her.

"Thank you, Gran."

I kissed her cheek and moved on to Dylan, hugging him and thanking him before I buried myself against Ashe's chest, where he held me so tightly that I couldn't breathe.

But I didn't want to.

I just wanted to get lost in his arms.

"Blown away," he whispered against my neck. "Literally blown the fuck away by what you did up there."

I clutched him back. "Thank you."

"I couldn't believe that was my girl on that stage." He kissed my cheek, breathing against it. "You amaze me, Pearl."

My eyes were threatening to tear up again, the smile on his face everything I needed to see as I pulled away. "I love you," I said, looking at all three of them. "Thank you for being here."

I hooked my hand through Gran's, knowing the plan was to grab some dessert before taking her home, and I was just about to help her across the parking lot when I heard, "Excuse me, Miss Daniels?"

I halted at the sound of my name and turned around. The man standing behind Ashe was the one who had spoken it. He was dressed in an extremely impressive suit, a briefcase hanging from his shoulder.

"Yes?" I responded.

He held out his hand for me to shake. "I'm Brett Young, an agent and one of the owners of The Agency, the largest talent firm on the East Coast."

I felt my eyes bulge as I put his face to his name—one that had been whispered throughout our department since the first day of my freshman year.

"I'm extremely impressed with what I saw on that stage. I'd heard you were phenomenal, but I wasn't expecting a performance like the one you just delivered. Do you have a few minutes to talk?"

I'd heard there would be a few agents in the audience tonight.

But I hadn't heard Brett Young was going to be one of them. An agent every actor in the country would give up anything to sign with.

"Yes," I replied quickly. "Of course I do." I turned toward Ashe, trying not to freak out when I said, "I'll be just a minute."

"Not a problem," he said, taking Gran's hand from mine, smiling with so much encouragement. "We'll wait for you over by the car."

As they began to walk away, I faced Brett. "It's an honor to meet you. I've been following you for a long time." I realized how that sounded and corrected, "I don't mean *following*, following."

He laughed and moved us over to the side of the stairs. "I understand, Pearl, and the honor is mine." He adjusted his jacket. "I normally send my team to some of the top-performing schools, looking for new talent, but everyone raved about you, so I had to come see you for myself." He shook his head, the streetlights showing me how pleased he was. "You certainly made the trip worth it. Could you meet with me tomorrow morning? I'd like to talk about your goals and see if we can find a place for you in our company."

I didn't have to act.

I was positive the shock and emotion were covering my face.

This was the moment I'd been waiting for.

The moment where everything was going to change. The dream I had of making a better life for Gran, of getting her out of Boston, had the potential of coming true.

My lips parted, a breathlessness in my chest. "Just let me know where and when, and I'll be there."

FORTY-FOUR

AFTER

ASHE

The clock on the wall was digital. Rather than hearing the constant tick of the second hand, I had my eyes glued to the countdown. Each minute that passed meant we had that much less time to find the motherfucker who had blown up our city.

When it came to acts of terror, time was of the essence.

That was why our captain and the director of the FBI had immediately called us back in before any of us had even reached ground zero. The two of them stood at the head of our conference room, a whiteboard behind them that showed the breakdown of the last several hours. Diagrams of the finish line depicted the location of each detonation, and camera footage was running on a wall-mounted TV, replaying the last minute before the explosion.

Once the video ended, it started over.

Tactical teams were on the ground, forensics were scouring every inch of the area, crews were monitoring phone lines that had been set up for tips from the public. And we were here, coming up with the plan on how to identify the bastard and take their ass down.

Every few minutes, we were updated on the number of deceased, the amount injured, how the hospitals in the area were handling the sudden intake.

Mentally, Boston was a fucking wreck.

But everyone in this room, along with teams that were being flown in, was tough as hell, and we were going to do everything we could to heal those wounds.

Since the explosion, my phone had been vibrating nonstop from my pocket, and I'd dodged all calls, aside from my family, letting them know I was safe and ensuring they were as well. But as I took a quick glance at the screen, Alix's name was on it.

She had just called a few minutes ago and not left a message.

I sent her to voice mail, hoping she would leave one this time, and looked at the FBI director. He was outlining how far the fragments of the bombs had flown. But as I tried to focus on his drawing—the details of this important, as it helped us figure out the exact spot of ignition—Alix was calling again.

As a paramedic, if she hadn't already been on the schedule for today, I imagined she would have been called in to ground zero. I was sure she was phoning to get information on the bomber, probably on her way to the hospital with an ambulance full of wounded.

I didn't have time to answer those questions.

They needed me here, in this room, paying attention.

I sent her to voice mail again, my eyes back on the board, the anxiousness in my stomach heightening as the FBI director began circling the placement he was estimating as the location of the first bomb. Once that was determined, footage could be reviewed to look for unusual activity and movement, bringing us one step closer to finding the suspect.

My phone vibrated, this time with a text message.

Alix: CALL ME RIGHT NOW.

There was something about her words that set off an alarm inside my body.

The urgency.

The demand.

Things I'd never seen from Alix before.

I glanced up when there was commotion in the hallway—it happened every time the door opened, someone coming or going. Now, it was from two agents making their way inside, finding seats behind the large table, and again as I rushed out the already-open door.

Once I was outside the room, I found Alix's number and connected the call, holding the phone to my ear.

Within a ring, she answered, her voice coming out as a gasp. "As-she."

"Alix? Are you all right? I'm in the middle of—"

"As-she!"

She sounded worse, a mix of weeping and hyperventilating.

I rushed down the hallway several paces, finding a bare wall to push my back against. "What's wrong?"

"A-sh-sh-e," she stuttered, and I was hardly able to make out what she was saying. "H-he's gone."

I pressed the phone even harder against my ear, making sure there was no space in between the speaker and my skin. "I don't know what you mean. Who's gone?"

"Dy-lan."

My heart lodged into the back of my throat; my free hand flattened against the wall to hold my balance. The weight in my legs felt so heavy; they didn't want to hold me anymore.

"What do you mean, he's gone?"

"We were at the m-marathon, and he was st-standing at the finish-sh line." She tried to inhale, but her lungs wheezed. "I-I held him in m-my arms, Ashe. H-he's gone."

My back lowered as my feet gave out, landing me on my ass. "No, Alix." The room was too bright, too loud. I placed my hand over my eyes to block some of it out. "Tell me this isn't fucking true." My stomach was revolting, my heart stopping while I waited for her answer.

"When I-I held him, he was already d-dead." Her voice quieted, but there was no mistaking what she had said. "I-I rocked h-him until they to-ok him from me-e. Oh God, A-Ashe. Oh God."

My hand left my eyes and clenched into a fist, pounding on the floor. "No." My fingers were threatening to break. "No, Alix. *Nooo!*"

I couldn't process this.

I couldn't comprehend it.

I couldn't believe it.

My best friend ... couldn't be gone.

No.

"Ashe!" she screamed, like she was fighting for her life. "I s-still have his blood o-on my hands. I-I can't wash it off-f." She gasped in a breath. "Help me, A-Ashe. H-help me!"

My eyes dripped, and I swiped it away before I punched the floor again. "No."

"Every time I-I look down, I see h-him. His lifeless body. Those b-beautiful eyes closed. Oh God-d, Ashe. I c-can't ..."

My teeth ground together, the tightness in my chest expanding to the rest of my body.

I couldn't feel.

I couldn't think.

I couldn't ...

My eyes shut, squeezing together, the air not moving well through my lungs. "No."

"You're the first person I-I've called. I haven't even t-told his parents." She let out a cry that was even louder than the others had been.

"Alix ..." I had no breath. No thoughts. I was a pit of emptiness, trying to work my way through this news. "No."

"I have t-to go relive this all over again when I-I tell his mom and d-dad."

"I'll do it." I paused, trying to swallow. "I'll call them."

"I was-s there, holding their son. It-t feels like it sh-should come from m-me." She took several breaths, almost choking after each one. "Good-bye, Ashe."

The phone went dead before I could tell her I was leaving for the hospital, to be there for her, my cell now dropping from my hand. As it hit the floor, the screen turned on, showing a photo of Pearl, Dylan, and me.

It was eleven years old. The morning of graduation.

Dressed in our caps and gowns.

"No." My fingers clenched, hitting the hard floor, unable to stop. "Nooo!"

FORTY-FIVE

KERRY

"*He'll forgive you.*"

The words that man had spoken from the other side of the wall stayed with me.

I didn't know who he was.

I didn't know how he fit into this equation.

But I'd said more to him and not gotten a response. I'd even begged for conversation, and each request had gone unanswered.

The more time that passed, the more his words repeated in my head, the more the punishment sank in.

And it came on immediately.

No food.

No light.

No emptying of my bucket.

I was stuck in the dark, in the cold, with nothing, except for the cot and Beverly.

Not even a drip of water to wet my tongue.

I'd experienced dehydration in the past—when I went running on hot summer days and didn't drink enough water.

But this was a dryness that took over my entire body, like a hose had sucked out every drip from inside me.

My head pounded.

My stomach churned.

I didn't think I could survive another minute.

Yet this was what I'd wanted, wasn't it?

For it all to end?

If I'd thought I was living in hell before, nothing compared to this.

The total darkness was terrifying. Consuming. It took my brain to places I didn't want to be in.

I screamed.

As loud as I could, I shouted, "*Ahhh!*"

I wanted to see my hands. The floor. The walls. Things I'd taken for granted while I'd been down here.

Beverly wasn't enough.

She couldn't make this tolerable.

I needed him—Ronald—to make this better.

I barely had the strength to lift my head from the mattress.

To open my mouth.

To shout, "I'm sorry!"

I saw stars in my vision the moment my lips closed.

They were the size of freckles, and they moved.

Danced.

I followed them with my eyes, connecting their shapes, listening to their quiet buzzing sounds.

I tried to wet my lips, but my tongue was so dry, like I'd coated it in flour, that I couldn't.

"I'm sorry," I whispered. "Ronald ..." I choked, gagging on the thickness in my mouth. "I'm so sorry." I coughed, trying to make it easier, to feel better. Nothing worked. "I'll be a good doll." My eyes closed—even that was too much. "I'll do whatever you want ... just make this stop."

FORTY-SIX

BEFORE

PEARL

Only three months until graduation. I was keeping a countdown on the calendar that hung above my desk, each day in red marker, showing how many I had left in Boston. That meant only three more months until Gran and I moved to Manhattan, where I would be auditioning for Broadway, where Brett, my new agent, wanted me to begin my career. He was going to have his assistant send me some apartment listings, so I could find us a place that I could afford. And as soon as I arrived, he was going to start having me audition for commercials and voice-overs, jobs that would bring in a steady income until I could land a permanent role.

Things were happening.

Fast.

And my heart was trying to process all of these new opportunities, the dreams that were on the verge of coming true. But while that was happening, something was weighing down my excitement.

Ashe.

He had applied to three medical schools and was waiting to

hear where he would be going. It didn't matter where he landed; none of the schools were in New York, all would be several hours away from me.

This was exactly what I had been trying to avoid when he pursued me last year, why I hadn't dated in the past.

The thought of leaving half my heart in Boston—or somewhere that wasn't minutes from where I lived, like our apartments now—was a thought I could barely handle.

I loved this man.

A love that I'd never expected to happen, but one I was positive I couldn't live without.

And each time I stared at the countdown, like I was doing now, the number decreasing so rapidly, a wave of anxiety would move through my chest, digging a hole right in the center.

How was it possible that part of me was dreading this move when it was all I'd ever looked forward to?

"Dollface?" Gran called from the living room, dragging my eyes away from the numbers—a break I so desperately needed.

I got up from my bed and wandered down the hallway, sitting next to her on the couch. "What's up, Gran?"

"Are you feeling all right?" She put her hand on my forehead, checking to see if I was running a fever. "You usually spend your nights off with Ashe; it's unlike you to be home."

Her fingers slid to my cheek before she acknowledged that she felt no temperature.

I caught her hand before it dropped, holding it between mine. "I'm fine, Gran."

"I could tell the second you walked in here that you were not fine." She sat up straighter, and the blanket fell from her chest, which I immediately fixed. "When you hurt, baby, I hurt. Tell me what's bothering you."

I exhaled as I looked toward the window, unable to hide

anything from her. "I was just in my room, thinking about the future."

"Always the worrier." She gently moved her thumb across my palm. "You were in this same place right before you two became a couple and again when your feelings for him grew." She lifted my chin, causing our eyes to connect. "You have to realize, you can't change the outcome. What's meant to happen between you and Ashe is already written. So, stop stressing about the what-ifs and the unknowns." Her eyes moved back and forth between mine. "Life is going to happen; you don't have the power to stop it, dollface. So, tuck your body into a ball and roll with each bump."

"But I love him and ..."

"And he's madly, deeply in love with you." She leaned forward, getting closer, lowering her voice when she said, "I promise you, whatever is meant to be will be. But neither of you has the power to control fate, so stop trying." Her lips went to my cheek, where she kissed me so softly.

I kissed her back and continued staring at her, even after she pulled away, watching her take a drink of her tea.

She had a point. There were certain things I couldn't control, and this was one, but that didn't ease the emotions in my chest.

"Are you going to Ashe's?"

I nodded. "I'm supposed to be there now."

"Dollface, what are you waiting for?"

"Answers. Clarity." I shrugged. "A crystal ball."

"When you stumble upon one of those, will you send it to me?" She lifted my hand up to her mouth, kissing the backs of my fingers like a hen would peck at grain. "You're forgetting to live in the moment because you're so stuck in the future." She turned quieter. "Stop it, baby."

"You're right. Again."

She smiled. "Now, go along. I don't want him to worry."

I stood from the couch and was heading toward my room to grab my things when she called out my name, causing me to turn around.

"Bring those boys some of the cookies you made me yesterday. Lord knows I won't be able to eat them all."

I grinned suspiciously. "Are you sure you want to share?"

"Just save me a few. The ones with the extra peanut butter hunks on top."

I laughed. "I love you, Gran."

"From the sun to the moon and every star in between, baby."

FORTY-SEVEN

BEFORE

ASHE

All three envelopes sat on my desk, unopened. They hadn't arrived on the same day. In fact, two of them had come a few weeks apart. But I had promised myself I wouldn't break their seals until all decisions came in. I didn't want to get my hopes up or let down. I didn't want to start planning my future until I knew every option that was available.

Dylan had threatened to open them. He was just so fucking excited for me; he wanted to start celebrating and was positive I'd gotten into all three med schools. But I'd applied to the toughest, most challenging programs in the country with the hardest acceptance requirements. There was a good chance I hadn't gotten into any, and I didn't have a backup plan. It was either one of these three or I wasn't going at all.

That thought alone was enough to make my chest ache.

But that was also another reason why I'd waited. I didn't want to be punched in the face on three different days. I wanted one hard smack, and then I'd move on.

I'd waited long enough.

It was time.

I slid my finger under each envelope flap and set the letters on top, still folded.

The first I opened was from UPenn, and I scanned a few sentences, *congratulations* immediately popping out at me.

"Fuck yes," I whispered, my eyes closing as I processed what this meant.

The hard work, the long nights, the no sleep, the endless studying to get the best score I was capable of achieving on my MCATs.

All of it had paid off—at least for one of the schools.

I moved on to the next, Harvard's emblem printed at the top of the paper. I held my breath, reading the beginning lines, not believing what I was seeing. Harvard had accepted me too. I went over the words once again, just to be sure, and was just as shocked the second time.

I picked up the last one. The one from my top choice, Johns Hopkins. Once I had it opened, my eyes jumped past the introduction, the answer italicized on the second line.

The paper fell from my hands, landing on my desk.

"Holy fucking shit," I exhaled, staring at all three.

"I hope that's a good *holy fucking shit*," Pearl said from my doorway. She rushed in and wrapped her arms around my neck. "Sorry I'm late. I had a few questions for my professor, and then I ran into one of the girls from the play and ..." Her voice trailed off as she picked up one of the letters. "Oh my God, is this what I think this is?" She held it up to her face, her eyes widening as she read. She quickly grabbed the other two papers from my desk, giving them a scan before shouting, "Ashe, holy fucking shit!" She threw herself down on my lap, hugging me against her. "I'm so incredibly, ridiculously proud of you." Her lips were hovering over mine, hands framing my face. "You got into every school, just like I had known you would."

CHAPTER 47

"I can't believe it."

"I can." She kissed me. "You work harder than anyone I know. You hardly sleep. You study and study and study even more." She rubbed her nose over mine—something I loved to do to her. "If anyone deserves this, it's you. Now, which one are you going to pick?"

I didn't immediately answer, still trying to process what had just happened. "Man"—I took a breath—"I don't know."

She smiled, a light laugh coming out. "Yes, you do. Your dream school has always been Johns Hopkins." Her arms tightened around my neck. "That's where you're going."

"You're right."

"I know." She giggled, and it was a sound I could inhale; it was so delicious.

We turned silent, the news still unraveling, my brain taking me to Baltimore, Maryland, where I would soon be living. I already knew that distance from New York—I'd looked it up long before I received those letters.

"I'll be over three hours from you." I stared into her eyes, assessing them. "I hate how little I see you now. I can't imagine what it's going to be like when I hardly see you at all." I paused. "When you're acting every night of the week and I'm drowning in a relentless workload."

"I've tried not to let that weigh on me, but it has."

"Baby ..." The worry was so clear in her eyes. "You've been thinking about this too?"

She nodded. "I didn't know where you'd end up, but I knew it wasn't going to be in Manhattan."

I brushed the hair out of her face, holding her stare steady. "I'll have a car while I'm there. I'll come see you every chance I get."

"You'd better."

"And when you have a few days off in a row, you can take the bus to come visit me."

My suggestions didn't relieve the look in her eyes. And I knew why. This was going to be different than anything we'd ever experienced. We were going to be in two different worlds with a hell of a lot of space between us, and it was going to test us in ways we hadn't anticipated.

I could already feel the pull.

"It's going to be all right," I promised. "We'll figure this out." I held her cheek, making sure her eyes stayed on me. "We have to because I'm not letting you go."

She buried her face in my neck, so I couldn't see it, eventually breaking the silence with, "Let's go out."

"Where?"

She reached for the letter from Johns Hopkins and held it in the air. "Where we can celebrate this. You." She kissed my cheek. "And the monumental moment that happened today."

She stood from my lap, holding out her hands to help me rise from the chair. Once I was on my feet, I pulled her into my arms, gripping the back of her head to keep her close.

"I love you." I breathed in the cinnamon, my eyes closing. "For every reason."

"I love you more."

I heard her words, but I didn't believe them. It was impossible for her to have feelings that were stronger than the ones I felt right now.

FORTY-EIGHT

AFTER

ASHE

I stared at my phone while it rang, not wanting to answer the captain's call, thinking of every goddamn excuse not to. Once I'd told her what happened with Dylan, she'd left me alone for three days, giving me the space I needed to be with Alix and his family. Not a single person in my life was holding it together, including myself. But if I didn't answer her call now, it would be my ass.

I looked at the empty bottle of whiskey next to my bed, the dark room spinning as I sat up. I held the phone to my face, clearing my throat. "Flynn."

"I don't have time to ask how you're doing. I'm calling to tell you I need you in Watertown as fast as you can get there."

My hand stretched across my forehead, rubbing the top of it, and then raked through my hair. "I don't know. I'm not in good shape—"

"Flynn, we found them."

Them.

Her voice told me exactly who she was referring to.

Tamerlan and Dzhokhar Tsarnaev, the brothers who had

bombed our city and killed my best friend.

My hand dropped, and my eyes shot open—I hadn't realized I'd been keeping them closed. "Where?"

"I'm going to text you the information. Get there quickly. We'll assign you once you arrive."

A surge of adrenaline shot through my chest, my empty hand clenching the blanket, revenge building with each second that ticked. "I'll leave in five minutes."

"Flynn ... we need you there. We can't do this without you."

"You can count on me."

I disconnected the call and went into my closet, dressing in tactical gear. I ensured each tie was bound and every strap was pulled tightly, and I spent a good amount of time brushing my teeth before I grabbed my wallet and keys and rushed out the door.

When I got into my car, my hands on the steering wheel, only one thought was in my mind.

The next time I was behind this wheel, those motherfuckers were going to be in custody.

I wanted nothing more than to put bullets through both of their heads. But a punishment far worse was having them sent to a supermax facility, where seeing the sun for an hour a day would be the only privilege those bastards got.

"Police," my team yelled as they kicked in the front door of the house we'd been assigned. "Hands up where we can see them."

Several different police forces, the FBI, SWAT, and National Guard had been divided into a twenty-block area, as the brothers were suspected to be hiding somewhere in those borders.

As I stepped into the home, there was a man sitting on the couch in the living room, the TV on, his hands raised in the air, one clenching the remote.

Helicopters were circling above in the air, and blue lights were flashing through the windows.

The newscasters were covering every second of this manhunt.

There wasn't a fucking person in this state who didn't know what was going on right now.

"Don't move," one of my team members yelled at him. "Are you alone? Who else is in this house?"

"Just me," he replied.

The team split—half running upstairs to scour the second floor, the other staying on the main level—dividing to cover each room.

I approached the man, showing him a photograph of the bombers. "Are you housing these men?"

"No," he answered. "You're not going to find them in here."

"We'll be the judge of that," I told him.

As I entered the kitchen, there wasn't anything in the sink, the counters were mostly bare, and nothing was underneath the small table. Everything in here had a place.

"Clear," I yelled and went back to the living room, a cat weaving between my feet as I gripped my rifle with both hands.

"Clear," one of my guys yelled from the back of the house.

"All clear," an agent said from the front.

Once we had been assigned areas, we had been given blueprints to review each home, so going in, we would know the layout, how many floors, whether the house had a basement or attic.

This house only had the latter.

While we waited for the team upstairs to report back, my training caused me to study the living room. There were framed photos sitting on the TV stand, a few more on the end table by the couch. Several peculiar, abstract art pieces were on the walls, which I had a hard time dissecting. I stepped closer to the television to get a better look at the pictures and the faces that were in each one.

"When was the last time you were outside?" one of my team members asked the homeowner.

He continued to hold his hands in the air. "When I came home from work."

"Has your doorbell rung this evening? And have you answered it?"

He shook his head. "No."

The man's chest was rising and falling rather fast, his eyes darting to each of the agents, his foot bouncing on the floor. With his shoes still on, the heel made a noise each time it landed.

All very normal movements, given the situation.

"Where do you work?"

He used his head to point behind him, as though he were giving us directions. "L & S Accounting in Watertown."

"What do you do there?"

One of the agents who had been on the second floor just reached the bottom of the staircase when the man answered, "I'm an accountant and the owner."

The same agent stepped in closer and said, "Then why do you have an engineering degree from Wentworth in your office?"

No question was off-limits, not when every clue had the capability of leading to something much larger.

"Answer the question," I said to the man.

His arms dropped a few inches, and I sensed he was getting lazy. "I got bored of surveying land, decided to shift gears into something more profitable."

"When was the last time you—"

The agent's voice was cut off when, "Black down, black down," was shouted from the street.

Hearing the name of the mission—code that the suspects might have been located—caused every agent in this room to freeze. We all glanced at one another, needing a third announcement that would serve as confirmation before any of us moved a goddamn inch.

Anxiousness pounded through my fucking chest, my feet ready to rush out the door as we waited.

"Black down!" was finally screamed from the road.

My hands squeezed the butt of the rifle, relief flooding my body.

They got the motherfuckers.

"Clear out," I shouted.

Once we were down the front steps of the house, the agent running next to me said, "That guy was a fucking freak."

"Yeah?"

"We weren't able to finish searching upstairs because there was so much shit to look through."

"Do I want to know?"

He shook his head as we came to a stop in the center of the road. "No way, man." His eyes went wide. "Some people are into some weird shit, and I'm not one of them."

I didn't respond as we joined the large team of law enforcement, the director of the FBI at the head. As he detailed the plan of attack, my ears were buzzing, my fingers shaking.

A hand clamped down on my shoulder, and I glanced behind me to see Rivera standing there.

His grip tightened as he leaned into my ear and said, "For Dylan."

I released my gun just long enough to pound my hand on top of his, glancing up at the dark sky. "For Dylan."

FORTY-NINE

BEFORE

ASHE

"Gorgeous ..." I groaned as Pearl walked into my apartment, the shorts she had on showing those delicious legs. "Did you get it?" Even though the bag on her shoulder told me what I was asking about was more than likely inside, the excitement on her face also giving it away, I'd still had to ask.

She hurried over, locking our lips, the cinnamon so profound that I licked my mouth after she pulled away, just to taste her again.

"Yep." She giggled. "I still can't believe it. The whole thing is honestly so surreal." She reached inside the bag and pulled out her cap and gown, holding it against her body to show me what it would look like, the stole she had achieved for magna cum laude resting over the shoulders. "Now that we're only a week away from graduation ..." She shrugged, breathing heavy. "I don't know. It's a lot to take in and process."

"Nothing to process." I pulled her into my arms. "You've crushed the last four years; you've gotten sick grades and every lead in the play. You've teased the patrons who have come into the bar when you run around there in your see-through tank tops." I tickled her waist, kissing both cheeks and behind her neck, listening to her laugh the whole time. A sound so contagious and satisfying that I hated that I was mostly only going to hear it over the phone now. "It's time for you to crush the next best thing, and that's New York, baby."

A smile covered her face when she asked, "Did you get yours?"

I nodded. "It's in my room."

"Show it to me."

I locked our fingers together and walked her down the hallway and through my door, the cap, gown, stole, and tassels hanging on my closet door.

Her eyes widened as she stared at it. "Wow."

"It's identical to yours."

I could feel her eyes on me.

"I'm just envisioning what it's going to look like on your incredibly sexy body—that's all."

I chuckled. "Get over here." My hands went to her waist, and I pulled her against me, my lips taking ahold of hers.

"Is Dylan here?" she whispered.

Since our trip to Maine, when Dylan had made the comment that our rooms shared a wall, Pearl had been extra careful about how loud she was during sex.

"No."

"*Yesss.*" She jumped into my arms, wrapping her legs around my waist, her hands circling my neck.

I carried her to my bed, and once I rested her on top, I immediately began working on her clothes, peeling off each layer, along with my own, until we were both naked. With my lips back on hers, I palmed her tits, running my thumbs over her nipples.

Needing more, I kissed my way down her chest until I took

one of those scorching peaks into my mouth. I flicked the end, gently scraping the width, pulling it with my lips. Switching to the other side, I rubbed my stubble across the skin in between. Her back arched, and her breath came out in slow, steady moans, especially when I began teasing her nipple with my tongue. Each tug caused her to lift further off the bed, each nibble making her exhale a louder moan.

"Pearl," I hissed as I traveled down her navel, every inch I kissed even sexier than the last.

When I reached the center of her pussy, I glanced up, looking across her stunning body, at the dips and curves, skin that was so incredibly soft.

A body so fucking perfect that I still couldn't believe it was mine.

Goose bumps rose over her skin as I kissed her inner thighs, bursts of short breaths, long and deep inhales coming out of her.

"I need to taste you." I licked her entire length, her thick wetness coating my tongue. "And smell you." My nose pressed into the top of her, inhaling the cinnamon, rubbing up and down her slit so I could get her all over my face. "*Mmm* ... fuck me."

As I looked up at her again, her eyes were feral. Her expression hungry, telling me she was seconds away from begging for my tongue.

I wouldn't make her wait.

"Oh my God," she groaned as I gave it to her in one long, slow swipe.

My dick was so fucking hard and throbbing as I wedged my tongue between her lips, starting at the base of her clit and licking until I reached the top.

"*Yesss*," she breathed, her hand releasing my hair, her head leaning back to fall against the bed.

She liked that.

She was going to get a hell of a lot more.

I pushed her legs apart and circled the entrance of her pussy, plunging a finger deep inside. She was dripping, soaking my skin, a feeling that couldn't be sexier.

I arched my hand, reaching that special spot at the same time I licked her clit.

I wasn't gentle.

I didn't take my time.

I ate her like I hadn't put food in my mouth for days.

I added a second finger, working my way through her tightness, focusing on only the top of her clit, flicking it back and forth. I read her body, knowing when to increase my speed, when to slow down my hand. When she was getting close to coming.

Her knees bent, toes digging into the mattress. She gripped the sheet beneath her. "Ashe ..."

I sucked her into my mouth, massaging her clit with my tongue, and her sounds got louder each second. When she couldn't breathe without moaning, that was when I knew she was desperately close.

My mouth moved faster, my fingers thrusting harder, and her entire body clenched as a new wave of wetness began to drip. Her moans transformed into light screams, her stomach shuddering, and she came as I licked.

It was a sight.

One so fucking beautiful that I couldn't have pictured it in my mind even if I wanted to.

I turned down my speed, knowing she was probably extremely sensitive, and gently pulled my fingers out. I kissed around her pussy, gradually working my way up her body, mine now hovering on top of hers.

"Holy fuck," she breathed against my lips before kissing

me. "Your mouth … there are no words for what that thing can do."

I smiled as I pecked her, carefully slipping her legs around me, the tip of my cock teasing her.

"*Mmm*," she groaned as my teeth found their home around her nipple.

"I'll be gentle." I surrounded it, biting but not enough to cause her pain.

She reached into my hair, nails raking through until she found my shoulders, digging into my skin, urging me for more. "I don't want you to be."

Once that suggestion hit my ears, I was driving into her. "*Fuuuck.*"

I lifted her ass off the bed, going in even deeper. I positioned myself on my knees, holding her hips in the air, and she met me with each pump. As her tits bounced, her hands stretched behind her, holding on to the pillow as I increased my speed.

"You're so fucking wet."

She was tightening around me, clenching, each pulse making me want to move in further. I spread her legs wider and upped my stroke, rotating my hips, hitting every one of those sensitive places inside.

"Ashe!" she shouted. "Fuck!"

I knew how she was feeling. I wasn't that far behind.

I lifted her off the mattress and moved her toward the head of the bed. Once her back hit the wall, I held her there, her hands clinging to my shoulders, mine gripping her ass.

With the wall taking a majority of her weight, I dived in and out, kissing her. "Goddammit," I roared. "You're getting even wetter."

She kept me hugged against her, owning my lips with the same dominance that I was using to fuck her.

Each time she pulsed, telling me she was close, I would slow down my movements, teasing her orgasm even though my own was begging for a release. But she was starting to fight me, holding me tighter, rocking her hips back and forth, so when I tried to slow, she would take over.

"You want to come?"

I knew the answer. I could feel it from inside of her. I could hear it every time she took a breath.

I just wanted to hear her say the words.

"*Yesss.*" She drove her fingers into my shoulders. "Oh God, please."

I reared my hips back, and with more speed, more power, I deepened my thrusts, burying myself all the way in. And when I reached that spot, I twisted my hips before I pounded into her again.

She was milking me.

Her pussy goading my cum.

My balls tightened, a sensation moving through them and into my stomach, and I pressed my lips to hers, moaning, "Pearl," as the intensity began to peak.

She was bucking against me, hips slapping mine as she rode my cock with the same speed I was driving into her.

"Fuck," she hissed as our bodies began to tremble. "I'm coming."

We were locked in each other's arms, shuddering, our breathing in sync and equally as loud. The pleasure was spreading so fast that I couldn't control it.

And when it hit that highest point, I gripped her even harder, shouting, "*Ahhh,*" as I shot my load inside her.

We slowly came down, our sounds turning to shallow pants until there was just stillness between us, smiles building across our lips.

"*Mmm.*" She cupped my face. "I'm going to miss these afternoon sessions."

I chuckled even though the thought hurt, knowing someday, very soon, we would be living in different places.

I lifted her off the wall and set her on the bed, pulling her against me as I lay down. I kissed the top of her head, rubbing my hand over it, smelling that scent I loved so much. My eyes closed. "I'm going to miss everything about you, Pearl."

She said nothing. She just held me tighter.

FIFTY

BEFORE

PEARL

"I'm afraid I don't have the best news," Ashe said as I walked into his room that evening and collapsed on top of his bed.

Only two days had passed since graduation, and I'd been cut early from the bar due to how slow it had been tonight. Now that everyone had gone home for the summer, we weren't getting slammed with college kids.

I'd only made thirty dollars the whole shift.

And the stress was coming on thick.

In a little over a month, Gran and I would be moving to New York—a date I'd extended because with finals and graduation, I didn't have time to go to Manhattan to look at the apartments Brett's assistant had sent over. But whichever one I picked, I would have to come up with two months' rent—first and last—and a security deposit.

Meanwhile, our electric here was just days away from getting shut off for non-payment.

I yawned as I pulled his pillow into my arms. "Maybe you should wait and tell me in the morning." I rubbed my eyes, knowing I was smudging my makeup but too tired to care. "We have four hours to kill on the bus to New York, and I'm positive I'll be in a much brighter mood then."

He got up from his desk and sat next to me on the bed. His hand dived into my hair, holding the back of my neck. "I don't know how to tell you this ..." He paused, and my stomach started to act up as I saw the look in his eyes. "But I can't go with you to Manhattan tomorrow."

I squeezed the pillow tighter. "Please tell me you're kidding."

We'd planned this trip when Brett's assistant had sent me all the apartments that were within my budget. Seeing the photographs weren't enough. I needed to visit the small two-bedrooms in person, making sure they were in locations I liked and close enough to the train station. For the first time in my life, I would have a real bedroom, but before I signed a lease, I wanted to feel them out and choose which one felt best.

Ashe had promised to help, escorting me during my very first trip to New York, so I wouldn't have to do all of this alone.

His thumb was swiping my cheek. "I wish I were, baby." He glanced down, showing me how hard this was for him. "You know it's my dad's sixtieth birthday, and I thought he was going to have a small dinner at the house tonight, but he planned a trip for the entire family, along with Dylan's, to go to Maine instead. I told them I couldn't make it, and they laid on the guilt pretty thick." He turned silent for a moment. "I just don't feel right about missing it. Every year my dad is in remission, I feel like it's a birthday we need to celebrate, especially since this is the last one I'll be home for, for a while." His eyes met mine again, his filled with a deep sorrow. "I'm sorry, Pearl. This is not what I wanted, and I feel fucking awful about it."

Tears pricked the backs of my eyes.

Aside from the one trip we'd taken, I had no experience with traveling. Leaving Boston, navigating a whole new city, was so far outside my comfort zone that my body started to shake. I knew I would soon have to do it, and I'd be responsible for Gran, but this felt different. This was almost like a vacation that I was now taking by myself.

"I ... don't know what to say," I whispered.

"I know you're disappointed."

I couldn't get mad at him; this wasn't his fault. But I was angry at the situation, at the thoughts that were monopolizing my brain. At the shitty day I'd had and how this escape with Ashe was the only thing I'd been looking forward to.

"I'm a lot of things," I replied.

He lifted my leg to drape it across his, massaging my thigh once it landed. "I don't want you to be upset."

My mind was fast-forwarding to tomorrow. The bus ride, finding the hotel, eating at a restaurant, auditioning for upcoming roles—three days of that, alone, when I was supposed to be doing it all with Ashe.

A knot was slowly building in the back of my throat, an uneasiness moving into my chest.

Maybe this was just a taste of what was to come. Ashe would soon be in Maryland, and Gran would mostly be bound to our apartment.

Me against the world.

Like it had always been, except the stage wouldn't be familiar. This script unknown. The setting and backdrop completely foreign.

I wanted this, but I was still petrified of it.

"How can I make you feel better?"

I pushed myself to the edge of the bed. The comfort of his mattress, the fluffiness of his pillows, the way he was closing in on my leg—it all felt so suffocating.

"You can come with me," I told him.

There was pain in his eyes when he replied, "You know, more than anything, I want to."

That should have counted for something. And maybe it did, but at this moment, I couldn't feel it.

"You're going to kick ass this weekend," he said, his voice so soft. "You're going to nail your auditions and find an awesome place to live, and Brett is going to be there to make sure it all goes smooth as hell."

I had five auditions in total—two voice-overs, one commercial, and two fairly large roles in long-standing Broadway plays.

I needed Ashe there to calm me. The nerves were already taking hold, and I hadn't even gotten on the bus yet.

I shook my head, trying to push down whatever was blocking my throat. "I'm terrified."

Just because this was my dream, the only thing I'd ever wanted, didn't mean I wasn't scared to death to make it a reality. That I wasn't worried about landing a gig and being unemployed for too long and how I was going to afford our new place and the cost of living in this extremely expensive city. I had a fear of falling so hard on my ass that we would end up in a home that was worse than the one we lived in now.

"I just need you there, Ashe."

His hand was on my cheek. "I'm sorry I'm letting you down, but you're so strong, Pearl. I know you're going to be just fine, and you're going to nail those tryouts whether I'm there or not."

What I also needed was for him to stop being so positive and admit how much this sucked. What I needed was for him to be angry about the situation, like I was.

What I needed was for him to be in New York with me.

"Where are you going?" he asked as I climbed off the bed.

"Home."

"This is your home."

His statement caused tears to move into my eyes. This place would be theirs for only a few more weeks, and then all of us would be going in separate directions.

"My other home."

He followed me, reaching for my arm. "Why are you leaving?"

"I need some time to think. My head ... feels like it's going to explode." I put my free hand on my chest, pushing against my lungs. "And I'm ..." I swallowed, the words not coming to me. "I feel like I can't breathe."

"Pearl, don't go."

His fingers tightened on my wrist, and I pulled out of his grasp.

"I have to. I ... need things to feel right, and they don't at this moment." I moved to his door. "I'll call you the second I get home from New York."

"Pearl—"

"I love you."

I was halfway down his hallway when I heard, "I love you too."

Air wheezed through my lungs, my chest throbbing as I opened his apartment door, and once it clicked behind me, the tears finally fell.

FIFTY-ONE

AFTER

ASHE

One of the brothers was dead, the other taken into custody, where he would battle out the death penalty in court. He would either die from lethal injection or behind bars as an old man, but prison was where that motherfucker was going to spend the rest of his life.

And now that I was home, I couldn't get a goddamn minute of the last several hours out of my head.

I stripped off my tactical gear and locked my gun in the safe in my closet. My only wish as I walked back into my room was that it had been my bullet that caused Tamerlan Tsarnaev to take his last breath.

Now that it was all in the attorneys' hands, it was time to repair our city. Lives had been lost; hundreds had been wounded. Even more were going to suffer from PTSD.

The spirit of Boston was in turmoil.

And my best friend was dead.

His fiancée and family inconsolable.

My plan was to drink until I couldn't think.

I picked up the bottle of liquor that I'd placed on my nightstand on the way in, making sure the drapes were closed on every window before I climbed into bed. I unscrewed the top and held the glass mouth to my lips, swallowing until my throat burned so badly that I couldn't take another sip.

I wanted to erase.

Forget.

Even if it was for a goddamn hour, I just needed a break from this pain.

It had been relentless, not letting up when I was in that fucking weirdo's house, not when we were getting fired at by the bombers, not even when we took the sole survivor into custody.

It ate.

Soiled.

Churned.

And I couldn't take it.

Before I began guzzling again, I shot off a text to my family, letting them know I was okay, and then I clicked on Alix's last message.

> Me: *I don't know how much news you're watching right now, but it's over. One dead, one in custody.*
> Alix: *Just tell me you're all right.*
> Me: *I'm home. Safe. I'll check on you tomorrow after my hangover.*

"I didn't think you were going to make it in today," Rivera said when I took a seat at my desk the next morning, gripping a large coffee, a headache throbbing from inside my skull.

When I'd woken up, the room spinning, the floor unstable beneath my feet, I'd thought about calling in. But I had known what would happen if I stayed home, and the booze and dwelling weren't going to help me move forward. The best thing for my brain, what I knew how to do better than anyone, was bury myself in work.

"I'm not going to lie; I feel like shit." I held the coffee to my lips, wincing as I swallowed.

"Not surprised. I can smell the whiskey all the way over here." He rested his arm on his desk, chin leaning against his palm. He was quiet, stuck in his thoughts until, "I can't get last night out of my head. Every time I close my eyes, I see those bastards' faces." He brushed his hand over his forehead. "What they did to Dylan, our city, every person involved—it makes me fucking crazy the more I think about it."

The anger inside me was certainly unhealthy.

The ache in my chest, creating an even bigger hole, would never heal.

But there was something else about last night that was bothering me.

Something that had trickled into my mind after I got home from Watertown and was drinking in bed.

"You're not alone, buddy." I gripped my temples to ease the ache on each side. "There's this feeling inside me that I can't shake."

"Of course you can't. You just lost your best friend."

I took a drink of the coffee and set it down. "Not about that. About one of the houses we infiltrated last night."

"In Watertown?"

I nodded. "The guy ..." I tried to think of the right description. "I don't know. There was just something off about his place, and I was too fucked up over Dylan to really take it all in the way I should have."

"What's your gut telling you?"

I looked around my desk, at the piles of folders, the stapler, some random paper clips—anything that would trigger that nagging feeling I'd had when I got back to my condo. "I can't put my finger on it, but it's not going away."

"Lay it all out. Maybe I can help."

I chugged a few more mouthfuls of coffee, forcing the fog out of my mind so I could unfold each of the minutes we had been inside his home. "There was nothing striking about the house," I started. "Typical colonial style, sparsely decorated. He graduated from Wentworth with an engineering degree hanging in his office and now owns an accounting firm. He was watching a show on crafting when we came in."

"Crafting?" His brows rose.

"You know, stitching or whatever that shit is that older women like to do."

"Interesting." He shifted in his seat. "Keep going."

"When we aborted and we were on our way out, one of the agents who had gone upstairs told me the dude was into some kinky shit and it was taking them forever to look through it all."

He shrugged. "People have strange interests. That doesn't alarm me."

"Me neither. We've seen our fair share of it in the homes we've been in over the years, but, man ..." I put my mind back there—to the feeling I'd had when everything inside was so fucking perfect. "Not a single thing was out of place. Not just tidy. I mean, no clutter, not even a wrongly tilted piece of art."

"Canvases or sculptures?"

I crossed my legs, my foot beating in the air, like his had drummed on the floor. "Canvases, and they were bizarre and moody. Abstract. Almost cartoonish, but I could see the shape of a woman's body in the swirls of one."

"What other details did you pick up?"

"Just the photos in his living room. There were some by the TV and a few more by his couch." I recalled their black frames, how there hadn't even been a speck of dust on the glass that covered them. "They were of the same girl—a blonde, roughly twenty years old or so."

"Anything particular about the photographs?"

I continued to remember them—the poses she was in, the smile that looked forced on her face. "I don't know ..."

"What else you got?"

I reviewed it all again in my head, wondering if the loss of Dylan was what had caused me to feel that way and I was making something out of nothing. "That's it."

"Keep thinking. It'll come to you." He linked his hands, resting them on the back of his neck. "Do you want to get some drinks later? I know I could use one, and by then, you should be ready for round two."

Home was the last place I wanted to be, lost in the darkest of thoughts, agony taking ahold of me. "Yeah," I agreed. "Tell me where, and I'll be there."

FIFTY-TWO

BEFORE

ASHE

E ven though I hadn't gone to New York, I assumed Pearl's itinerary stayed the same, and she planned to take the late morning bus back to Boston. Before leaving my apartment, she'd told me she was going to call once she got home, and I knew that would be around the middle of the afternoon. So, when Dylan had asked me to go out to lunch and stop by a pub after, not returning to our place until early evening, I'd expected the light on our answering machine to be blinking when we got back.

But it wasn't.

Instead of waiting for her to call, I phoned her number.

There was no answer.

Gran had a hard time getting around, and if Pearl wasn't home, most of my calls in the past had gone unanswered. I assumed her audition had just run longer than planned, and she was taking a later bus, or maybe she was so exhausted when she got back that she went straight to sleep.

I still tried again a few hours later, and no one picked up.

But by the next afternoon, I was done waiting. I went to

Pearl's apartment and knocked on the door. When I heard no movement inside, something in my gut sent me into the stairwell, where I knew she hid a key.

"It's Ashe," I called out once I unlocked the door and walked in.

"In here," Gran replied. "Hurry."

I let the door slam behind me and found Gran on the floor of her bedroom, only a few feet from the bed.

"Shit, Gran." I knelt on the carpet in front of her, checking her face and arms, seeing if she was hurt. "Are you all right? What happened?"

Emotion filled every breath, pain deeply etched into her face. "Oh, thank God you're here."

"Careful. Something could be broken," I said, holding her lower back, taking all of her weight as she tried to get into a seated position. "Don't move. I'm going to call 911."

I was about to run to the phone when she said, "I think I'm all right. Just give me a moment to catch my breath."

I kept my hand on her, watching the way she was breathing, looking for signs of pain or a concussion. "How long have you been on the floor?"

She touched her face and looked at her hands after to see if there was blood. From what I could tell, there wasn't any.

"I don't know ... a while. Maybe a day. Everything is a bit fuzzy since I fell."

The scent in the air told me it had been that long. I didn't want to mention it and embarrass her, but I also wanted her to know I would help in any way.

"Do you want me to run you a bath? Or grab you a change of clothes?" I paused for a few seconds. "Whatever you need, just tell me, Gran."

Her eyes softened, her hand now on my arm. "I can see why she loves you so much." She tried lifting herself a little and winced, her lack of energy getting her nowhere. "Bed. Let's start there. I'll have you run me a bath once I rest for a little bit."

I was still unsure if anything was broken, and I didn't know if moving her was the right thing to do, but I figured anywhere would feel better than the floor.

I slid my arm under her knees, the other stayed around her back, and I hauled her into the air, carefully setting her on her bed. I adjusted her pillows, trying to make her more comfortable.

"I'm fine," she said, reading my concern. "Just shaken up—that's all."

I sat next to her, assessing each of her movements, still undecided about calling an ambulance. "How did you fall?"

"I was on my way to the kitchen to get something to eat and lost my balance. It's happened before." She tapped her hands on the tops of her legs. "These frail things don't boogie like they used to, but Pearl has always been here to pick me right up."

"Where is Pearl?"

She shook her head. "Honey, I don't know."

"Has she called?"

"*Hmm.* You know, I don't recall the phone ringing."

If Gran hadn't heard any of my calls, that meant she wouldn't have heard Pearl's either.

"Give me one second," I said, and I went into the kitchen, checking the answering machine.

There weren't any messages, the light a solid red.

My heart started to race as I returned to Gran's bedroom, sitting in the same place as before. "I'm a little worried, Gran. She was supposed to be back yesterday."

"Yesterday?" she gasped, telling me she'd most definitely lost track of time since her fall. "That's not like my dollface. She's always late but not by this much."

I racked my brain, trying to come up with where she could be.

But none of this made sense.

Pearl was one of the most considerate, protective people I knew, especially when it came to her grandmother. If she was going to spend an extra night in New York, she certainly would have left a message to tell Gran, and she probably would have called me and asked me to go check on her.

Assuming they didn't have long distance on their phone, I took out my wallet, finding my calling card, and said, "I'm going to try the hotel in New York and see if she's still there."

She nodded, urging me on, and I returned to the kitchen, first calling information to get the hotel's number and then the direct line to their Midtown location.

Once the front desk answered, I said, "Hi. I'm hoping you can help me. My girlfriend checked in late Friday morning. The room would be under Pearl Daniels. Can you tell me if she extended her stay?"

"Sure, just give me one moment," the clerk said, the sound of typing filling the background. "Our records show Ms. Daniels never checked in."

My hands started to shake. "What do you mean?"

"The reservation shows Ms. Daniels was scheduled to arrive Friday and depart on Monday, but she never checked in. Our no-show policy states that a one-night payment is still required, so that was charged to the Visa that was used to book the room."

That was my credit card. I was the one who had called to get us the room, never bothering to change the payment when I'd gone to Maine instead.

What the fuck is going on?

My hand went into my hair, pulling at the roots. "So, you're saying Pearl was never there?"

"Yes, sir. That's what our records show."

"Could she have checked in under a separate reservation?"

"One moment. I'll check."

I stretched the phone cord, walking to the stove and to the fridge and the front door, circling the small space again.

"I'm sorry, sir. There were no other reservations made by that name. I tried several different spellings, and nothing came up."

"Thank you," I said and hung up, hurrying into Gran's room.

I knelt on the floor right next to her bed, so she could hear me.

"Is everything all right, honey? Were you able to get in touch with Pearl?"

I didn't want to alarm her, so I kept my voice calm and asked, "Did Pearl leave you the number to where she was staying?"

"It's on a piece of paper on the table out there."

Before she could say another word, I went into the living room, lifting the small note into my hands. Pearl's writing covered the whole sheet, where she'd jotted down the same hotel I'd booked for us and the phone number I had just called.

My stomach was in my fucking throat as I moved back over to Gran's bed. I rubbed my sweaty hands over my shorts, trying to breathe. "I don't know how to tell you this ..." My chest pounded every time I inhaled. "But Pearl never checked into the hotel in New York."

The lines in her brow deepened. "Where is she, then?"

I shook my head, the worry now eating its way into my arms and legs, my entire body feeling weak. "I don't know."

FIFTY-THREE

AFTER

ASHE

Most of my days were a blur, each one marked by a number that signified how many had passed since Dylan's death. I no longer called them Monday, Tuesday, or even Wednesday. They were day six, twelve, eighteen. Somewhere in there was his funeral, and I immediately went to Dylan's parents' house after the service.

It felt impossible to be there without him.

A strange silence that he would have always filled.

I held his mother while she broke down in my arms. As soon as Alix saw her crying, she was next. I couldn't get her to stop. I couldn't even get her to the bathroom in time before she vomited all over my suit jacket. Once she emptied her stomach, the panic attack set in. She couldn't breathe. Couldn't see.

That was one of the hardest moments of my life.

I was surrounded by mourning. I'd been to his gravesite; I'd traced my fingers over the engraved letters of his headstone.

Still, it hadn't hit me because in my mind, there was no way he could really be gone forever.

Dylan had been invincible.

The pilot who had flown through storms. Who had loved to be in the air, who could survive anything.

Even a bombing.

So, every time my phone rang, I expected him to be on the other end. When I looked at our pictures in my condo, I reminded myself to buy more frames for the trips we would have in the future. Every time I checked his last text, my mind created new conversations to fill in the gap of days.

I knew the reality.

I knew it would slam into me.

And when it did, I reached for the bottle, or I went into work to bury myself a little deeper.

Just like I had done this morning—sleep, once again, something I no longer had in my life.

But caffeine and carbohydrates were what I could fill myself with to keep me going, so I stopped at the bodega on the way to the police station to buy their largest coffee and a toasted bagel.

As I got out of the elevator on our floor, rounding the corner into the main space, the captain was heading down the same hallway, several files gripped in her hand.

"Morning," I said, stopping a few steps into the unit, leaning against the wall as she caught up.

"How's everything going, Detective Flynn?"

I wondered if she was referring to the dark circles under my eyes that had become a permanent fixture or the booze breath I'd tried to brush away this morning. "I'm all right."

She crossed her arms, pushing her shoulder into the wall once she reached me. "Are you?" Her eyes told me she had seen straight through my lie. "You know, you did excellent work in Watertown. I couldn't be prouder of you and my entire Boston team. But since the bombing and the loss of your friend, you've been"—her stare turned harder, as though she was assessing

249

which word would better describe me—"off, and in our line of work, that can be extremely detrimental. I want to make sure you're where you need to be or if you need some time off to let things settle."

Time off would lead to more sitting around with the shades drawn, covering the pain in morning hangovers. I knew what that would eventually look like after a few weeks—boxes of takeout piling high that wouldn't make it into the trash, the stench of unwashed skin, empty liquor bottles on every surface, as though my condo were a giant game of booze pong.

But she wasn't out of line for questioning me. Just because I was here, in this office, on the road, at crime scenes, it didn't mean my brain was. Parts of me were missing, and I wasn't sure when I would get them back.

Or if they would ever return.

I sighed, shifting my posture, and the paper that was taped to the wall, underneath where my arm was resting, threatened to tear.

Printouts had lined this area of the department for as long as I had worked here. Ten rows high, running almost the entire length of the unit, were white pieces of paper, spaced less than an inch apart. On each one was a most recent photograph, their name, identifying characteristics, and where they had last been seen.

The missing persons wall.

An area that everyone passed when they came on and off our floor.

A place that every detective, including myself, looked at weekly as a reminder that we weren't doing our job if these papers continued to grow.

I went to fix the printout that I'd almost torn, and the photo in the center caught my attention. I couldn't stop staring at it, the face suddenly so familiar. I tried to remember where I'd last seen those eyes, that blonde hair, the look of innocence on her face.

I dug through my brain, trying to locate this girl in my memory.

When it clicked, a chill ran through my entire body.

"Detective?" the captain said.

My gaze slowly met hers again, and my feet started to move. "I have to go. I'll stop by your office later, and we can talk about this." I tossed the coffee and bagel into the nearest trash can and jogged to Rivera's desk, the top of it as unorganized and chaotic as my own.

I took out my phone and pressed his number.

"Are you all right, buddy?" he asked, answering after a few rings, his voice scratchy from waking up.

I used my shoulder to hold my cell against my face and started looking through the pile of folders on the side of his desk. "Where do you keep your old files?"

He yawned. "Which one?"

Not having luck there, I switched to a new section, checking the names on those. "The young girl who went missing from Dorchester several months ago."

"Bottom drawer, right side. Last name is—"

"Mills," I said, bending down to be eye-level, sifting through until I reached the *M*s and found hers.

I took it out, and a picture of Mills was stapled to the inside flap, all of Rivera's notes written below.

"Holy fuck," I whispered, my brain on overdrive, my hands shaking so hard that the file was vibrating. "It was her."

"Who was her?" He waited for me to answer, and when I was too busy reading through the notes, he added, "Speak, Flynn. It's too early for me to try to guess what the fuck you're talking about."

FIFTY-FOUR

BEFORE

ASHE

"What other information can you give me?" the detective asked Gran and me while he sat on the couch in her living room, looking at the small pad he'd been taking notes on.

I'd gone over every detail in my head, repeating each of those thoughts to the detective the moment he'd walked inside her apartment.

The pieces I didn't know, like when Pearl had left my place upset and gone home, Gran had filled in those blanks. She'd told the detective that when Pearl returned that night, they'd had a brief conversation, Pearl never mentioning that she was going to New York alone. She then went into her room and packed and said good night. The next morning, she'd stopped by Gran's bedroom to kiss her good-bye, telling her that she'd left the information of the hotel on the table.

Before I'd called the police, I'd phoned her agent, Brett Young, and asked if he'd heard from Pearl. He'd confirmed what I feared—that he hadn't spoken to her since the day prior to when she was supposed to leave and that Pearl hadn't shown up to any of her auditions.

I'd told all of that to the detective as well, and that was where our knowledge came to a screeching halt.

We knew nothing more.

I dug my fingers into my scalp. "I can't think of anything else," I said to him.

The detective looked at Gran. "How about you?"

"Please find my granddaughter and bring her home to me," she replied.

He shut his notebook, placing it on the inside of his jacket. "The first forty-eight hours are crucial in missing persons cases. Normally, that's the window in which they show up—sleeping off a bender, finding cash to use a pay phone, realizing they stayed the night at a place they shouldn't have been at and they come running home."

"That's not Pearl," I informed him, sitting up from the floor. "She's not that person you're describing."

He looked at me and said, "Since this case has passed the forty-eight-hour mark, I would say things look a bit more serious. My team and I will start by retracing her steps." He leaned forward, rubbing his hands together, like he was washing them at the sink. "We'll send out a report, letting all local and state officials know that she's gone missing. We'll speak to the bus station and the hotel, every place we can think of in between. I have both of your numbers, and I'll follow up when I have some information."

My stomach was in a fucking knot, my arms wrapped around it, trying to alleviate some of the aching. "What do you think happened to her?"

He shook his head. "There's no way for me to speculate."

"Will you find her?"

I had been hesitant to ask this question in front of Gran, but we needed answers.

And hope.

"I've been doing this a long time." He glanced down. "Every case is different, and many still surprise me."

"What does that mean, Detective?"

His stare was haunting when he replied, "It's been over four days without any contact. The statistics aren't in your favor at this point."

"She had everything going for her," Gran said, the emotion clear in her voice. "A big move to New York, a career on Broadway." She dabbed her eyes with a tissue. "She was going places, making a name for herself."

He nodded impatiently, standing from the couch. "We'll do everything we can."

"I don't understand this." My voice rose even though I was trying to stay calm. "How does someone just disappear?"

He sighed, sounding like this job exhausted him, the bags under his eyes confirming it. "Responsibility can make or break a person, and Pearl certainly had a lot on her plate. Maybe her plate was full, and she took matters into her own hands. Maybe someone was jealous of her success. Maybe I've missed the nail entirely. We'll find out ..." He breathed loudly again. "And oftentimes, we don't." He handed me his card. "Call me if you remember anything else."

I glanced at the bottom, where Detective O'Connell's name had been printed with the police station's address and his direct line, before shoving the card in my pocket. When I looked up, he was walking out the door.

"Ashe ..." Gran whispered.

She was squeezed into the corner of the couch, her body the size of a small pillow.

I could only imagine the thoughts running through her head right now.

Pearl was her life.

She counted on her granddaughter for everything, including paying for the home they shared.

"We'll find her," I said softly.

We both needed to hear those words for entirely different reasons, but love was what we had in common.

"He didn't sound convinced."

I took a few breaths, pushing the emotion away so Gran wouldn't see it. I needed to be strong for her even if I wanted to fall the fuck apart. "He doesn't know her like we do."

I'd spent two full years of college with this girl; there wasn't anything I didn't know about her. She wouldn't have gotten so overwhelmed with her future that she would just take off. She would have called; she would have left a different note.

She would have told us she needed a break.

I was certain.

But for some strange reason, something the detective had said was repeating in my head, and I couldn't get it to stop.

"Responsibility can make or break a person, and Pearl certainly had a lot on her plate."

That was something I'd always said about her.

But that still didn't explain this.

FIFTY-FIVE

KERRY

He'd forgiven me.
        Just like the man on the other side of the wall had said.

I didn't know how long it had taken. I'd lost track of periods and nail-biting.

I just knew that after loads of groveling and begging, he'd accepted my apology.

The light then turned back on.

Food was left for me on the stairs, paperbacks in my possession again.

His playdates resumed, like there had never been a pause at all.

When I sounded as though I enjoyed the playing, when I was wet instead of him having to use his spit, he would make my plates of food extra full.

I would gag in the bucket the moment he went up the stairs.

But his good side was the one I wanted to stay on.

The side that rewarded me.

CHAPTER 55

The side that was hopefully making me something to eat right now as I heard him banging around on the floor above, the light in the ceiling shaking from his movements.

With Beverly in my arms, I crawled across the floor and huddled in the corner.

That was my favorite place down here.

Even though the walls were cold, I could widen my shoulders and feel the cement on both sides, like I was getting a hug.

The sounds above got louder.

I squeezed Beverly and waited, wondering if I was going to get a break from the hell today.

I worried that I wasn't.

The footsteps got heavier.

Pounding.

It sounded like there was more than one person up there.

I held my breath.

I clutched Beverly as tightly as I could.

The noise roared.

Almost ... like thunder.

And then there was silence.

I jumped as the latch clicked.

Followed by one, two, three locks.

I could feel my heart pounding all the way in the back of my mouth.

Is he alone?

Is someone else coming down?

Will he hurt me too?

But as he got farther down the stairs, I saw that it was just him, his black boots making all the noise.

He had the white dress in his hands with the wide straps.

"Get over here," he said, standing in front of my cot.

He was winded, unable to catch his breath.

His gobbler jiggled.

He pushed his glasses even though they were already at the top of his nose. "Hurry, goddammit. I'm not in the mood to wait."

I knew these moods.

I'd experienced them in the past.

They usually resulted in blood.

FIFTY-SIX

BEFORE

ASHE

I'd asked the detective how a person just vanished, and he'd given me a response. But with each day that passed, Pearl still not found, I asked myself the question again.

It was like she had disappeared into thin air.

And each time I repeated that question in my head, I took a sip of booze. The bottle was already half-gone, and I could still feel the hurt. It wept inside my blood, in my muscles, bones. It didn't matter how much I drank; my body wouldn't let me forget, the presence of Pearl as strong in there as she was in my head.

Still, I only had one plan.

Drinking this fucking nightmare away and waiting for the detective to call with news.

For a clue to appear.

For Pearl to walk through my door.

But after twelve days, there was still nothing.

Just me, a bottle, and a hangover in the morning.

When I pulled myself out of bed, I'd throw some scrambled

eggs down my throat, not even bothering to pick out the shells, and I'd take a shower before I went over to Gran's.

The only person she had in this world was me. Even though it wasn't any of my business, I offered to help in any way I could, and we had an extremely honest conversation about her finances.

Within a week, she would be served an eviction notice with no means to pay her rent.

And with limited options, especially where she needed so much physical assistance, she had no other choice than to enter a state-run nursing home. I'd found several for her to look at, and I'd brought her to each place, helping her choose the best one.

She would live there until Pearl returned.

Tomorrow, Dylan and I were going to move her out of Roxbury and into her new home.

Therefore, today's agenda was more drowning.

I lay across the couch, lifting the bottle to my lips, the burn long gone by the time Dylan walked through our door. There was a bag in one of his hands, a twenty-four pack in the other.

He held the case in the air. "Figured it was time for a switch-up." He shrugged. "I don't know. Maybe the beer will be nicer to your liver."

I laughed—something I hadn't done in days. "Nice of you to look out for my organs."

He set the bag in the kitchen and reached for the bottle that I was gripping. I took a swig before handing him the whiskey in exchange for a beer. The can was cold, the taste bitter.

I banged the back of my head against the pillow. "Fuck, man. Today has sucked."

He went back into the kitchen, returning with a to-go container that he placed next to me with a napkin on top. The meaty, greasy smell caused me to open the lid, and I saw a cheeseburger inside with a mound of fries.

"Ketchup?" he asked.

"Yeah, please."

When he returned with some, I squirted it on the inside of the bun and across the fries, taking bites of both. "You're a good man, Dylan Cole." I swallowed, shoving in the pickle that had fallen.

He sat next to me and clicked his beer against mine. "I've got you, buddy." He waited until I took several more mouthfuls before he added, "You know, you're supposed to leave for Maryland in two weeks. Have you thought about packing, or are you going to crash at my new place?"

He'd already started packing. There were boxes all over his room, several more in the living room and kitchen. Since he now had his pilot's license, he'd landed an incredible gig with a private airline, earning a large starting salary, and he'd be moving into a one-bedroom in the Back Bay.

And I was going to med school.

At least, I was supposed to. The plan was to head there before the term started, so I could get acclimated to the area and my new apartment and have meetings with the professor who would be my mentor for the next four years.

Every morning that I woke up, my head fucking pounding, I tried to put myself there mentally.

Boxing up my life.

Leaving Boston.

Studying for up to twenty hours a day, running on no sleep.

Not knowing where the fuck Pearl was.

I was going, but I thought when I left, it was going to look so much different than this.

Medicine just didn't feel the same anymore.

My chest was constantly tight. My hands grabbing air, like

she was within reach. My eyes moving to the doorway every time Dylan walked through it, as I hoped like hell it was going to be her.

I felt like I was abandoning Gran and Pearl.

Even though that made no goddamn sense.

I just missed her.

Fiercely.

"I'm going to start tomorrow after we move Gran," I finally said. I set down the cheeseburger, the heaviness not feeling right in my stomach. "I've put it off long enough."

"You're not driving there alone," he said, digging into my fries. "I'm going to go with you and catch a flight back."

I didn't ask why.

The same way I hadn't asked why he'd brought me home lunch ... or dinner—whatever the fuck time it was.

They were just things he did for me—a trait I'd learned a long time ago about my best friend.

Instead, I lifted the beer off the table and tapped it against the side of his. "To Maryland."

He drank the rest of his can and clenched it in his fist, bending the metal in the middle before he got up to grab another. "I need about nine more of these before I catch up to you."

He wouldn't even let me drink alone.

I was one lucky bastard.

FIFTY-SEVEN

AFTER

ASHE

I sat in the back of the van, the search warrant tucked tightly under my fingers, Rivera at my side, along with the team of police who were going to help me infiltrate Little's home in Watertown. In order for this piece of paper to be in my grasp, I needed a motive.

My visit to Little's house yesterday had given us that.

When Rivera and I had gone to his home, I'd told Little we were there to conduct a follow-up interview regarding the bombers' case. With his residence being only a few doors down from where the brothers had been captured, asking additional questions to help connect evidence seemed like a justifiable reason for a visit. Reluctantly, he let Rivera and me inside. While I was keeping Little busy with the interrogation, Rivera took pictures of the room with a hidden camera he had clipped to his tie, specifically of the framed photographs that were by the TV and side of the couch.

Most of the photos were too dark and grainy to make out, but forensics were able to match one of the pictures with several we had on file of Mills, the girl who had been taken from Dorchester, who had been missing a few days shy of six months.

Rivera also took several pictures of Little, and we presented those to Mills's mother to see if she could identify him as someone who'd had a relationship with her daughter. The mother had had no knowledge of him or their relationship or a reason why he would have multiple photos of her daughter in his home.

We were back to get that answer.

Before we'd gotten in the van this evening, we'd done our homework. We researched his accounting firm and the hours he spent there and the ones he was at home. We pulled registration on the two vehicles he had in his driveway, and we knew he had made his final mortgage payment almost a year ago. He paid his taxes, had voted in the last four elections, had graduated from Wentworth and UMass.

After speaking to the detective who had been on the second story of Little's home the night we captured the brothers, I now knew Little had a secret fetish. An affinity for dolls—life-sized, petite, and every length in between. The detective had told me they were in Little's bed, on every surface upstairs. One guest room was a dedicated space for crafting these dolls, another for fucking them.

The man certainly had kinks, but what didn't make sense was why this fifty-two-year-old guy had multiple photographs of Mills in his home.

While the team waited a block away in the van, listening through hidden microphones, Rivera and I knocked on Little's door.

As soon as Little opened it and saw us on his front steps, his stare narrowed, and he snapped, "I told you everything yesterday. I know nothing more. This is harassment."

I raised a photo of the missing girl, observing Little's face as

I said, "We're here to question you about Kerry Mills." I showed him the piece of paper I had in my other hand. "And this allows us inside to ask you anything we'd like."

A tic quivered through his chin as his eyes moved from the photo to me. "I don't know where she is."

I hadn't asked him that.

In fact, I hadn't said a word about her disappearance.

"Let us in, Little. Or we'll let ourselves in."

His chest rose, nostrils flaring, as he took several deep breaths, gradually stepping aside.

Remembering the space well, I pointed at the couch. "Why don't you take a seat over there?"

I waited for his ass to plant before I walked over to the closest framed photo, holding it in my hands. Easily identifying the girl, I pointed the picture toward him while Rivera scouted the rest of the room, and I asked Little, "You obviously know Kerry Mills has been missing for six months, so why don't you tell me why you have photographs of her in your home?"

He shrugged. "She's someone I knew."

"How?"

"I took a few classes at Northeastern. Kerry was in one. We hung out a few times."

We knew Mills was a part-time student. If Little had taken classes at Northeastern, we would have found that information, and it would have been flagged.

"We have no record of you enrolled in any class at Northeastern."

"And that's my problem?"

There was something so smug about this asshole, and I wanted to punch the look right off his fucking face.

"I'm asking why you're not registered in their system."

While I waited for him to respond, I took my time in studying the photo. Mills was on her knees with her hands behind her back. A white dress covered her body that almost resembled a maid's costume. Behind her was mostly darkness, beneath her a dirty, bare mattress.

"I don't know why I'm not," he answered.

I didn't believe that.

I met his eyes again and said, "How many classes have you taken there?"

"Just the one we were in together."

His story was already changing.

In my earpiece, one of the guys in the van said, "I'm digging into the school's system right now. Give me thirty seconds."

I turned the framed photo toward Little and said, "Explain this picture."

"What's there to say?"

I walked closer to where he was sitting and dropped the photo on the table in front of him. "Don't play fucking games with me. When I ask a question, you answer." I pointed at the frame. "Why are her hands behind her back? Why is she in a dress that's unlike any style we saw in her closet at home? Where was this picture taken?"

He sighed, like I was wasting his goddamn time. "She liked to be dominated. She wore that outfit, and it was a little game we used to play."

A team member said in my ear, "We're reaching out to her mother right now to see if she can locate the dress in Mills's room."

"How long were you two intimate?" Rivera asked him.

"Couple of months."

"Did she bring you home? Did you meet her family?"

He laughed, and even though his glasses didn't fall, he pushed them high against the bridge of his nose. "I'm thirty years older than her. I'm not the guy you bring home to mama."

"Then, what kind of guy are you, Mr. Little?"

He tilted his head, almost like a dog. "The one who likes to fuck after the bell rings and not speak again until the next class."

"There's zero record of Ronald Little at Northeastern," my team member said in my ear. "We've tried running his address, phone number, work line, and Social Security number. He doesn't exist in their system."

I glanced at Rivera, who had just heard the same information in his earpiece, and then looked back at Little. "When was the last time you saw Mills?"

He crossed his legs, his hands folding in the center. "I'm not positive, but it was before tax season. She stopped coming to class, and I never saw her again."

"Did you try to call her?"

"I didn't have her number."

"Did you stop by her house to see if she was all right?" Rivera inquired.

My thoughts were interrupted again as a team member came through my ear and said, "The mother has never seen that white dress before, and it's not in Mills's closet."

"I didn't have her address." Little scratched his bald scalp. "Like I told you, we were fuck buddies, nothing more."

"Tell me how someone—a business owner, a homeowner, a man who, on paper, seems to follow all the rules—attends class at a university, and the school has absolutely no record of him being there."

He stared at me for several seconds before replying, "The school needs to take better records."

He was lying.

Rivera knew that; the team listening to this conversation knew that.

A stranger off the fucking street would know that.

Little could have used an alias, so nothing could be traced back to him, or he'd never attended the class in the first place.

"Mr. Little, what class was it that you took with Miss Mills?"

There was another pause and then, "A business course."

"Mills was enrolled in *Communications II* and *Basic Algebra*," the team member said in my ear.

Now, I knew this entire story was a facade.

While Rivera began another trip around the living room, I asked, "Where was that photo taken?"

Little scratched his arm, his stare on Rivera, eventually saying, "Some house she took me to in Dorchester. I don't know where it was."

"So, your relationship extended beyond sex?"

"We went there to fuck. So, no, it was just sex."

Rivera stood next to the end table, only a foot from Little, and said, "Where were you on the evening of September twenty-seventh?"

Little laughed, his head falling back against the pillow, the movement causing his glasses to slip toward the tip of his nose. Interestingly, he didn't lift them. "You honestly want me to remember that? I can hardly recall yesterday. I certainly can't remember a date that long ago."

There was something about this man that rubbed me the wrong way, like the needle of a mosquito inserting into your skin. It wasn't just his voice. It was his entire demeanor. I had this throbbing feeling that every word that came out of his mouth was a goddamn lie.

But I knew from experience, if we just kept him talking, those lies would eventually unravel.

Men like him could only hide in the dark for so long before the sun revealed their integrity.

That was what Rivera, my team, and myself were today.

The fucking sun.

"So, you don't know where you were on the evening of September twenty-seventh," I began, feeding his dishonesty. "How about we ask you something simpler, like, are you enrolled in any classes this semester?"

"No."

"Why?"

"I'm taking the semester off. Work has become extremely busy, and I want to relax at night."

"You mean ... to redecorate?" Rivera said, now standing by the wall that lined the staircase to the second floor.

"Excuse me?" Little inquired.

Rivera knelt down, looking around the bookcase that was against the wall. "Do you move your furniture around a lot?" He looked at me and then to Little. "You know, move the couch here"—he pointed at the wall on the right side of us—"and switch the bookcase to over there." He used his finger to aim at the spot where the couch was presently placed.

I had no idea where Rivera was going with this, so my gaze was focused on Little.

"No. I don't move anything."

"Your hardwood floor says otherwise," Rivera said. "In fact, it appears that this bookcase has been moved quite frequently from the amount of wear you have underneath."

Little's foot started to bounce. The heel that was on the floor now making a noise. Once he noticed, he stopped. But his breathing still increased, his chest rising and falling.

The same floor was throughout the entire room, and I reached down to feel its texture. The material was quality, durable. It would certainly hold up unless there was a constant grinding or movement, like Rivera had suggested.

"These scratches are significant, Mr. Little," Rivera contin-

269

ued. "And I see that this bookcase is on wheels, which is an odd addition to a piece of furniture like this."

Rivera gave a slight push against the side of the shelves, and the bookcase rolled forward, slowly revealing a metal door behind it.

One that was large enough to fit through and was dead-bolted shut with three padlocks hanging from the side.

"Sit the fuck back down!" I shouted at Little as he stood and tried to take a step, my gun out of its holster and pointed at him. "Put your fucking hands in the air."

"We're on our way in," the team member said in my ear.

Little returned his ass to the couch, his hands raised.

"Where does the door lead to?" I pressed him.

The team came charging inside, guns pointed at Little.

"Answer the question," I barked.

He was quiet, looking at every person in the room.

All of us waiting for an answer.

"The county records show this home has no basement, that your house is sitting on solid dirt," I said. "So, for the third time, tell us where the door leads to, Mr. Little."

He took several breaths, his eyes darting from the front door to the metal one, like any of us in here was stupid enough to let him escape. "I want my lawyer."

The words every guilty motherfucker declared the moment they were caught.

I looked at the team and shouted, "Get him cuffed and get him out of here, and let's get that metal door open!"

While one of the team members put handcuffs on Little and brought him outside, the others were working on the metal locks. Cutters eventually snapped them off one at a time, and Rivera was standing in front of the door when it was opened.

"What's down there?" I asked from behind him.

"I can't see anything aside from a set of wooden stairs." He shifted a few inches to the side, handing me a flashlight. "You do the honors, Flynn."

I shone the light into the hole and crouched through the small opening. I was careful when I stepped down, not sure of the stability of the steps. Something told me Little had used his engineering background to construct this staircase along with whatever was below. That meant, I didn't trust it. There could be traps, false stairs—anything was possible.

I slowly descended, checking the stability of each stair, and halfway down was when I saw the shape of a woman, huddled in a corner, making it difficult to distinguish more than just the outline of her body.

"Someone is down here," I yelled up.

Rivera was already on the top step, using the same speed as me, an officer behind him waiting to climb down as well.

Still cautious about the remaining stairs, I finally reached the bottom and did a quick scan of the small space. Slightly larger than a typical dorm room, there were no windows, a single bulb dangling from the ceiling providing the only light.

The girl's knees were tucked against her chest, face buried beneath her arms. Her eyes, the single part of her that showed, were glued to me.

"Kerry Mills?" I asked as I took a few steps closer.

As her arms loosened, a doll appeared that she'd been hugging to her chest.

Her forearms dropped even lower, her whole face now revealed. Even though there was dirt and muck on her cheeks, her body much frailer than her photos, there was no question who I was looking at.

"Yes," she whispered, her voice hoarse. "That's me."

I took out my wallet, showing her my badge, hoping that would give her a piece of comfort. "I'm Detective Flynn." I turned, pointing to my partner, who had just reached the bottom of the stairs. "That's Detective Rivera. Kerry, we're here to take you home."

"Home." It sounded more like a breath, and once the single syllable was out, tears began to roll down her cheeks. She gripped the doll, like I was going to yank it from her. "You're really going to t-take me home?" Spit pooled on her lips as the tears fell faster.

"Yes."

"Oh God. Oh God." She put her hands over her face, the doll now lying across her legs. "It's o-over. Dear God, it's over-r."

I made sure to make plenty of noise as I came closer.

In situations where victims were held in captivity, it couldn't be determined how they were going to react to anything; what trauma they had faced could cause them to process everything differently. It was important she knew my location at all times; surprising her in any capacity would be extremely detrimental.

"Kerry," I said, kneeling a few feet away, "once we get you outside, we're immediately going to take you to the hospital and get you the medical care you need." Her fingers dropped from her face as I added, "We'll call your mom on the way and make sure she meets us there, okay?"

She nodded. Slow at first and then harder. "My mom-m." More tears dripped. "I miss-s her so-o much."

"You're going to see her really soon."

Her head dropped, shoulders sagging, hands holding the doll so tightly. "I'm free." Her voice was still no louder than a murmur.

"The man who was keeping you down here—Ronald Little —he's now in custody, and he'll never be able to hurt you again."

Long, dirty pieces of hair stuck to her face. "Lock him up."

I was getting the sense that she couldn't physically speak any louder or she'd been trained not to.

She held the doll to her chin, adding, "And throw away the fucking key."

"An ambulance just arrived," a team member said in my earpiece. "They've been briefed, and they're on standby to take Mills to the hospital."

I looked around again, seeing that there was absolutely nothing down here aside from a book and a bucket. With the stench of urine so strong in the air, I knew exactly what that bucket had been used for.

My heart broke for this innocent girl.

"Would you like to get out of here now?" When she nodded, I held out my hands to show her I had nothing in them. "I would like to carry you if that's all right?" Before she could respond, I continued, "I will not hurt you, Kerry. Neither will Rivera. We just want to help you, and we're asking you to trust us. Can you do that?"

Her response was delayed. "Yes-s."

She wasn't sobbing, like when a victim was pulled from a car wreck and the person they loved was sitting dead next to them. These tears were like a sickness that she was finally healing from.

The feeling looked far deeper than relief.

"I'm going to lift you up," I said.

When she gave me the approval, I gradually closed the gap between us. With no space left, I very gently slid my arm under her legs and another behind her back, holding her against me as I stood.

She felt weightless.

The smell of the basement permeated from the filthy clothes she wore.

"Once I get you outside and into the ambulance, the paramedics are going to drive you to the hospital."

I wanted her to know each step, and I repeated them, so she felt comfortable. In this scenario, there was no such thing as too much communication. The last thing I wanted was to cause more anxiety than what she was already feeling.

I moved only a few inches and asked, "Are you all right?"

"Yes-s." Her arm wrapped around my neck, the doll resting against her stomach—an accessory she wasn't ready to part with.

Rivera led us to the bottom of the stairs, and just as I was about to start climbing, her fingers bit down on my shoulder, stopping me from moving any farther. Her face leaned into my ear, lips pressed close to it.

She whispered.

And the words that I registered sent a chill through my entire fucking body.

FIFTY-EIGHT

BEFORE

ASHE

The sound of the phone, ringing only a few inches from where I sat, caused me to jump at my desk. I had been so focused that I had to pull myself out of my *Pathology* textbook to hold the phone to my face and say, "Hello?"

"Is this Ashe?"

The voice on the other end gripped me, instant memories flashing through my mind, like a movie reel was playing in my head.

The same thing happened whenever I reached out to her, but in the three months since I'd left for med school, this was the first time she had ever called me.

"Yes, it's me. Hi, Gran."

"It's good to hear your voice," she said. "How's school?"

In some ways, the days had crawled by, and every one felt like a year. In other ways, I couldn't distinguish one from the next. If I had thought premed was difficult, nothing I'd ever done compared to this.

I lived and breathed medicine.

And I didn't even have a second to contemplate if it was still something I loved.

But without this program, I would have been on Dylan's couch, drunk, swallowed in a depression over Pearl. Even though I felt her absence every second, that dark, miserably intoxicated place wasn't where I needed to stay. I could miss her and long for her return while not drinking myself to death.

"It's ... daunting." I closed the book I'd been reading and dropped the highlighter from my hand, standing from my chair to pace my small bedroom. "How are you, Gran? How's everything going at the nursing home?"

I tried my hardest to call her once a week, but there were instances when a few had passed before I phoned her. This was one of those times. It wasn't because I didn't want to. I just returned from the library so late every night, and I knew she would be sleeping if I reached out. The next morning, I'd tell myself I'd try harder, and the same thing would happen all over again.

Groundhog Day.

That was med school.

"Things aren't going so well, I'm afraid. That's why I'm calling."

I paused in front of my window. "What's wrong?"

"I've been having these episodes where I get light-headed and fall, and it's been happening quite often." She cleared her throat, her voice already quite raspy today. "They put me in the hospital."

My heart was breaking.

For her, for this situation.

For the fact that she had no one but me, and I was all the way in Baltimore.

"You're there now?"

"Yes."

I ran my hand through my hair, the throbbing in my chest not lightening one bit. "Gran, what can I do? I want to help."

"You sweet, sweet boy, there's nothing you can do. I'm reaching out because I haven't been home in over a week, and I was worried that if you called to give me news about Pearl, you wouldn't be able to reach me."

I held my forehead, hoping the pressure would make the hurting stop. "I call the detective every couple of days, Gran. He still has no news for us."

"I was scared you were going to say that."

I rushed over to my notebook, where I kept my schedule, quickly reviewing what I had planned for this week. "I'm going to come home this weekend. I'll leave early Friday afternoon, and I'll head to you once I get into town. Which hospital are you at?"

It was only Monday. Assuming she would still be admitted and I could get enough work done over the next couple of days, there was a chance I could even skip out a little earlier.

"Oh, honey, I hope you're not coming home just for me."

I didn't want to lie, but I certainly didn't want her to feel any guilt either.

"I've been needing a break for the last several weeks, and home is the perfect place to go."

"It really will be wonderful to see a familiar face." I could hear her smiling, and that caused my heart to ache even more. "Boston Medical, honey. Room 226."

"I'll see you on Friday, Gran."

She was silent for a few seconds and then, "Take care of yourself, Ashe, and drive safely."

"I will."

I hung up and placed the cordless phone back on the receiver.

I needed to call Dylan and tell him I'd be crashing on his

277

couch this weekend. I wasn't sure he'd even be home—he could be flying. I didn't want that to be the case. I really needed some time with my best friend. And I also had to phone my parents, who would be disappointed I wasn't staying at their house, but I'd promise them a dinner in Chinatown for at least one of the nights.

I hadn't thought I'd make it home until the end of the semester, even planning to spend Thanksgiving here.

But this trip was what I needed. A break from the monotony and a reminder that there was life outside of medicine. Maybe it would even make me miss it a little since I could hardly stand the thought of it at the moment, especially as I looked at my desk, knowing how much work I had ahead of me today.

Most importantly, after seeing Gran, it would give me a chance to stop by the police station.

Phone calls weren't getting me anywhere. It was time I paid this detective a visit.

———

Since I had been able to leave Baltimore several hours early, I arrived in Boston shortly after dinnertime and headed straight to the hospital. With Gran's room number written on a small piece of paper in my hand, I took the elevator to the second floor and found the correct hallway, the numbers next to the doors decreasing the closer I got to her room. I checked the paper one final time and slowed as I neared her doorway, trying to be quiet in case she was sleeping.

When I walked in, I expected to find the outline of her thin, petite frame covered in a blanket, her gray hair feathered across the pillow, her arthritic hands resting on top. But the person lying in her place was the right age, just the wrong sex.

Assuming they had moved her room, I went to the nurses' station, waiting for the RN to get off the phone before I said to her, "I'm a friend of Esther Daniels. She was in room 226. I'm wondering if you can tell me which room she's in now."

She stared at me, her shoulders perfectly still, the lines around her eyes deepening the longer she was silent. When she took a breath, I saw something I didn't want to.

Pity.

Compassion.

"I'm so sorry," she said. She glanced at her hands that were clutched on top of the desk. When she looked back at me, her expression had intensified. "I was Esther's nurse for most of the time she was here. She passed away two evenings ago."

My heart stopped. The air in my lungs was stuck, not releasing and not able to take in any more. "She ... *what?*"

She gently nodded. "You're Ashe, her granddaughter's boyfriend, aren't you?" She didn't need for me to confirm; her face told me she knew that answer already. "She told me all about you and that you were coming to visit today." Her hand went on top of mine, holding it for only a second. "I hate that I have to deliver this news to you. Esther was the most wonderful woman."

"I can't"—I looked at the floor, my shoes, the long hallway, anywhere, just trying to find something that would take this feeling away—"believe she's gone."

"She fought hard, but she was extremely sick. We did everything we could to keep her out of pain."

I looked at the nurse again, confused. It was like she was speaking a different language. "She was sick?" I shook my head. "I just spoke to her on Monday. She told me she'd been falling and feeling light-headed."

"She planned on telling you when you arrived; she didn't want to worry you while you were at school. I know this because I was in the room when she called you—she needed help dialing and holding the phone to her ear."

The emotion was brewing in my chest, whistling like a goddamn teakettle.

"She had stage four small-cell carcinoma."

"Lung cancer," I sighed, my hand in my hair, barely feeling the grip I had on each piece. "I can't believe this ..."

"Poor thing was diagnosed two months ago. She started chemo treatments immediately, hoping to help with the pain, but there was nothing we could do to stop the progression." The lines around her eyes caved with sympathy. "She didn't have the strength to fight it."

Gran had been here all alone, no one to hold her hand through her diagnosis or chemo treatments.

No one to give her any hope.

And every one of my phone calls had told her they weren't any closer to finding Pearl.

Fuck me.

My arms felt too heavy to hold, and I rested them on the counter, my face wanting to fall too. "I think I need a minute." My throat was tightening. "I wasn't prepared for this."

She rolled her chair several inches away to a different part of the desk and reached inside a large purse. When she returned, her hand landed on my arm. The same place Gran had touched many times in the past with her small, fragile fingers. "She asked me to give you this. If you didn't show up today, she left me your phone number, and I was going to reach out to get your address."

In her other hand was an envelope, my name written in very shaky writing on the front.

"She wrote that part." She nodded toward the cursive. "I helped her with the rest."

I placed the envelope in my pocket. "Thank you for being there for her."

She smiled. "She was the loveliest woman. She sang your praises and was so grateful to have you in her life. She was trying to hold on—she told me that every time I came in for my shift." She breathed, her voice softening. "I'm sorry you weren't able to say good-bye."

I didn't try to speak.

I just held my hand against the envelope, pressing her last words against my body so I could feel closer to her.

And when I felt like I had the strength to move, I took a step back, mouthing, *Thank you*, and I forced myself to walk in the direction in which I had come.

FIFTY-NINE

AFTER

ASHE

"There's someone on the other side of that wall," Kerry whispered in my ear, her fingernails loosening, no longer stabbing my skin.

I leaned my head back to look at her tortured expression.

"A man who spoke to me sometimes, helping me through the roughness."

I glanced at Rivera, and within a second, he was speaking into his microphone, telling the news to the team.

"Do you know the man's name?" I asked her gently.

"No."

The look my partner gave me told me he was on it, and I said to Mills, "We'll take care of it. I'm going to carry you out to the ambulance now."

With her arm securely around my neck, I carefully brought her up the steep steps and took her outside, setting her on the gurney that was in front of the ambulance. Two female paramedics were standing next to it, ready to check her vitals.

"They're going to examine you," I told Mills the moment I knew she was safely on the bed. "And then they're going to bring you to the hospital." I held my finger up in the air, letting her know I just needed a moment, and I said into the microphone, "Can I get an update on Mills's mother, please?" A team member responded in my ear, and I looked back at Mills and said, "Your mom is on her way to Mass General Hospital. She'll be there before you even arrive."

She was nodding, her hair making a sound as it scratched the pillow behind her head. "Okay."

"Before I leave, is there anything you need? Anything I can do to make you feel more comfortable?"

"No. B-but ..." Her chin quivered as it rested on the doll's head, her stare darting around outside. Knowing she'd lived in that cell for six months, I was sure the brightness and sounds were overwhelming her senses. "Th-thank you."

I tapped an open spot beside her bare foot. "My partner and I are going to follow up. This isn't the last you've seen of us." I held her eyes for a moment more. "You're going to be all right, Kerry."

One of the paramedics placed a blanket across Mills's legs, the other one warming her stethoscope to place on Mills's chest, and I turned to head back into the house.

The police had blocked off the entire road, and yellow tape was surrounding the front entrance. Multiple cruisers were parked along the street with their lights flashing, and news reporters were already filming from the sidewalk.

Within an hour, every channel in New England would be covering this story.

"They're looking for another door," Rivera said as I got inside the living room. "The room Mills was in was all cement. If someone else is down there, it has to be from a different access point."

The team was analyzing the staircase, the one where Rivera had found the metal door on the side.

"I'm not saying that was easy, by any means," Rivera continued. "But I didn't think he had her imprisoned in his fucking house."

We stayed close to the team, watching them bring in machinery, tools that would help aid them in their search.

"I knew he was lying," I said. "But I really thought he'd killed the poor girl. I had no fucking idea we were about to uncover that."

He crossed his arms over his chest. "When you were bringing Mills outside, I took a look upstairs." He shook his head, sighing. "That dude is one sick puppy."

"We have something!" one of the team members shouted.

They had broken through the bottom of the staircase, lifting the first four steps and tilting them backward toward the others, a hinge between that allowed them to move. As I got closer, looking through the large gap, there was another hidden staircase below that led to a different section of the basement.

"That shifty motherfucker," I said to Rivera as he stood next to me, looking at Little's construction.

"A brilliant design from a raging psychopath," Rivera replied.

The team handed Rivera and me flashlights, and I was the first to go through, my feet hitting the wooden step.

As I slowly descended, I shone the light in all directions, trying to get an understanding of the layout and what we were about to walk into. From here, I could only hear silence aside from the buzzing of the single bulb that hung from the ceiling above.

Once I eventually reached the bottom, the room appeared to be a hallway of cement with a door just off to my left. A padlock kept it closed, and the door wouldn't budge when I tried to pull.

"Bring down a pair of bolt cutters," I said into the microphone.

An officer rushed down the stairs, positioning the tool around the lock, and snapped it off, the door loosening enough that we could slowly slide it open.

I sucked in a mouthful of air, holding it in my lungs, preparing myself for what we were about to find.

I hoped like hell if there was a person in there, they were still alive.

The door widened enough, giving us a full view of a cell that was identical to the one Mills had been in. A bucket was in the corner, and a single light dangled from above. There were three paperbacks on the floor and a dirty cot in the middle of the small room.

And sitting on top of the bed was a thin, scared, shivering man.

His hair was long, his eyes haunted.

His arms wrapped around a doll.

"Detective Flynn," I said, showing him my badge. "We're here to save you. Can you tell me your name?"

He lifted his face, showing a bushy, extremely long beard. When he cleared his throat, a sound as loud as a cough came out. "David." He was so quiet that I barely heard him. "David Cohen."

Relief, I had learned, didn't always come out in sounds. It didn't always reveal itself in tears. In Cohen's case, it came out in breaths. A chest that was rising and falling, like we'd just given him a new set of lungs.

"David Cohen, thirty years old, taken from Brookline almost six years ago," a team member said in my ear. "Last seen on the evening of February seventh, wearing a gray sweatshirt and jogging pants. His mother said he was going out with his friends and never returned home."

Cohen's legs were spread out straight, ankles turned toward the ground, hands holding the neck of the doll.

"We're going to call your family and let them know you've been found, and we're going to get you out of here and take you straight to the hospital," I told him.

He dropped the doll and put both hands on his chest.

It was as though we had disconnected the cables and removed the oxygen from his nose, and for the very first time, he was finally breathing on his own.

SIXTY

BEFORE

ASHE

I found myself wandering Boston Medical, not ready to leave, but unsure why I was still here. My hand didn't move from my pocket as I yearned for the closeness of Gran's words even though I hadn't read them. Aside from a few pictures she'd gifted me from her old apartment, this letter was the only thing I had of hers.

It didn't feel like enough.

She was gone.

So was Pearl.

And I had nothing to grab on to.

Each hallway I walked down felt endless. A corridor of squeaky white floors and the swishing of lab coats and scrubs. Name badges with the letters *DR* at the front.

Clothes I'd wanted to wear just months ago, initials I'd envied.

Now, they were just men and women who hadn't been able to cure Gran.

An emptiness poured through me with every step.

An ache.

A burning that started in the center of my chest and moved into the back of my throat.

My other hand clenched and released the air, keeping me present but sending my brain far away. During one of the pumps, when my fingers were in the shape of a ball, I pushed against a closed door. I needed some privacy, a place where I couldn't hear the hospital sounds, where no one could stare at me.

I found myself inside a room with several benches that spanned the width.

Alone.

I threw myself in one of the seats, everything inside me so tight—the air in my lungs, the stiffness in my limbs, the way my heart was barely beating, like hands were closed around it. I'd thought sitting would help. I'd thought taking the pressure off my feet would alleviate this feeling.

It only made me feel worse.

Slowly, I reached into my pocket, resting the envelope on my palm. I traced my finger over my name on the front, seeing the squiggles in each letter, how her hand had trembled when she wrote.

Up until the end, she'd still tried so hard.

Fuck, Gran.

How can you be gone?

We were in this together, and now ...

It's just me.

My head dropped as I peeled open the sealed lip, taking out the paper that was inside, the hospital's emblem at the top of the stationery. I inhaled as much as my lungs would allow, and I began to read.

My sweet boy,
If you're reading this, that means I wasn't able to hold on until

Friday—something I wanted so badly because I didn't want another good-bye to be taken from me. I wanted to thank you in person for giving me so much peace and comfort these last several months, for helping me when it wasn't your place or responsibility.

Not often in this world do you find someone, especially your age, who's willing to sacrifice like you have. Who steps into roles they didn't sign up for, who has so much goodness in their heart.

I knew that about you from the minute I laid my eyes on you.

You weren't just perfect for my dollface. You're a kind, good-natured, warmhearted young man with a presence that causes everyone to smile the second you walk into a room.

That's what scared her the most, you know. That she had found someone so wonderful and she wasn't equipped to accept all that you had to offer, that her heart was too scarred to return the love. My baby had all the confidence when she was acting for a role, but that's where it ended—and it's not her fault. Her upbringing had taught her how to run—that's all she knew how to do. Never in her wildest dreams had she imagined someone as incredible as you coming into her life, standing at the bottom of the stage, waiting to catch her if she fell.

I knew it would happen, but never in my dreams could I have picked someone more perfect than you.

I'm leaving, knowing one thing: you won't stop until you find her.

I know she's alive.

I've had this connection to Pearl from the moment she was born. When she hurts, I hurt. When she cries, my eyes shed the same tears. That's how I know that if she were gone, I would feel it in my body. My heart would have shattered and stopped beating long before the cancer took me.

Find our girl, Ashe, and bring her home. Don't stop looking until you wrap your arms around her. And after you tell her how much you love her, tell her how much I do too. Hold her face with the palm of your hand and look into those precious, gorgeous blue eyes. Tell her that I held on for as long as I could, but even if I'm not here, I'm watching over her.

I'm standing from my seat, clapping my fragile hands from heaven.

Take care of yourself, sweet boy. Chase every one of your dreams. Don't ever let anything cause your beautiful smile to dim. Life is too short to stop running after the things that make you happy. Before you, my dollface had been running in circles for a long time, wearing sneakers that were too tight and never able to catch her breath. You were the reason she took off those shoes. The reason she learned how to really live. The reason her heart is overflowing with love.

My Pearl has always been more breathtaking than a diamond, and you made her sparkle as though she were standing in the sun.

All my love,
Gran

SIXTY-ONE

AFTER

ASHE

"Flynn, I need you ..." Rivera said after I got to the top of the basement stairs with Cohen, the paramedics standing by with a gurney.

I made sure Cohen was comfortable and that he knew where he was being taken and didn't need anything from me before they wheeled him off.

Then, I finally turned toward my partner.

"Come with me," he said and began walking back down the steps into the basement, his shoes making a sound each time they landed on the wood.

I didn't understand.

Forensics had a lot of work to do down there. Pictures had to be taken and processed, samples had to be collected—it was going to take them all night and probably half of tomorrow morning. And they would want us completely cleared out before they started, so entering again was just delaying their work.

"Where are you going?" I asked halfway down the steps.

"Just follow me."

My stomach fucking dropped at the thought of what he could be showing me.

Two victims, powerless, whose voices had been taken away, whose lives had been tortured and trashed.

I couldn't stand the thought of finding more.

As I reached the bottom, he led me past Cohen's cell and through the rest of the hallway. When I'd been down here the first time, I'd assumed it was a dead end. That was because everything—the walls, floor, ceiling—were the same color, masking the dimension, and the lack of light didn't show that the hallway actually turned, leading to another door on the right.

He stopped several feet before reaching it and faced me. "I had the officer cut off the bolt."

"Is there anyone in there? Are they alive?"

He shook his head, breathing deeply, loud enough that I heard every exhale. "Damn it, Flynn ..."

This was the first time any emotion had shown on his face. I hadn't seen it when we entered Little's house or found Mills or even Cohen.

We had been trained to hide our feelings. In our jobs, they could cost us our lives. But my friend was breaking down, and this was the first time I'd ever seen that from him.

"Are you all right, man?" I put my hand on his shoulder, squeezing.

He wiped his face. "Fuck."

He didn't say another word for several seconds, and I tried to figure out what had shaken him this badly, how ugly things could be behind that door ahead of me.

"Go look for yourself," he said, nodding toward it. When I didn't move, he said, "Please ... go."

I held in my breath as I walked toward the door, pausing before I reached it to get control of myself. Seeing Rivera crack wasn't something I had been prepared for. This was hard enough, and to keep myself emotionless was even more challenging. But he had put me in a headspace I needed to get out of, so I took the little time I had to set myself straight, and then I turned to the entrance.

An officer was kneeling next to the victim, tending to her while her face was pointed to the floor, hair covering most of it. Her condition and cell were just like the previous two—deplorable, filthy—and her clothes and feet were covered in muck.

I reached into my back pocket, taking out my wallet and opening it to my badge. "I'm Detective Flynn," I said to the girl. "We're here to help you, and we're going to bring you home."

She gradually looked up at the sound of my voice, her hair parting, her eyes showing through the few greasy strands that stayed.

I took in their size.

The shape of her thin face.

Lips that I could never forget.

There was no mistaking who I was seeing.

I heard myself gasp, reaching for the doorway, needing something steady to hold on to as my heart launched into the back of my throat. A pain shot through my stomach, another inside my chest. My entire body shaking as I whispered, "Pearl …"

SIXTY-TWO

BEFORE

PEARL

The ache was still in my heart when I woke up the next morning, knowing I was about to go on this trip to New York alone. Fear was threatening to hold me hostage, but I knew it was something I had to push through, especially because Manhattan would soon be my new city. The place where I'd be moving Gran and getting steady work, where every one of my dreams was going to come true.

Getting on that bus in two hours was going to be the start of something much larger, something wonderful.

A whole new life.

But it was also when Ashe and I would be living in two different worlds.

The love I had for that man would somehow keep us whole. It could take several acts and a residency, but we would find our way back to the same city one day. By then, I hoped it would be in a shared apartment.

In the meantime, the way I had left his place last night felt terribly wrong. I didn't want to start my vacation that way. I wanted to tell him how much I loved him and hold him in my arms and kiss his handsome face.

I couldn't do those things over the phone.

It had to be in person.

So, once I was showered and dressed, I grabbed the duffel bag I had packed my things into, and I went into Gran's room. I knelt next to her bed, my lips close to her ear to ensure she could hear me.

"Gran ..." I waited for her eyes to open, for the grogginess to settle a little before I continued, "I'm getting ready to leave. I just wanted you to know I left you dinner in the fridge for each night I'll be gone. Your cereal is already poured for breakfast; you just have to add milk. The tea bag is in a mug right next to it."

"Thank you, dollface."

"I left the name and number of the hotel on a piece of paper on the table. I'll be back Monday afternoon. I love you."

"Love you too, baby. Good luck, and have a good time."

I leaned into her face, giving her a soft kiss on the cheek, the scent of the baby powder so strong when she was in bed.

I pushed myself off the carpet and grabbed my jacket on the way out. I rushed down the flights of stairs and into the coldness of the early morning, the wind wrapping around me the moment I stepped outside. I wasn't normally out at this hour—six was even early for me—but I wanted to make sure I had plenty of time to stop at Ashe's and still make it to the bus several minutes before it was scheduled to depart North Station.

The nice thing about Roxbury this early in the morning was the quietness. The only sounds were my own footsteps and breathing and the soft whistle of the wind. The dark, cloudy sky hung over me, holding me like a hug—Boston's way of keeping me in until I soon pulled myself out.

At the crosswalk, I turned the corner, the train station now only a few blocks up ahead. If I kept up this pace, I would even be able to fit in some snuggle time. And I wouldn't even have to wake him to get in; fortunately, I knew where they hid a spare key, so I could keep this visit a surprise.

That thought brought a smile to my face, knowing how happy he would be when I woke him with a kiss.

I picked up my speed a little and was just adjusting the strap of my bag, the duffel incredibly heavy on my shoulder, when I heard my name spoken from somewhere close to the street.

I was sure it had been in my head. I saw no movement, and there was no other sound.

I ignored it and kept going until I heard it again, a tone that was deep, gritty, immediately slicing through my thoughts.

My feet halted as a man stepped onto the sidewalk, through the darkness of two vehicles parked along the curb.

"You are Pearl Daniels, aren't you?" A tool belt hung from his waist, the van behind him telling me he was here to repair something in one of the buildings.

"Yes," I answered. "How do you know that?"

His arms crossed, and his back leaned into the van. "Sorry. I hope I didn't startle you. I just went to your play a few weeks ago, and when I saw you under that light"—he pointed at the streetlamp behind me—"I instantly recognized you." He pushed his glasses higher on his nose. "You are the lead actress for BU, aren't you?" When I nodded, he grinned and scratched his bald head. "That's what I thought. My wife and I are huge fans. We've seen every performance you've been in for the last couple of years."

"Wow." The wind was whipping even harder, and I pulled my jacket closed, shifting the strap of the bag to a spot that didn't ache. "Thank you ... I'm flattered."

"No, I should be thanking you." He unbuttoned the wrist of his long-sleeved flannel, rolling the cuff up to his elbow. "It's quite an honor to have someone from my hometown be as talented as you. You're going to make it on the big screen someday soon—I feel it."

I smiled and waved, my time extremely limited; therefore, I kept walking and said over my shoulder, "I sure do hope so."

I wasn't more than a few paces away when I heard, "Can I get you to sign something for my daughter?" I turned around as he opened the door to the van, where he pulled out a notebook and pen. "She's seven, and she's been coming with us to your plays." Now that I'd stopped, he closed the gap between us, reaching forward to give them to me. "She would be so grateful. Hell, it'll make her whole year when I tell her I ran into you."

I'd been asked for my signature a few times, each instance from a kid who had come to see one of our performances. It was a humbling experience, and this was no different. "Of course." I took the pen and paper into my hand. "What's your daughter's name?"

"Dolly." He gave me a crooked smile, rolling up his other sleeve. "I call her Doll for short."

"That's cute."

I thought of the name Gran called me as I wrote *Dolly* across the top, telling his little girl to always reach for her dreams, and signed my name below before I handed it back to him.

"That's real nice of you, Pearl." He read my note. "She'll be so pleased."

"Happy to do it." I waved again. "Have a good day."

I was headed toward the train station again, my smile still so wide, wondering if running into that man was a sign. Maybe of good things to come, like the auditions I had tomorrow morning. The thought of that, of reading lines in front of a room full of people, made me so nervous. But visualizing that man telling his daughter about me, how he'd seen me on the street, could definitely shake some of my anxious energy.

A moment from a monumental day, and that was what I would concentrate on instead of the anxiety in my chest.

But those plans were quickly interrupted when a hand slapped over my lips. There was something on the inside of his palm that he shoved into my mouth, holding it between my teeth, that stopped me from screaming. A blindfold was then tied over my eyes. The bag dropped from my arm, and he pulled my hands behind my back, shackling my wrists with rope.

I couldn't use them.

I couldn't ...

"You're coming home with me." His laugh was more like a cackle. "Won't my dolls be pleased when they see someone as beautiful as you in their dollhouse?"

My body stiffened, becoming dead weight. My knees buckled. My stomach churned, panic filling each of my crevices. Emotions I never knew I had came rippling out as he began dragging me backward toward the van.

I couldn't breathe.

I couldn't see.

I couldn't even shout for help.

"My, my," he growled seconds before he lifted me into the air. "You're even pretty when you cry."

SIXTY-THREE

AFTER

ASHE

"Pearl," I whispered again, needing to say her name out loud to make this moment feel real.

I didn't instruct my feet to move. I didn't feel the rush of wind as I ran to her. I didn't feel the pain when my knees smacked the cement, my body falling to kneel in front of her.

"It's me ... Ashe."

She cleared her throat, the noise like she was filled with smoke. "Is it"—her voice was so soft, barely audible. She lifted her hand, slowly reaching across the space between us, her fingers landing on my cheek, gently pressing against it—"really you?"

"Yes."

I knew I should wait. I knew I should follow the steps.

Every year of training was flashing through my head.

I ignored it all and wrapped my arms around her, pulling her against me. I held her hair, the grease coating my skin, my other hand on her back, the bones of her spine like the neck of a guitar. "My God, Pearl, you're alive."

My eyes closed, and I could finally take a long, deep breath.

I rocked her body, using a lazy pace, gripping what felt like only half of her.

Long ago, I had memorized every inch, each dip, all of her gorgeous curves. Most of them were missing as I clutched her tiny frame.

A shell, just like the other two victims.

"Is ... this ... real?"

I leaned back, so she could view my face, watch my lips, take in the honesty of my eyes. But while I was in this new position, I saw that her hair had doubled in length, her eyes were sunken, hollow. Her lips cracked and pale.

She shook like she was cold.

"This is real." I rubbed her arms, attempting to warm them. "I'm taking you out of here. That monster will never hurt you again."

Her lungs rattled when she inhaled, a hoarseness present, even in her breaths. "This feels like a dream." She tried clearing her throat again. "I've had so many. I can't tell when I'm having one ... and when I'm not."

Her hand had fallen, but she lifted it again, crawling through the air until it found me. The pads of her fingers moved across my face like she was a pianist, my cheeks her keys. "Ashe." It didn't sound as though she was asking, more like convincing herself that this was really happening. And I let her take her time, the moment unraveling as she studied what had now been eleven years of separation. "You c-came."

My hands tightened as I said, "I never stopped looking for you."

There was noise behind me, and I was sure it was Rivera and our team coming to assist. I didn't know when, but a message had come through my earpiece that another team of paramedics was on standby.

They were ready for Pearl.

"I'm going to carry you out and take you straight to the hospital." I paused, her face so aloof that I couldn't tell what information was hitting her brain or what was bouncing right off. "Is it okay if I lift you and bring you outside?"

She swallowed, the thinness in her throat showing each part that moved. "Outside ..." Her head nodded, and I could tell it took so much energy. "Yes." Her lips closed, and she tried again, "Yes, I want that."

What I wanted was to pick her up and run her out of here. But she couldn't handle that speed, so I forced myself to take it easy, to make sure that comfort was all she felt while I carefully tucked her into my arms and lifted her.

I waited for the cinnamon to hit me.

I searched the air for it.

A knot bulged in my throat when I couldn't find even the smallest hint.

Once I was standing, resting her like a baby in my arms, I nodded toward the doorway, where Rivera stood. "That's my partner."

I held his stare as I brought her closer, the emotion he had shown several minutes ago now making perfect sense.

"Paramedics are waiting at the top of the stairs," he said, reaching for my shoulder, holding it as I made my way through the door. Each squeeze of his fingers told me he knew what this moment meant.

With her arm wrapped around my neck, the other on my chest, I brought us through the narrow doorway and into the hallway. She stayed silent, folded against me, as I began ascending. Looking up at the entrance from the halfway point of the stairs, I saw the gurney and two female paramedics next to it.

Protocol was to place her down on the bed, and they would roll her outside.

But I was the boss of this investigation, and Pearl Daniels wasn't leaving my fucking arms.

"Move out of the way," I told the paramedics before I reached the top. "I'm carrying her to the ambulance."

As the wheels of the gurney began to back up, the metal legs squeaking, Pearl cowered against me. I grabbed the blanket that was at the end of the gurney, and while she rested her face on my chest, I covered her with it.

"You're okay," I whispered. "Close your eyes and think of something warm, beautiful ... the top of Cadillac Mountain."

The officers parted, and the paramedics did, too, the team following me as I made my way through the house, stopping at the front door.

"It's going to be extremely intense out there. This covering will cut some of it out." I lifted the blanket over her face, and she said nothing in response.

I opened the door, and it was even crazier outside than it had been before. Choppers were flying overhead. There were double the amount of camera crews. Neighbors had gathered on the nearest lawn to watch.

I paused in the entryway, speaking under the blanket, "Pearl, I need you to breathe for me. The noises are going to be much louder than you're used to, but within three breaths, I'm going to have you in the ambulance."

She crouched closer to my body.

"Take your first one"—I made it onto the first step—"right now."

Questions were being shouted, and there was a hum from all the murmuring. I tried to block her from most of it with the blanket, hurrying down the rest of the steps and down the walkway and driveway to where the ambulance was parked in front. The moment I reached the back, the double doors were flung open, and I set her on the gurney inside.

"I'm right here," I told her, holding her foot from the sidewalk while the paramedics climbed in, beginning their routine.

Wires were hooked onto her chest, an IV was inserted into her arm, a stethoscope was moving up and down her back.

"She's stable," a medic said. "Let's roll out."

Another paramedic climbed out next to me and said, "We're taking her to Mass General."

I placed my foot on the step, gripping the handle on the door. "You're taking me too."

She waited for me to get in before shutting the doors and pulling away from the curb.

While the other paramedic worked on her, I sat on the opposite side, taking Pearl's fingers into my hand. "Are you doing all right?"

Her arm was resting across her eyes, most of her face hidden, her knees tucked into her chest. "I don't know," she whispered. "This is ... so much."

I ran my thumb across the back of her palm and over her knuckles. "We'll be at the hospital soon, and they'll give you something to calm you."

Goddamn it.

I wanted to run the tests and review the results and determine what she needed.

I wanted to heal her.

But my medical background was a lifetime ago.

A few months shy of eleven years.

Now, all I could do was hold her hand and stay by her side and help her try to forget.

If she even wanted me to.

I glanced down at her fingers, skin that was dirty, nails that were broken. I was sure her hair hadn't been cut since she'd been kidnapped. She certainly hadn't been properly fed. I hoped there wasn't anything too serious going on internally, but at her current weight, I feared her numbers were terrifying.

That was only half of it.

Inside her head, things were probably far worse.

I pulled her hand up to my face, breathing into it so she could feel my warmth, listening to her breaths as we rode in silence the rest of the way to the hospital.

A team of doctors and nurses rushed toward the doors the minute we were parked, lifting the gurney out of the back, ripping my hand from Pearl's.

"I'm sorry," one of the nurses said once we got in the hospital, her fingers pressing the center of my chest, stopping me from following them through the double doors. "Only medical staff is allowed beyond this point."

I could see the top of Pearl's head as they rushed her down the hallway, and I didn't take my eyes off her, trying to move past the nurse to get in. "I need to be with her."

"You will be once they're done with the examination."

"You don't understand what she's been through." My jaw tightened, clenching. "She needs me."

"Detective ..." She shook the spot she was holding, trying to gain my attention. "Detective!" When I finally looked at her, she continued, "There are no exceptions. I'll come and get you once they're done." She nodded toward the row of benches behind me. "Make yourself comfortable; it's going to be a little bit."

"Pearl," I shouted before the doors closed, making sure she heard me, "I'm not leaving you. I'm right here!"

I continued following the darkness of her hair until they turned the corner, and she was gone. I then backed up several steps, the nurse's hand dropping from me.

"Hey ..."

I found her eyes again.

"We're going to take good care of her. Don't you worry."

———————

"How's she doing?" the captain asked as I stood with her in the doorway of Pearl's hospital room, my eyes fixed on the bed, watching Pearl sleep soundlessly.

I kept my voice low, looking for any signs of movement. I didn't want her to open her eyes and not be sitting in the chair next to her. "The few times she's been awake, she hasn't said much. But she's medicated and calm; I guess that's all I can ask for at this point."

The IV attached to her hand was giving her fluids that she desperately needed. The cocktail of other meds was helping her numbers rise. Her lack of weight, vitamins, and nutrition had wreaked havoc on her organs, causing them to work over-time. Her kidneys and heart needed improvement, and her blood cell counts were terribly low. Within time, she would make a complete turnaround—physically.

Mentally, there was so much to be determined.

"How are you?"

I shrugged. "Doesn't matter."

Her hand went to my arm, and my stare slowly left Pearl to glance at the captain as she said, "Your health most certainly matters right now. First you lost your friend Dylan and now this."

I couldn't talk about Dylan.

I couldn't even put my brain there right now.

"I just want her to be all right—whatever that means and whatever that looks like. Once I have an idea, I'll be doing much better."

She took her hand back and crossed her arms. "I checked Daniels's file." She paused, her stance shifting. "Her case was before my time at the department, but I've heard of Detective O'Connell. He's been retired for quite a while."

"He was gone a week after I started working. He was a useless motherfucker. Lazy, uninterested. He didn't care enough."

"I saw your notes—every call that you made, every angle you pursued. Even up until a few weeks ago, you continued to search for her." Her gaze moved between my right eye and left. "Is Pearl the reason you joined the force?"

I checked on Pearl again. She hadn't even stirred.

"Mostly," I sighed, leaning into the doorframe. "I was in med school, miserable, missing home, missing her." I hated putting my brain back there, the pain so immense that it hurt to even think about. "I knew I could do a better job than O'Connell. I just needed the resources. The department opened up those gates."

There wasn't a smile, but a look of understanding was on her face. "And we're lucky sons of bitches to have you. Take all the time off you need, Flynn. You've certainly earned it with everything you've been through." She nodded toward Pearl. "You also have a lot of work ahead of you." I was stepping back inside Pearl's room when the captain added, "I hope once things relax a bit, we're not going to lose you?"

I hadn't thought about my future. I hadn't even considered what things would be like in an hour. Pearl was minute by minute at this moment. But I was certain of one thing. "I don't want that missing persons wall to gain any more photos."

She reached over, patting my shoulder. "That was the answer I wanted to hear."

SIXTY-FOUR

AFTER

PEARL

B rightness.

Something I hadn't seen in eleven years—a mind-blowing and terrifying number—that would take me a long time to get used to again.

The only colors in Ronald's prison had been the white dress he made me wear and the cement-colored walls.

But in this hospital room, I was surrounded by so much more.

The warmth of the sun that came in through the window was yellow. The heat from Ashe's hand red. I felt both penetrate me, even when my eyes were closed, the exhaustion taking hold, not even having an ounce of energy in me to keep them open. But when I was awake, I felt the colors too. During the moments when my eyelids would flutter open, expecting to be met with another white dress and a demanding, roaring, gray Ronald.

But that wasn't what I saw.

I saw Ashe.

And the dream that I'd kept in my head for all of those years was now the reality playing out before me.

Safety.

Freedom.

Security.

When the panic set in again, the machines behind me singing a nasty song, Ashe would remind me that the nightmare was over. His fingers would hold me extremely tight, and I would try to calm the anxiousness in my body.

Just like I was doing now as my eyes moved from the white walls to the yellow window.

To him.

"Good morning," he whispered.

The room smelled like coffee, and he was holding a large paper cup, the same way he had done in college.

I cleared my throat, the thickness moving down, my voice slowly returning. "I used to fantasize about different flavors, wondering if I'd have them again." I swallowed, the back of my tongue still so permanently dry. "Coffee was one."

He held out his cup for me to take. "Would you like some?"

"No." I rested my arm over my stomach, my gut so bloated and full of whatever they were pumping me with. "Thank you."

He moved his chair a little closer, and I jumped from the noise—a grinding, almost shrieking—the same sound the door would make when Ronald would come in.

"I'm sorry." He paused midair, squeezing my fingers, the machine behind us screeching. "I'll move it back."

"No—" I started but cut myself off when I didn't know how to continue. How to describe how I was feeling. How to even process what it all meant in my head. It had been so long since I'd been allowed to speak. I only knew how to keep it in. To let it eat. Scorch. Bolt in every direction. "You're fine."

He waited until I calmed and asked, "How are you feeling?"

"I"—I reached inside me, searching for that answer. Freedom was what I'd wanted for so long, but with it came things that terrified me, and they were as scary as being inside the prison—"don't know."

"That's understandable." He set down his coffee and pulled at the collar of his button-down. It was a light blue, the color of his eyes, more beautiful than the ones I'd seen in my head for all these years. They had the tiniest hint of aqua, a gaze more piercing and precise than I remembered. "You've been sleeping on and off for three days."

"Three days?"

I cleared my throat, the burn making me cough. He handed me a light-pink plastic cup, and I looked inside at the clear waves of the water. I took a drink, swishing it around before swallowing.

It tasted ... heavenly.

"I spoke to your doctor this morning, and he's extremely pleased with how you're responding to the meds. He wants to talk about discharge plans. There are several options for you to consider."

"I'm going to Gran's." I paused to cough again. "I hoped she would come here to see me, but I know that's probably hard for her at this point." My eyes shut, recalling how she used to hold on when she walked, her hands so delicate that she would squeeze me with her whole arm. "That's my plan—to go to her."

Ashe was silent, his thumb rubbing the tops of my knuckles. "Pearl, we have to talk about Gran."

I couldn't miss the compassion in his tone, the way his stare turned sympathetic, just like every nurse who woke me when they were checking my vitals.

Both made me hurt.

Even worse.

"Ashe ..."

He shook his head, his Adam's apple bobbing. "I don't want to have to tell you this."

I coughed, opening my lungs, the air feeling stuck. There was a hole in my chest so large that I didn't know how it would ever repair. How this hurt would ever stop burrowing.

"Don't." I put my hand over my mouth, needing to filter the cleanness that was going in. "I can't hear it." I pulled my other hand away from him and held it against my chest. Pushing. "I ... can't." I tasted a tear on my lip. Something I hadn't been sure would ever drip again because I didn't think I could possibly have any left. I tasted another, remembering that, for a long time, they had been the only things I had to drink. "I c-can't." I crawled onto my side, tucking my legs to my chest and reaching for her.

My doll.

But she wasn't there.

Another pillow was instead.

But I had known the doll. I had known what to expect from her. What I needed from her in that prison and what she was able to give me.

The pillow was a stranger.

I still pulled it against my chest, burying my face in what would have been the doll's hair.

Silence passed through the room as I tried to breathe, pushing thoughts of Gran far out of my head to a place where I would visit them again—maybe tomorrow or in a week or when I could process time in increments that were longer than a second.

"We don't have to talk about this now," Ashe said, and my eyes opened to the sound of his voice. "But you do have lots of options. We can find a small place for you to rent or an inpatient program or you can stay with me." He paused. "My place isn't huge, but you can have the bed, and I'll crash on the couch."

The pillow was turning wetter. "I don't know ..." It smelled clean. Sterile. Not like any of the prison's scents. "I don't know anything."

There was pressure on my shoulder. It took me a moment to realize it was his hand.

"You're not supposed to. It's going to take time, but you'll get there."

"Where?" I said softly. "To a place that's ... normal?"

Normal.

My eyes closed again as I swallowed that word, feeling it swirl around my chest like water going down a drain. I couldn't remember what that felt like. I hadn't even seen glimpses. The girl I'd been in college, the one heading to New York to act, the one who wrapped her arms around Gran for comfort and love —she was long gone.

This was who I was now, jumping at loud noises, choking over my own voice, not being able to take in more than a few sips of water.

It was as though I were made of glass that was so thin that even a tiny breeze could chip me.

Normal wasn't just far.

It was impossible.

"No, Pearl," he said, pulling me from my thoughts, "to a place that's perfect for you."

———

"My name is Marlene," a woman said as she stepped into my room.

Ashe had already told me she was coming, so her presence wasn't a surprise. Her frizzy, curly hair was like a halo around her head, and she took a seat on the other side of my bed, her chair a good distance away.

"I'm a therapist, specializing in sexual assault." A category she was telling me I now fit under, causing me to process this new characteristic of mine. "I'll be working with you today as well as outside the hospital when you continue outpatient therapy."

Ashe's fingers squeezed to get my attention. "I'm going to leave for an hour while the two of you talk. Are you okay with that?"

Every time I woke, no matter what time it was, he was there. Sometimes on his phone, sometimes looking at me. Sometimes asleep. He hadn't left, not even once.

"Yes," I answered.

He gave my fingers a little pulse. "I'm just going to the cafeteria to make some calls and grab something to eat. I'll be back once you're done."

I nodded, watching him rise from his chair and move through the door.

"Pearl ..." the therapist said.

My stare eventually found hers, the brown a color that was oddly soothing.

"You seem comfortable with having him here."

The light from the window made me squint. I rested my arm across my forehead to shield some of it, immediately feeling guilty for denying myself the rays.

When my arm went back to the bed, I scrunched my lids again.

I didn't want that.

But I didn't want to be blinded by the sun either.

I didn't know what the fuck I wanted.

"I ..."

She slowly rose from her chair and went over to the blinds. "I'm just going to close them a tad—I can tell you're struggling with the glare." Once they were turned enough, my eyes getting a break from the beating, she returned to her seat. "The light is going to take some getting used to."

I cleared my throat. "Everything is."

She crossed her legs, lifting the pad from her lap and setting it back down, adjusting the pen at the same time. "I want this to be a space where you can talk freely and say absolutely anything. Share your emotions, fears, concerns—whatever comes to you. We'll take our time, working through each one."

"I haven't spoken." I coughed. The tightness like a chain that was never going to be unlocked. I took a drink of water. "He ... wouldn't let me."

"There were no words shared at all?"

I swallowed, the burning so intense. "Some. Not many."

"That's a lot of trauma to hold in over a long period of time. Now that you have the opportunity to get it out and share, how does that make you feel?"

Her voice was soft, calming. Not the storm that used to unlock my door and stampede inside my prison or the high-pitched wailing on the other side of my wall.

"Overwhelmed." I was gripping the top of the blanket, squeezing it into my palms. "Everything is so loud. Bright. And I'm so foggy, like ... I'm floating."

"Detached."

I chewed on the word for a while. "Yes." I rinsed my mouth with more water and added, "My brain is here"—I set down the cup, pointing to the spot next to me on the bed—"my body over there." I aimed at Ashe's empty chair.

"That's very normal for what you experienced. Your brain allowed you to escape the terrifying situation you had been placed in. Now that you're free, separating those moments from reality is going to be something we'll work on." She tucked a large chunk of curls behind her ear, most of them staying for only seconds before they sprang right back. "I would like to talk about your discharge plans. With it coming up soon, it's one of the more pressing matters."

"Gran," I whispered, fighting the breathlessness in my chest. "My dream was always to return to her."

"I know this is difficult." Her eyes didn't hold sympathy, but they told me she knew what I was referring to. "Would you like me to describe each of your options?" When I didn't reply, she said, "Our goal is to have you in an environment where you feel the highest sense of security. That's vital for your recovery."

I glanced at the window, how the blinds created a shadow over the wall that looked like zebra stripes. There was a whiteboard next to it. If the date hadn't been written at the top, I wouldn't have known it was April.

"It's spring," I whispered, my tongue so dry that it didn't want to work. "Ashe and I used to go to this coffee shop. We would order one of those." I lifted my finger, pointing toward the paper cup that was on the table by my bed. "We'd sit outside and drink them."

I heard her writing on her notepad—a noise that didn't make me want to scream.

"Living with Ashe is an option—an invitation that's open indefinitely. I know he's told you that. He lives alone, and the bedroom would be yours."

Spring.

The scent of rain.

The sound of the birds, how they would chirp outside his window when I was just waking up for class.

As I dug inside my head, the smell was so faint, the squawking so distant.

"Okay," I said softly.

Her pen paused. "Pearl, is that your decision?"

He'd kept me safe from the moment he had come into my prison. I didn't know what that meant, but it was a feeling I wasn't ready to lose.

"I think so."

When I turned toward her again, she was grinning.

"You've just climbed your first step. That's a huge accomplishment—I hope you know that."

I didn't know why that made me want to cry.

But suddenly, tears were dripping from my eyes.

SIXTY-FIVE

AFTER

ASHE

After Pearl was released from the hospital, so many firsts followed. She had to relearn how to do everything again, like navigating a computer and using a washing machine and a TV remote. It wasn't like watching a young child attempt things they had never tried. This was like learning Spanish in high school and not using it until you moved to Spain eleven years later.

While she was getting reacclimated, I was adjusting to her triggers—how the condo could never be dark, the sounds never loud, setting a schedule so she could feel the comfort in staying mentally busy. I took a month off from work and didn't leave her side—bringing her to therapy every day, to get her hair cut, to the dentist, and to visit her attorney to help build the case against Ronald Little. Then, there was the media to deal with, the interviews that were offered, the television programs they wanted her to appear on, the magazines that wanted features.

Everyone wanted Pearl's story, and she wasn't ready to tell it yet.

But after four weeks, I had used up all my vacation, and it

was time for me to return to work. With Pearl being by herself a lot more, we developed a new schedule. One where I popped in at least twice a shift to check on her and where I called every few hours.

Not only because it helped her, but it helped me too.

Even when she showed progress, I still worried. I just wanted to make sure she was getting everything she needed, and I constantly consulted with her therapist to make sure I was giving her that. Marlene trained me on how to assist with Pearl's growth.

And each day, I noticed a change.

Gradually, she was finding her footing, taking on new challenges, and I was there to admire each one, like the evening she cooked for the first time.

She'd been living with me for about nine weeks when it happened, and I could smell the tomato sauce as I returned from work and unlocked the front door. Once I had it open, she was standing at the stovetop, a wooden spoon in her hand, dipping it into several different pots. A dish towel hung over her shoulder, her wet hair twisted in a long braid.

I watched from the doorway, frozen.

A million memories hitting me at once.

She looked over her shoulder, catching me staring. "Are you hungry?"

"Yes." I dropped my bag by the door and took a seat across from her on one of the barstools. "What are you making?"

Maybe it was the way she was moving through my kitchen, or maybe it was just the bright lighting in here, but I noticed the weight she had gained and how healthy she was starting to look. The color was coming back to her cheeks, her eyes not so sunken and hollow.

"Some pasta and garlic bread. Nothing too fancy."

I smiled, knowing the answer before I asked, "Did I have that food in the pantry?"

She was stirring onions and peppers into the sauce. "Marlene and I went to the grocery store today."

"How did that go?"

She moved to the counter in front of me, cutting a large loaf of French bread. "It was really loud in there, and the options were overwhelming." She glanced up. "I chose something I was comfortable with—or at least, I used to be since pasta was one of Gran's favorites." Her hands paused from cutting, and she took a deep breath.

Gran was a topic she hadn't begun discussing in therapy. She just wasn't ready to tackle that pain. There were still so many other heavy items to get through.

"Hey ..."

Her eyes met mine.

"You're doing great, and pasta is one of my favorites too."

She didn't smile back, but there was light in her eyes. "Aside from the stage, the kitchen used to be one of my happy places. Marlene wants to see if I can get that feeling back."

"It smells incredible in here. I'd say you're doing something right. How's it feeling?"

She finished cutting the bread and began swiping butter over each piece. "I think I've missed it." She turned her head to cough. "And I'm surprised how quickly it all came back to me."

"Tell me about your day."

She set down the knife to sprinkle garlic on top of the spread. "Therapy, grocery store. I used your laptop and did this meditation video that I'd found online. I took a nap and journaled while I sat on your balcony to get a little sun. I got out of the shower and only started cooking about fifteen minutes before you got home."

There was a warmth across the bridge of her nose and the tops of her cheeks, showing me she'd been outside.

The tan looked beautiful on her.

"You took control of a meal."

Up until this point, I'd been making all the food decisions. This was another huge step and a moment that needed to be recognized.

She nodded. "I hope that's okay."

I reached forward, my hand surrounding hers. "It's more than okay." We didn't move for several seconds. Our fingers stayed linked, our stares fixed. "I'm extremely proud of you," I said softly.

Her thumb swiped the side of my hand, back and forth.

And then she returned to the pot and stirred. "I didn't grab anything for dessert, thinking there was ice cream in the freezer. But when I got back, I looked, and I guess we'd eaten it all last night."

"I'll run down to the bodega in a little bit. Ice cream or cupcakes?"

I wanted her to continue making decisions, to build back the control she had lost, even if each step was small and the decisions were minor.

She lifted the pot of pasta and drained the water in the sink. "Cupcakes." She paused. "Yep, cupcakes." She scooped a pile of noodles onto two plates before covering it with the simmering sauce.

Since I didn't have a dining table, she joined me on the other side of the bar, and we began to eat.

"Pearl ..." I groaned, the garlic she'd added to the onions and peppers making the sauce so rich and delicious. "This is amazing."

"Thank you."

I put my hand on her back, causing her to look at me. "No, it's really, really amazing."

Her eyes lightened even more. "It makes me happy to hear that." She took a bite of her bread and slowly set it down, twisting the paper napkin in her hands. "I want to talk to you about something." She cleared her throat. "It's something I discussed in therapy today." She wiped her mouth with the napkin and then twirled it through her fingers. "I know you mentioned no one would be coming over here, giving me the space I need to heal, but this is your home, and I don't want you to feel like a guest. If you want to bring your friends over, a girlfriend, whomever, I will support it."

Marlene had thought it was important for Pearl to hear about the events that had led to capturing Little, so over the course of several weeks, we had addressed Dylan's death, letting that news gradually unravel in Pearl's head. There were several ugly moments and a setback—she felt as though she had lost everyone she loved. But we made it through, and when we were able to move on to other topics, I described what had led to me walking into her cell that night. During those conversations, I had told her I'd dropped out of med school and joined the academy to find her, but we hadn't discussed my personal life aside from the fact that I lived alone.

Marlene had told me that even conversations between Pearl and me needed to have the right pacing in order for her to process their importance and depth.

This one had been avoided for long enough.

"In the future, I might ask Rivera to come over. I know he would like to see you. And a few of the guys we hung with in college—all names and faces you would recognize. But that's it, Pearl. There is no one else, and there's no girlfriend."

She lifted her fork again, diving it into the spaghetti. "I spent so much time wondering what your life looked like." Her voice changed to an almost-raspy tone whenever she spoke about the basement. "What area of medicine you had chosen, what hospital you were working at." She looked at me. "How many kids you might have." A wrinkle formed between her brows, more on the sides of her lips. "I didn't picture this." Emotion was moving in, a storm gathering in her expression. "That you would be the one who walked through my prison door."

I turned my body toward her, ignoring my plate. "The moment I realized you were gone, so was my love for medicine. I needed to find you, and there was only one way I knew how." I rubbed my hands on my pants, stopping myself from reaching for her. "In my closet is a bin that's dedicated to you. It holds all the notes I took over the years, the people I interviewed, every dead end I hit at the bus station, the hotel in New York. I even spoke to every employee who had been on that day. I documented all of it."

Until I heard Pearl's testimony to the police and her legal team, I hadn't known that she had been on her way to me the morning she was kidnapped. That she had been rushing to the train station to come to my apartment when Little stopped her on the sidewalk, making up a bullshit story to lure her in.

When I had heard that, it'd made me feel even worse.

"You and Gran—that's all I thought about," she whispered. "You two were the only things that kept me alive." Her voice turned even softer. "There were times I wanted to end it. Times I could have forced him to." She shook her head, tears dripping with each pass. "But I would think of you and Gran, and I couldn't do it."

I wiped the drops that fell from her chin and the new ones that formed under her eyes. "Pearl ..."

Her lips were quivering. Her chest more labored as the tears increased.

"I want to hug you."

"Please." She nodded. "Hurry."

My arms circled around her, and I lifted her into the air, holding her body against mine. I'd been close to her over the last nine weeks, but this was the first time she'd been in my arms since I'd carried her out of Little's house.

My hands pressed into her back, her spine no longer protruding now that she had more meat on her bones. And as I held on, I buried my face in her neck, pieces of her wet hair tickling me.

But there was something else.

Something so strong that grabbed ahold of me immediately.

It was her scent.

The cinnamon.

"I'll never forget that day," she whispered. "There was the sound of heavy footsteps above. The pounding and sawing followed, filling my head with so many questions. The door unlocked, and then suddenly, you were there. A moment. And I knew this was ... when darkness ends."

A pain tore through my chest, one that shot into my throat and grew with each breath. "I've waited so long to do this." I felt a wetness move through my eyes and lids, and something broke from inside my throat. And with each inhale, the smell of her grew even stronger. "I never lost hope that I would find you again." I squeezed tighter, feeling her arms do the same around me. "N-never."

SIXTY-SIX

AFTER

PEARL

Five and a half months later, and the hole in my chest was becoming lighter. I wasn't seeing the world in hot-pink tones or wearing rainbow-colored glasses, but the darkness was lifting, and life was starting to make a bit more sense.

Ashe always mentioned when he saw a new change in me.

I was noticing them too.

I would wake when the sky was still dark and open the blinds, going out onto his small balcony with a mug of coffee to watch the sun rise. I wouldn't squint when the brightness hit my eyes. I wouldn't use my arm as a visor either.

I would let the luster and warmth melt into my body. Tasting the freedom. Even if that came with decisions and emotions—I was learning to handle both a little more each day.

But I wasn't doing it alone. Ashe was still here, holding my hand, so incredibly patient with me. There was no pressure, just an ease and rhythm that we had fallen into.

An understanding.

Hope.

But we knew there was healing that had to be done first,

trust that I needed to rebuild in my heart, scars that needed more mending, and he was giving me the time and space for that.

Still, we had so much fun together, especially on his days off. Even though each hour was arranged into a schedule, Marlene thought an important part of my recovery was spontaneity, and she encouraged Ashe to surprise me with adventures, knowing he would always respect my boundaries.

He had one planned for today, and as much as I wanted to let him sleep in, that wasn't usually possible the moment I got into the kitchen since his bed was the couch. But I was craving the taste of coffee, so I quietly opened the bedroom door and was shocked to see he was already up. The blinds were open, just the way I liked to arrange them, and I could smell coffee coming from the kitchen.

He tapped the spot next to him on the couch. "You have to see this."

I hurried over, and once I took a seat, he spread his blanket over my lap. While we faced the large balcony doors, the sun started to lift.

"Beautiful," I whispered.

He waited until it got farther in the sky before he broke the silence. "I was thinking of taking a drive today. Would you be up for that?"

"You usually don't ask."

"It's a bit of a long one, and it would require a stay in a hotel. You've never slept anywhere but here, so I want to make sure you're comfortable with the plan." Before I could say anything, he added, "I checked with Marlene; she knows all about it and has given me her okay."

Since I'd gotten out of the hospital, we'd only stayed within the city. A long drive told me we could be leaving Massachusetts.

I thought of tomorrow's schedule. "I do have that meetup with Kerry and David at five. They're coming here, and we're ordering pizza."

Every two weeks, I met with the others. We talked about our progress and failures. We encouraged each other and helped in ways that no one else could. While the both of them were also finding their footing in this world, we shared similar struggles. As heartbreaking as that was, it was also comforting.

"You'll be back in plenty of time," he promised.

"Then, let's do it."

He smiled, the blue of his eyes even sparkling. "You're sure?"

I nodded. "Should I go shower?"

"Yes, and then we'll leave after we've had some breakfast."

My lips tugged into a grin. "I'm looking forward to it."

I grabbed some coffee and brought the mug into the shower. I quickly washed my hair and body before I climbed out and wrapped myself in a fluffy towel.

Five and a half months, and I still appreciated the scent of soap on my skin. The feel of hair that had been shampooed and conditioned. Water that came out of a spout, hard like raindrops, washing the night away.

I had a small section in Ashe's closet, where I'd hung the clothes he had purchased for me. Jeans and sweaters, tank tops and shorts. Sneakers and shoes sat on the floor below.

Every time I tried to thank him for everything he did, he would say he wasn't doing enough. He was the most giving man, all the way down to his core. One day, I would make him understand what this all meant to me. He would see my appreciation rather than just hear it.

Until that day, all I had were my words.

When I finished getting dressed and came out of his room, I heard him in the shower, so I went into the kitchen and started on breakfast. I cracked several eggs right onto the pan and mixed them while they cooked. I added a second pan for the bacon and popped some bread into the toaster. I was plating it all when he walked in.

"You didn't have to do this," he said.

Even though we used the same products in the shower, the scents were so different on him, especially when he put on his cologne. My eyes closed, and I briefly took in the aromas, smells I had memorized long, long ago, but they didn't compare to the real thing.

"Hush," I said, my lids opening again. "I wanted to."

I set the plates on the counter, refilled our cups, and took the stool next to his.

"Man," he groaned. "You used to make the meanest breakfast in college, and it's even better now." He spooned in several bites. "These eggs are delicious."

I remembered the meals I used to cook for him and Dylan, and the darkness started to encroach into the edges of my mind. The sadness that I constantly tried to push away.

"I wish we could eat like that again—I mean, the three of us."

He glanced up from his plate, chewing a piece of bacon. "You have no idea how badly I wish for that."

"Even if it was for a short time, at one point, both of us were gone." I felt a tightening in my throat, an almost choking inside my chest. "The pain you must have felt—I can't even go there."

"No, Pearl ..." He set down his fork. "I lost all three of you."

Gran.

I didn't know what their relationship had looked like after I was gone, but I had a feeling there had been one. I wasn't ready to hear about her yet. I couldn't even handle talking about her passing—that needed strength that I still didn't have. But once I was ready, I knew Ashe would give me those answers.

"How are you still holding it together?"

"You." His hands dropped, and I reached for one, holding it while he said, "You think I pulled you out of the darkness. But, Pearl, you pulled me out too."

I squeezed his fingers, staring at them, his always so warm and kind. "Can I hug you?"

He nodded. "Hurry."

I knew that feeling well, and I got off my stool and fell into his open arms, holding him as close as I could. I couldn't take it away. I couldn't even make my own pain leave. But I could sympathize, and I could make him a promise. "I'm back," I said into his neck. I took a breath, holding it in while I let that thought settle in my head. "And I'm not going anywhere."

SIXTY-SEVEN

AFTER

ASHE

It had taken almost seven hours to get here, and it had been over eleven years since the last time we'd visited, but the moment I pulled into the base of Cadillac Mountain, the landscape and details all came rushing back to me. This was a place I couldn't forget even if I tried. And I was sure Pearl couldn't either, just like I assumed she had known where we were headed the moment we got in the car in Boston. But she never said a word about it during the drive until we reached Trenton. That was a town about twenty minutes from Bar Harbor, where we'd stopped once with Dylan to eat lobster, and when we'd passed that lobster pound, her smile had reached as far as her eyes.

"What a day that was," she said so softly.

This time, we drove up the mountain, and I reached across the front seat, clasping our fingers together, bringing hers up to my lips to kiss. "A perfect memory."

As we reached the end of the road, I parked, and we got out, walking the rest of the way to the summit. Our fingers were still tangled, the heat of her hand against mine, and we found the spot where the three of us had sat all those years ago.

But now, there were many differences. I could feel them in the air. I could see them every time I glanced at Pearl's side, the place where Dylan had landed his ass when we finished our hike.

"I miss him," I whispered.

"Me too."

That eager grin of his, a personality bursting with energy, fearlessness, and an equal dose of cocky and crankiness.

The world couldn't produce a better friend than Dylan Cole.

And as I sat with Pearl on this rocky edge, the view of the islands below, the endless mountains across from us, I knew I'd been led here for a reason.

Things had a way of coming full circle.

I had survived the worst pain of my life, and this was the other side.

"I feel her."

I put my arm over her shoulders and pulled her against my side. "That's because being up here makes us closer to heaven."

She rested her head against my chest. "The warmth feels like her arms."

"Maybe it is."

She turned her face up to look at me. "Do you believe that?"

I stared into her eyes—a miracle that I was even able to do that. That we were here. Together. "You came back to me. I believe anything is possible."

The truth was, I felt Dylan too.

I felt him protect me every day.

I felt him when I laughed.

I felt him when things got hard.

Just because Pearl had been rescued and she was living with me didn't mean things had been perfect since the day she had walked back in. There were moments that felt impossibly difficult, but I was gaining more strength, patience, and most of all, hope.

"Aside from your home, this is my favorite place."

Holding the top of her arm, I pressed my lips into her hair, the cinnamon scent causing me to close my eyes. "It's our home, Pearl."

"No ..."

I held her chin, turning it until she looked at me again. "If it takes finding a new place, one that feels like it's half yours, then that's what we'll do."

Tears began to fill her eyes the longer she stared at me. "I wouldn't ask you to do that."

"There isn't anything I wouldn't do for you." The knot that had been visiting my throat lately was back, the breaking inside my chest. Both intensifying as I gazed into her gorgeous eyes. "A wise woman once told me that you were still alive, that she would have felt it in her heart if you were no longer on this earth. Therefore, I knew you would return one day. I felt it every time I took a breath. And even if you were found and you had fallen in love with someone else and I had to live with the fact that you were his and not mine, at least I would have known you were safe, you were alive, and you were loved. For me, that would have been enough."

It took her several moments to control her cries enough to say, "I could never love anyone but you."

Her hands surrounded my face, and I held the back of one, kissing the inside of her palm. "What I want more than anything is to one day ask you to be my wife. To hear a beautiful, blue-eyed girl call you her mommy, to wake every morning with you cuddled in my arms. I will protect you, Pearl, until I take my last breath." Her thumbs were swiping near my lips, and I kissed one as it passed across my mouth. "We have nothing but time to make those dreams come true."

"A child." She swallowed, the emotion welling in her throat. "Our child."

I wiped under her eyes as they continuously overflowed. She slid her arms around my neck, and I held her tightly on top of our mountain. Our breaths matched, emotion pounding from our insides.

I knew things wouldn't always be easy. As the weeks passed, more challenges would arise. New fears would present themselves. Pearl's road to recovery would be rocky as hell. But I wasn't afraid of those unknowns. We would solve them together, and Dylan would help me with each one.

But I also knew something greater was in control, and it didn't take standing on top of Cadillac Mountain to feel it. I'd felt that sensation from the moment I had run into her in the hall at BU. When she'd glanced up at me with those innocent eyes and lips so pouty that I couldn't drag my stare away.

This girl was always meant to be mine.

"I love you."

It was as though I'd said those words myself.

But I hadn't.

They had come from Pearl's lips.

I squeezed her even harder and whispered, "Baby, I love you too."

EPILOGUE

PEARL

Sixteen months. That was how long it had taken for me to come here. Even though I'd envisioned this visit almost daily and I'd talked about it with Marlene several times a week, there were very few things I could have done to prepare myself for this moment. For what it would feel like when I saw the headstone of someone I loved so deeply. For when I would sit on the grass that grew above her casket, breathing in air that was so close to her body.

Like I was doing now.

My life was still so scheduled, but coming here had been spontaneous. A feeling I had woken up with while Ashe's arms were clasped around me. Now that I was here, I expected to feel a weight lift off my chest, my lungs to open and turn lighter.

That didn't happen.

But there was a warmth in the breeze as it passed over my face, and it reminded me of the way her hand used to hold my cheek. The sunrays were like her gentle kisses. The tingles in my ears like her tender voice.

Baby, I could hear her say in my head.

She knew I wasn't ready for *dollface.* Even if that man was spending the rest of his life in prison with no chance of parole, that word needed to be locked away.

At least for now.

Esther Daniels
Grandmother, mother, and best friend

I traced my finger over each of the engraved letters along with the dates in which she had been alive. The stone felt so hard and cold—things she was not. And so final. But the same way she had known I wasn't dead, I knew that she was.

I could feel it.

An emptiness where her breath used to live in my heart.

I rested my forehead on her headstone, my hand gripping the top, tasting the tears as they hit my parted lips.

Gran.

I know I don't have to apologize for taking so long to come here. You're watching; you know. Just like I know you were with me in the prison, holding my hand the whole time, giving me strength.

I took a breath.

I dream about your arms. They were different than anyone else's I'd ever felt. They had this way of holding me, like a shield, and when they were around me, I would forget every thought in my head. The softness of your skin would soothe me. The way your hand cupped my cheek would give me a peace where I knew, no matter what, everything was going to be all right.

I missed those hands.

Those hugs.

Oh God, Gran, I miss you.

I want you to know I've been channeling some of your

strength as I've been writing. For a few hours a day, I sit in front of my computer, and I type small parts of my story that will eventually lead to the entire tale. I don't know if I'm doing it just for me and the story will only ever live on my hard drive or if I'll accept the book deal that's been offered to me.

But I started at the very beginning, during the early years in Roxbury, the ones when I was living with Vanessa. Getting out all of that hurt has helped. It's allowed me to start healing. I've even sent Vanessa a few letters to the prison where she's finishing out the next couple of years of her sentence.

One thing I do know is that I miss the stage, but my feelings are entirely different than before. I yearn for the art, the team who works together to create that incredibly moving piece. I don't want all those eyes on me. I don't want to stand in the center and take a bow. I've done that, and I've survived. Now, I want to help create those productions, and I've gotten a part-time job at BU, working backstage to make that happen.

For now, that's enough.

I wiped my eyes, and when my hand returned to the monument, the sun caused the ring on my left hand to sparkle. It had been placed on my finger after a question Ashe asked me a few weeks ago.

In the middle of the setting was a large pearl, two diamonds hugging each side. It was the most gorgeous engagement ring I'd ever seen.

I got so lucky, Gran. To be raised by you, to be loved by him.

To have you and Dylan watching over me.

I know, on this day, we'd be eating your favorite foods—a big steak and a twice-baked potato, banana pudding for dessert. I went to the store this morning and picked up all the ingredients, and that's what I'm going to make Ashe for dinner tonight.

We're going to celebrate you.

I hope you're having a wonderful birthday. I hope you're

dancing across the stars and shimmying your shoulders through the clouds. I hope you're feeling the love because we're certainly feeling it in our hearts.

I pressed my lips onto the coldness and whispered, "I love you, Gran."

And then I leaned back and looked at the markings, the deepness of the letters, the rich blackness of the stone. The spot she was buried in was situated halfway under a tree and halfway in the sun, so she could have the best of both.

"The city really did a wonderful job. This headstone, the plot—I couldn't have picked a better spot for her," I said to Ashe, running my fingers over the letters once again.

Gran had nothing saved, nothing to sell, so there was no way her estate had paid for this. And knowing she had died in the hospital, I assumed the city had had to put her somewhere, and this was where they had chosen.

But the more I thought about that, the more it didn't make sense.

I turned to Ashe as he stood behind me, looking at his handsome face. "You paid for this, didn't you?"

He nodded after several moments and knelt onto the grass, holding me from behind. We sat in silence, looking at Gran's grave. At some point, I heard him unzip his jacket, and he placed something on my lap.

I glanced down, and there was a Polaroid with an envelope behind it.

I knew the picture well. It had hung in my bedroom in Roxbury, taken a few weeks after I moved in with Gran. We had been sitting in the park, reading one of the books she had gifted me, and she'd asked a stranger to take our photo. The memory was one of my favorites because it was when I had fallen in love with reading, and that had made Gran the happiest.

"You kept it," I whispered.

His hand went to my chin. "I kept all of them."

My fingers shook as I saw her writing on the front of the envelope. Her big, loopy letters, the squiggles in each line showing how badly her hand had tremored.

I lifted the flap and pulled the paper out from inside.

"The nurse told me it was too much for Gran to write the letter, so the nurse did, and Gran told her what to write."

Within the first sentence, I knew that aside from the handwriting being different, there was no question whose heart this had come from. Every word sounded just like Gran. And even though I had to stop a few times, I got through it, and I pressed the paper against my chest when I finished.

Ashe held my face with the palms of his hands, wiping my tears with his thumbs. He looked into my eyes, just like Gran had told him to, and said, "She held on, Pearl. She fought for as long as she could. She wanted so badly to be here when you got out. And now, she's up there"—he nodded toward the sky—"watching over you."

Even my lungs were quivering as I tried to take a breath. Wetness coated my lips. My chest ached, as though something were tearing through it. "S-standing from her seat, clapping h-her fragile hands from h-heaven."

Something at our side caught my attention. It was two birds, chirping from the branch of the tree that was next to us, their fat red bodies balancing on a thin limb.

I looked at my fiancé's face, etched with as much pain as mine. "Gran's taking care of Dylan. Neither of them is alone, I promise."

He pulled me into his arms, the letter wedged between my heart and his, and he pressed his face into my neck, his breath hitting my skin as he whispered, "She's holding his hand right now."

ACKNOWLEDGMENTS

Nina Grinstead, no one—and I mean, no one, aside from B— believes in me more than you do. You see things I just don't believe are possible, and you encourage me to reach for them. You show me dreams I never in a million years thought I'd achieve, and you push me to exceed them. Your belief, partnership, friendship are things I've written about but never experienced in my life. Until now. Love you doesn't even come close to cutting it. Team B forever.

Jovana Shirley, I'm beyond blessed and so grateful to have you as part of my publishing dreams. You're not just someone I trust implicitly with my words; you're a genius at what you do, and I continue to learn and grow because of you. Like I say at the end of every book, I wouldn't want to do this with anyone but you. Love you so hard.

Hang Le, my unicorn, you are just incredible in every way.

Judy Zweifel, as always, thank you for being so wonderful to work with and for taking such good care of my words. <3

Chanpreet Singh, thanks for always holding me together and for helping me in every way. Adore you, lady. XO

Kaitie Reister, I love you, girl. Thanks for being you.

Nikki Terrill, my soul sister. Every tear, vent, dinner, virtual hug, life chaos, workout, you've been there through it all. I could never do this without you, and I would never want to. Love you hard.

Sarah Symonds, I feel like we've been on this journey together for centuries, but, girl, it's only the beginning. Thank you for holding my hand through this ride. Love you.

Donna Cooksley Sanderson, another one down, my friend. Thank you for your endless support. I can't wait for the day when I can hug you again. xxx

Ratula Roy, being inside your head, especially with this book, was a true treasure. You always have my back, my heart, and my love. Forever, baby. Love you.

Dawn Fuhrman and Patricia Reichardt, thank you for being such a massive part of this process. I said this last time, and I'll say it again—no one has ears like you two. Heart you both.

Kimmi Street, my sister from another mister. There's no way to describe us; there's just something special when it comes to our unbreakable bond. Nothing and no one will ever change that. I love you more than love.

Extra-special love goes to Valentine PR, Kelley Beckham, Kayti McGee, Chris Fletcher, Tracey Waggaman, Sally Ilan, Elizabeth Kelley, Jennifer Porpora, Pat Mann, and my group of Sarasota girls, whom I love more than anything. I'm so grateful for all of you.

Mom and Dad, thanks for your unwavering belief in me and your constant encouragement. It means more than you'll ever know.

Brian, my words could never dent the love I feel for you. Trust me when I say, I love you more.

My Midnighters, you are such a supportive, loving, motivating group. Thanks for being such an inspiration, for holding my hand when I need it, and for always begging for more words. I love you all.

To all the bloggers who read, review, share, post, tweet, Instagram—Thank you, thank you, thank you will never be enough. You do so much for our writing community, and we're so appreciative.

To my readers—I cherish each and every one of you. I'm so grateful for all the love you show my books, for taking the time to reach out to me, and for your passion and enthusiasm. I love, love, love you.

MARNI'S MIDNIGHTERS

Getting to know my readers is one of my favorite parts about being an author. In Marni's Midnighters, my private Facebook group, I post covers before they're revealed to the public and excerpts of the projects I'm currently working on, and team members qualify for exclusive giveaways. To join Marni's Midnighters, click HERE.

ABOUT THE AUTHOR

USA Today best-selling author Marni Mann knew she was going to be a writer since middle school. While other girls her age were daydreaming about teenage pop stars, Marni was fantasizing about penning her first novel. She crafts sexy, titillating stories that weave together her love of darkness, mystery, passion, and human emotions. A New Englander at heart, she now lives in Sarasota, Florida, with her husband and their yellow Lab. When she's not nose deep in her laptop, working on her next novel, she's scouring for chocolate, sipping wine, traveling, or devouring fabulous books.

Want to get in touch? Visit Marni at ...
www.marnismann.com
MarniMannBooks@gmail.com

ALSO BY MARNI MANN

STAND-ALONE NOVELS

Even If It Hurts (Contemporary Romance)

Before You (Contemporary Romance)

The Assistant (Psychological Thriller)

The Unblocked Collection (Erotic Romance)

Wild Aces (Erotic Romance)

Prisoned (Dark Erotic Thriller)

MOMENTS IN BOSTON SERIES—CONTEMPORARY ROMANCE

When Ashes Fall

When We Met

When Darkness Ends

THE AGENCY SERIES (STAND-ALONE NOVELS)— EROTIC ROMANCE

Signed

Endorsed

Contracted

Negotiated

THE SHADOWS DUET—EROTIC ROMANCE

Seductive Shadows—Book One

Seductive Secrecy—Book Two

THE PRISONED SPIN-OFF DUET—DARK EROTIC THRILLER

Animal—Book One

Monster—Book Two

THE BAR HARBOR DUET—NEW ADULT

Pulled Beneath—Book One

Pulled Within—Book Two

THE MEMOIR SERIES—DARK MAINSTREAM FICTION

Memoirs Aren't Fairytales—Book One

Scars from a Memoir—Book Two

NOVELS COWRITTEN WITH GIA RILEY

Lover (Erotic Romance)

Drowning (Contemporary Romance)

Made in the USA
Las Vegas, NV
30 June 2024